I0687177

Timp and the Blueberry Vikings

Book 1

Written and Illustrated by

Shawn-Michael Monroe

Edited by Albert Pearce

Published by Flipbook Studios LLC

theShawno.com

Timp and the Blueberry Vikings: Book 1

Written and Illustrated: Shawn-Michael Monroe

Edited by Albert Pearce

Book formatting and cover by Shawn-Michael Monroe

ISBN: 978-0-9911362-6-1

First publication date 2024.

For the McClures

and Mom

CONTENTS

A NOTE FROM THE AUTHOR

WARNING! This book contains magic, mischief, wicked-horrible villains, and bees. While all of these things can be dangerous, one should be respected above the others: Bees.

Bees are fascinating insects that are vital to our eco-system, but they can also be deadly. After reading this book, you might decide to find yourself a bee. Don't do it. Bees are not pets. Bees can be territorial. If a bee feels threatened, it will sting you. If you happen to be allergic, you could die. You don't want that. So, DON'T MESS WITH BEES!

If you're interested in bees, first have yourself tested for allergies. If you're not allergic, contact your local apiarist. Apiarists raise bees and harvest honey. They're generally quirky, awesome, and friendly people who love to talk about bees (especially if you buy some of their honey—Mmm honey).

Some apiarists offer classes about beekeeping. It's a safe, interesting way to learn, and the best part is you won't die . . . most likely. That's good, right? Right. So, show bees some respect, and leave them bee. (Get it: "bee"/ "be"?) That's a very witty pun that I came up with—You're so lucky you're reading this book.

Also, avoid wicked-horrible villains. They're both wicked and horrible. You know what, just don't do anything in this book. It's all dangerous . . . but I do hope you enjoy reading about it, though.

– Blueberry Springs Farm –

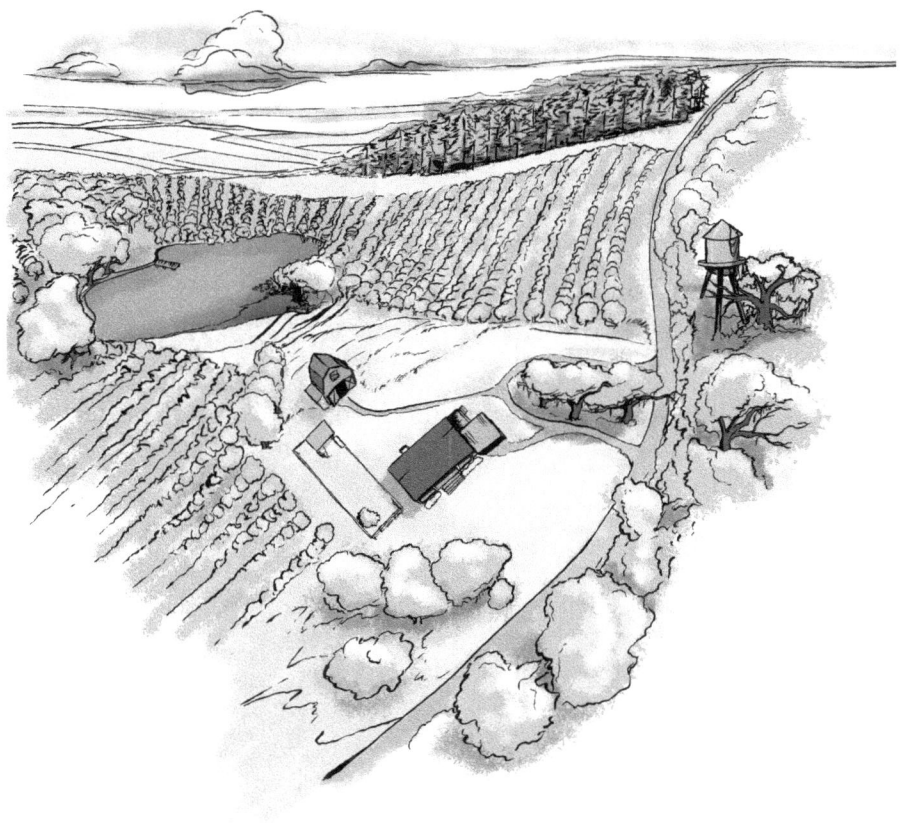

"If you don't know where you're going,

any road can take you there."

Lewis Carroll, Alice in Wonderland

PART I

The Land of Giants

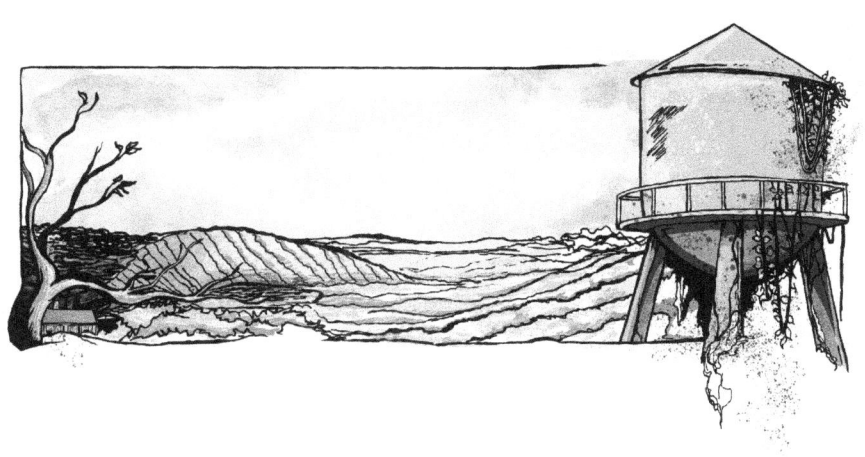

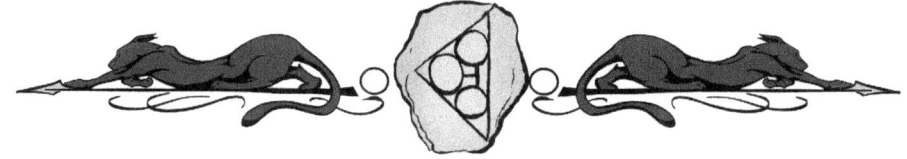

CHAPTER 1

MRS. MOLLY MOUSE CATCHER IS ONE CRAZY CAT

Mrs. Molly Mouse Catcher sat on the porch plotting murder as she licked a stark white paw and rubbed it over her folded black ears. It was a hot summer day at Blueberry Springs Farm, and the humidity caused Molly's fur to poke out in ways that—Mrs. Molly felt—gave her the appearance of a common alley cat.

But Mrs. Molly was most certainly *not* a common alley cat.

"Stupid humans. Stupid. Nasty. Servants. How dare they," she said as she pulled a stubborn tuft of fur with her teeth. *"How dare they do this to me! Betrayal, that's what it is. I've been betrayed by my very own servants. Me, a queen! I shall simply have to kill them all."*

Over the years, Molly had become confused—or maybe it was the Littletons who were confused. The Littletons believed Molly was their family pet, while Molly believed the Littletons were her devoted servants.

There was much more evidence to support the cat's claim.

After all, the Littletons fed and bathed Molly and had done so throughout her life. They brushed her hair, clipped her nails, and bought her toys. They even played with those toys whenever Molly seemed bored. She'd lay on the couch with yawns and stretches, watching her servants shake around feathered sticks for hours. *"Humans are so easily entertained."*

But if Molly ever wanted proof that the Littletons were her devoted servants, she need only check her litter box. Whenever Molly used the restroom, she found the remains so offensive that she quickly covered them with sand, sprang from her box, and ran away, pretending the refuse belonged to somebody else. *"Probably some smelly alley cat,"* she'd call from a safe distance away.

But on occasion, Mrs. Molly caught various members of the Littleton household combing through her box actually searching for her droppings! *"Gross! Disgusting! Ugh!"*

They sifted through the litter with slotted plastic shovels like archeologists through the sands of the Sahara, and whenever they found a stinky lump of disgusting, they dropped it into a brown paper bag—the same type of bag they used to carry their lunches! *Yuck! Yuck! Bad servants, bad!* What they did with the droppings after that, Molly was sure she did not know, but one thing was certain: The Littletons were definitely *her* devoted servants and not the other way around. And that's what made their betrayal all the more infuriating . . .

Just over a week ago, Mrs. Molly had an incident, or as the Littletons called it, "Mrs. Molly's Big Bad Incident." Since then, the Littletons forbade Molly from entering the house.

"Banished from my own palace." Molly pawed at the backdoor, then gave up and lay on the porch. *"The nerve!"*

She'd just begun daydreaming about torturing her servants one by one, when the farmhouse door swung open and smacked her square on her kitty-cat butt. *"Yeow!"*

"Oh, I'm sorry, Molly," Mrs. Littleton said. "I didn't see you there."

Molly spat threats and curses, but as usual, all Mrs. Littleton heard was "Meow. Meow," and, of course, "Meow." Molly hated that her insipid servants were incapable of learning the exquisite language of Cat's Meow. She needed new servants, there was no doubt about it, but how to get rid of these idiots? Before Molly could give it much thought, she noticed Mrs. Littleton had left the doorway wide open. She shook the dust from her coat and dove for the opening like a charging rhino, but Mrs. Littleton was quick. She blocked the entryway with her foot and shut the door.

"Now, now, Molly, you know better. You know you're not allowed inside. Not after Mrs. Molly's Big Bad Incident." She said that last part in baby talk, and Molly choked back the urge to vomit.

"I see I'll have to kill you first," Molly growled.

Mrs. Littleton walked to the end of the porch and scanned the orchard. Molly stretched and did the same. The sun tucked behind the trees in the final hours of its descent, casting a blue light that made the farm seem dream-like and tranquil. Rows of evenly spaced blueberry bushes curved around a large hill and disappeared into the distant pines. At the base of the hill, green pellets of duckweed floated on the calm black water of a spring fed pond. Crickets, frogs, and cicadas sang their evening song in a steady rhythm that sounded as if the earth itself was breathing. This was the good time.

Mrs. Littleton took a deep breath, and then shouted, "Timp? Tiiiiiiimmmp?" She waited, but there was no reply. "Where is he?" She wondered to herself. Her eyes scanned the farm until they stopped on the old, rusty water tower in the distance. Her jaw clinched and her lips drew tight. "He better not be . . ."

"Oh good," Molly meowed, *"the little one is in trouble. Always in trouble, that one. I can't wait to see what she does to him this time. Hey, wait for me!"*

Molly chased Mrs. Littleton as she trekked up the hill. Whenever Mrs. Littleton looked back, Molly stopped, licked her butt, and pretended to be uninterested in the goings-ons of her silly chambermaid. Mrs. Molly was a queen, after all.

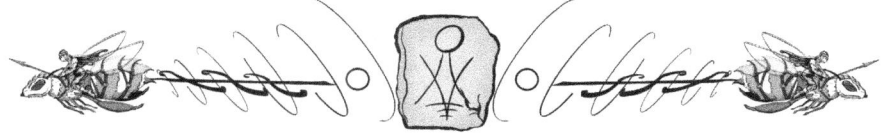

CHAPTER 2
THERE ARE SOME WHO CALL ME . . . TIMP?

Timp tried to steady himself on the limb of a 300-year-old oak. His knees trembled and the limb bounced up and down, threatening to catapult him to the ground 15 feet below. No. He couldn't think about that right now. He needed to block that out, to concentrate. He'd come here with a purpose. Timp widened his stance one tremulous inch at a time. His left hand clutched a wet ball of leaves, stripped from some forgotten branch, grabbed in desperation. His right hand held a thick rope tied into a knotted loop.

Timp followed the rope from his hand to the water tower, where it began around a rusty crossbeam 40 feet above. A flash of embarrassment ran through him as he remembered searching the Internet for the proper knot to tie a tree swing. It seemed the sort of thing a kid should already know, but he wanted to do it right —or maybe he didn't want to do it at all. In the end, he settled on a double running bowline knot. He followed the steps, tied the swing, and now he was going to use it.

Timp yanked the rope to make sure it was tight. The tower creaked in response. He rolled the rope to the side, centering it on the support beam high above, and yanked again, harder this time. The tower swayed and groaned a familiar sound that Timp found comforting; his tower was saying hello . . . or was it goodbye? No, he couldn't think about that now.

This was Timp's special place. True, the tower technically stood outside of the Littletons' property, but it was *his* all the same. It was his because he was the only one who cared about it, and that, more than any piece of paper or imaginary line, gave him ownership. Besides, who else would want it? The tower stood on three rusted legs—the fourth had surrendered to time and weather long ago. The tank still held water, but outside, the paint had faded until a once prominent message was no longer legible. These imperfections only deepened Timp's fondness for the tower. For reasons he couldn't explain, Timp felt he and the tower were connected.

Satisfied his knot would hold, Timp mentally checked the rope's length. He imagined slipping his shoe through the loop, holding tight, and jumping from the limb with a mighty swing. He'd fly under the tower, barely miss the ground, and soar into the air on the other side. Timp imagined that magical feeling of weightlessness that occurs just before going up becomes falling back down. His body would float—if only for a moment—then the rope would catch, and he'd swing back in the opposite direction . . . or maybe he wouldn't. What if he kept going? Flying up and away to someplace cold, someplace where he didn't have to work all summer, where he had friends. He'd just fly away. Timp wished the kids from school could see this unprecedented flight, but as usual during the summer months, Timp was alone.

Rope check complete, Timp was ready. At least, he thought he was ready. He guessed he was ready. Timp was reasonably sure, to the nth degree, that he might possibly be ready. His knees trembled and his palms sweat. He wiped his hands on his shirt. Wet leaves stuck for a moment, then fell to the ground, the ground so far below. Timp wondered if he'd be able hold the rope at all with those hands. He was not ready.

A hideous new story crawled from the dark recesses of his mind. What if, instead of flying, he crashed into the ground. His legs would snap like pretzel sticks, or maybe it'd be his back, or his neck. He'd die out there. Coyotes would drag his body into the woods. His parents wouldn't find him for days. They'd have to follow the stink. Timp edged closer to the end of the bouncing limb.

"I have to do it this time," he told himself. "I have to be brave, this time."

The ground swirled below. The tree seemed higher than it had ten minutes before. Had it grown? Was that possible? What if it kept growing? He needed to jump now, before it grew into the stratosphere. Timp wiggled his toes and dried his palms. He visualized the jump one more time. *Happy thoughts. Think happy thoughts.* He pulled the rope taut. His stomach churned, and he tasted metal. He had to jump. *Now!*

His feet remained fixed to the limb as if his body were another branch, twisting from the ancient oak.

"Who am I kidding?" Timp let the rope drop without him and watched as it swayed in the tower's shadow.

Timp never jumped.

He shimmied down the oak's thick trunk with the bark scratching into his forearms. He thanked the lord when his wet-noodle legs finally reached solid ground. His feet felt like two cinderblocks stuck in Mississippi river mud. He towed them to the abandoned rope beneath the tower, slid his legs through the loop, and sat down, dragging his feet in small circles as the tower swayed back and forth in the breeze. The rusted steel creaked as if to say, "Maybe next time."

"Timp Francis Littleton Michaelson, what in the blue-blazes do you think you're doing?" Mrs. Littleton said as she struggled to free her pants from the briars lining the roadside.

Timp's mother, like most mothers, believed she sounded more severe when shouting her son's full name. Unfortunately for her, Timp Littleton was Timp's full name. According to his father, Timp was named after Mount Timpanogos in Utah, which is where his father went on a spiritual journey to prepare his body, mind, and soul for fatherhood. Timp's grandmother said that was a bunch of hogwash. She claimed Timp was short for Timpleton . . . Timpleton Littleton. Timp prayed it was his grandmother's story that was hogwash.

He once asked to see his birth certificate in hopes of rooting out the truth, but his father said it was somewhere in the attic. In his father's mind, that was as good as lost, and that had ended the discussion. Timp supposed it didn't matter how it happened, facts were facts, and the fact was, Timp Littleton was his name. He had no middle name, not even a middle initial, just Timp Littleton, pure and simple. So, when Timp was in trouble, his mother invented new names to yell. Timp could always tell how much trouble he was in by the length of the name she created—

"Timp Don Durango Constine Littleton, I said get over here this instant."

Timp was in a fair amount of trouble, that day.

"How many times? How many times have your father and I told you to stay away from this tower?"

"I wasn't doing anything."

"It's not *what* you were doing, it's *where* you were doing it."

"*You tell him! Off with his head*," Queen Molly decreed as she hopped over some brush to get a better view.

Mrs. Littleton took a deep breath, and her fury melted into reason. "This tower is old and dangerous. Do you understand? I don't want you getting hurt."

Timp didn't see the problem. The tower had stood for his whole life, and that was 12 long years. If it could stand for a lifetime, then surely it wasn't going to fall any day soon. Timp searched for holes in this logic and found none. *Totally inarguable.* But he knew better than to throw that winning point at his mother. All in all, Timp Don Durango Constine Littleton knew he was getting off easy. At least she hadn't caught him about to jump. He couldn't imagine how long his name would have been then. So he cut his losses, apologized, and showed her an easier way through the briars.

As Timp and his mother crossed the dirt road back to Blueberry Springs Farm, thunder rumbled in the distance. Or was it thunder? A black limousine idled on the roadside, billowing a dark cloud of smoke from the tailpipe. The rotten stench of cigar clung to the humid air so heavily that Timp could smell it from 100 yards away.

"But how can they do that? How is that possible?" Timp's father asked, waving his hands at the shadowy figure sitting in the backseat.

"Come along, Timp," Mrs. Littleton said when Timp lingered. "Let's get cleaned up for dinner."

"Who's that?" Timp asked as he caught up to his mother.

"Uh, a friend of your father's," Mrs. Littleton trailed off. Timp noticed it was she who now lagged behind as they started down the hill.

She watched the limousine with worried eyes. Timp's mother was tough. She wasn't afraid of bugs, spiders, snakes, or coyotes. She even watched scary movies without covering her eyes. If whoever was in that limo worried her, Timp knew he must be uglier than a 500 year-old cannibal mummy and meaner than a giant spider-snake with acid fangs—both of which were in movies Timp had recently asked his mother to stop before the end. He preferred Star Wars. He even had a digital copy where Han shot first.

The limo's engine pinged into gear and left his father standing in a cloud of smoke. No, it wasn't thunder Timp had heard, but a storm was coming. He could feel it.

The back door slammed shut, and Molly's face smacked it with a *Thunk!*

"Heads are going to roll! Do you hear me? Roll! I'm your queen! Your queen!" But as usual, all the Littletons heard was, "Meow. Meow," and of course, "Meow."

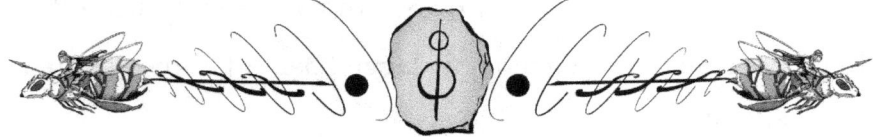

CHAPTER 3
BOLLOCKS TO BROCCOLI

Dinner that night began in silence. Unfortunately for Timp, it would not end that way. Before they joined him at the table, Timp overheard his parents arguing in whispers down the hall. He couldn't make out the entire conversation, but he heard his mother say something about needing money, then she seemed to get really excited about going shopping. It made no sense. Timp's mother mended her shoes eight times before she considered buying a new pair. "Making that dolla' holla'," she called it. Why was she so excited about going shopping now?

Timp studied his parents across a plate of burned chicken, runny mashed potatoes, and smelly broccoli. His mother stabbed at her potatoes with her fork, while his father stared into a glass of water.

"Eat your broccoli, Timp," his mother said without looking from her plate.

"I don't like broccoli," Timp said. This was an understatement. In truth, Timp *hated* broccoli. His parents knew he hated broccoli, yet every night when Timp came to dinner, there it was: disgusting-rotten-no-good-make-you-want-to-vomit broccoli. It bordered on child abuse.

Before she even opened her mouth, Timp knew what his mother was going to say next: "You know, there are children starving in Africa. I bet they'd like some broccoli."
Right on cue.

"Good, we can send them mine." Timp smiled. He'd finally come up with a solution to make everyone happy: his mom, the children of Africa, but especially himself.

"Don't be smart," his father said, waking from his thoughts.

I'll remember you said that next time I give you my report card, Timp thought, but he didn't dare say that gem out loud. He was on a roll tonight, but the sad fact was, Timp wasn't being smart. He really did want to send the starving children of the world his broccoli. Why not? He imagined himself dropping the horrid little trees into Ziploc bags, packing in some ice, and then mailing it all off with a note: "Dear starving kids, Please enjoy this broccoli. My mother tells me it's your favorite." Then again, why bother mailing it at all? Cut out the middleman and have farmers ship the world's broccoli supply to the starving kids directly. That was the way to do it. *Brilliant!*

"Well?"

Uh oh. Timp's mother expected something. What was it? Timp had been so busy figuring out new and ingenious methods of distributing the world's broccoli supply to the starving masses that he'd forgotten what his mother was talking about.

Mrs. Littleton gritted her teeth. "Eat your broccoli!"

Well, she didn't have to yell about it. Timp jabbed his fork into the pile of broccoli and speared the smallest piece he could find. In a moment of insanity, he thought about flicking a broccoli torpedo at his mother's forehead, standing on a chair, and shouting, "Freedom!" But doing so meant certain death, and Timp was fond of living. Nope, there was no way around it. He closed his eyes and braced himself for nasty-broccoli-barf surprise.

He popped the piece of broccoli into his mouth, and swallowed it whole so that he didn't have to taste the horrid flavor. But it was too late. Broccoli fumes filled his mouth and went up his nostrils. How did it get into his nostrils? He imagined little leafy pods exploding into a sickly yellow gas that crawled up his nose from the back of his throat. His face flushed, and his eyes burned. He gagged. He hacked and coughed, and banged his fist against his outer thigh, trying to choke the broccoli down before he spewed all over the table. Timp looked to his parents for sympathy, but found none.

"Stop acting like a baby," his mother said.

Stop acting—a baby? Couldn't they see he was dying? It wasn't fair, their taste buds were old and dead, his were young and hypersensitive. Timp had learned all about it in biology. His tongue had something like a trillion million more taste buds than theirs. They probably thought broccoli tasted like cotton candy ice cream, instead of what it really tasted like: freeze-dried barf trees. Timp choked down the broccoli and guzzled water to wash the taste away. He'd die before he ate the rest. *Die!*

Timp's father sighed. "Timp, we need to talk." Timp looked up while hiding his uneaten broccoli under his mashed potatoes. "I'm going to need you to get up an hour earlier every day to help me pick before the help gets here."

Timp stared at his father.

Mr. Littleton continued, "We need to harvest as much as we can for Summer Fun Fest. With the drought this summer, we're not getting enough berries, and I can't afford to hire more workers. I was also hoping you could help an extra week this summer."

It sounded like a request, but Timp knew it wasn't. Summer Fun Fest was the largest farmer's market of the season. The Littleton's sold their produce to anyone and everywhere that had need of blueberry deliciousness: walkup customers, restaurants, bakeries, coffee houses, yogurt shops, smoothie counters, juice bars, grocery stores, and ice cream parlors. The event was the main source of the Littleton's income.

Timp said nothing. His face burned as blood filled his cheeks. So this was how it was going to be. First, they tried to choke him to death with poisoned broccoli, and now, they planned to work him to death too. It was child abuse! He'd call Children's Services! But all he managed to get out was, "What about Colorado?"

Every year, after spending half the summer picking berries, Timp and his parents hauled up to Colorado to escape the Louisiana heat. They rented a cabin in the woods, fished for trout in the cold mountain streams, and roasted hotdogs on open fires. The air was 30 degrees cooler there, but best of all, Timp had friends—lots of them. He looked forward to seeing them all year long but especially after two mind-numbingly boring months as the only kid on the farm. By that point, Timp had to get away or he'd go nuts. His parents knew this.

Mr. Littleton studied Timp with sad crinkled eyes, "We just can't do it this year, Son."

He sounded sorry, he truly did, but Timp didn't want sorry. He wanted Colorado. He wanted his friends. Timp had only one response. "This is crap."

"Timp, language!" Mrs. Littleton said.

Language? Language! Who cared about language when his only chance at happiness had just been stripped away? He'd worked hard for that trip. He'd earned it.

"Timp, we're going to need you to act like a grown-up on this one," Timp's father said.

There it was again: "Act like a grown-up." "Don't be a baby." They kept saying that; yet, they were the ones calling him names and whispering about shopping sprees in the halls like gossiping schoolgirls. Yeah, that was solid. He'd go with that: "You're the ones acting like children: gossiping, calling people names. Didn't you just call me a baby a few minutes ago?" He had them now. Golden!

"No, we told you to stop *acting* like a baby."

Crap. That's true, they did. They were better at this than he was. Timp's frustration grew.

Act like a grown-up. It was absurd. He wasn't a grown-up, he was a kid, and he should get to act like a kid. He didn't want to work; he wanted to play. He didn't want to be alone during the summer; he wanted friends. And he didn't want broccoli, dadgummit! He wanted . . . anything other than broccoli! He should get to make his own decisions, like an adult. No. Wait. Not like an adult, like a kid. *Crap.* Now, he'd confused himself. Being 12 was tough.

If they wanted him to act like an adult, then they should treat him like one. Otherwise, he should get to be a kid. Yeah, that was it, that was what he wanted to say. But when Timp spoke, these points muddled together in a gibberish deluge. He tried to catch his breath and compose his thoughts, but new thoughts fell upon old ones until it all collided and slipped away, leaving only, "What about her?" Timp pointed at his mother in one last desperate grasp. "She's the childish one, getting excited about going shopping. Is that why I have to work harder, so she can go shopping?"

Yeah, secret knowledge bombs. Boom! Face explosion. He couldn't wait to see them argue that. But his words didn't have the "gotcha" effect he'd hoped for. In fact, his parents seemed completely lost.

"What on God's green earth are you jabbering about?"

Timp's confidence wavered, but he'd committed himself now. "If we need money, then why does she get to go shopping? I overheard y'all say she was going shopping."

Realization fell on his parents, and they glanced at one another. His mother covered her mouth, concealing a smirk. Mr. Littleton tilted his head to study Timp over his glasses. Timp knew that look well. It was the look his father gave him whenever he said something stupid. Timp's face flushed and his mother fought back a grin. "Timp, you don't know what you're talking about."

"You don't know what I'm talking about!"

Not his best comeback, he knew. Why did his brain always fail him when he needed it most? His eyes burned with the frustration and unfairness of it all. He didn't want to cry. He knew if he cried, they won. But Timp always cried when he got angry. He wasn't a crybaby, but when he grew frustrated, his eyes watered. His body simply couldn't hold all of that anger, and the only place it could go was to pour out of his deep brown eyes.

Timp hated himself for crying, and he hated his parents for making him cry. But he wasn't supposed to hate anyone, which made him even more frustrated and brought more tears. Timp's parents stared across the table with their mouths hanging open. Timp avoided their gaze. What were they looking at, anyway? Like they'd never cried before. Why were they staring at him? Didn't they have better things to do? He wanted them to look away. He felt small, powerless, and sick to his stomach. He wanted to explode with rage and force them to see things *his* way. It wasn't right; it wasn't fair. How could they not see that? Timp glanced at his plate of broccoli—nasty-stinky-make-you-want-to-throw-your-plate-and-scream broccoli.

It wasn't worth it. Timp threw down his napkin, ran to his room, and slammed the door. *Bollocks to broccoli!*

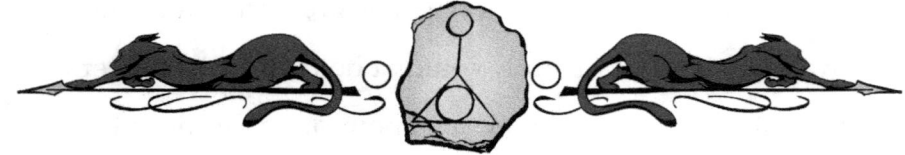

CHAPTER 4

SOMETHING WICKED THIS WAY PROWLS

It was a clear night. The moon climbed through the sky, casting a white glow on an otherwise blue world beneath. It was a perfect night for hunting, and Molly was on the prowl.

A week ago—just after "Mrs. Molly's Big Bad Incident"— Molly decided to show the Littletons who was *really* boss. And since her ridiculous servants refused to learn the exquisite language of Cat's Meow, Molly left the traditional message of the Kitty-Cat Mafia: a dead rat on the doorstep. Now, anyone who isn't a stupid alley cat knows that a dead rat on the doorstep is a clear message to the servants of the house: "Get out, or you're next . . . just as soon as I call my cousin the lion. He's a king you know, and oh my, have you seen his teeth?" But it turned out that the Littletons were humans of below average intelligence. They didn't understand her message at all. Though at first, the result was far better than Molly could have ever anticipated.

Mrs. Littleton stumbled onto the patio to collect the newspaper as she did every morning: wearing a satin nightgown, pink cotton robe, and socks. Molly watched from the azaleas as her chambermaid registered something out of place. Her maid sniffed and Molly did the same. The air was cool and moist, and smelled of morning dew on burned grass. "*Not that*," Molly said. Her maid squinted and Molly ducked back, giggling. She needn't worry; her chambermaid was blind without her contacts. The maid tilted her head.

"*Does the patio seem uneven, deary?*" Molly sniggered, and then covered her mouth.

The maid shifted her weight and something cracked. She tried to lift her foot, but lost her balance, and stepped down harder than before. A dozen more cracks and snaps, then squishy, red wetness soaked up her starched white sock. She leaned down and squinted. She didn't seem to see it at first, but Molly saw. Oh, yes. She saw. Molly held her breath in suppressed delight. Then the chambermaid saw it too. A lifeless grey rattail stuck out from beneath her foot.

Mrs. Littleton freaked.

She screamed and kicked her foot high into the air. The rat, wet and sticky from a night on the porch, stuck to her sock like a half-licked blow-pop in kitty litter. She threw her foot out and clawed desperately through the doorframe, but the rat-glue carcass remained fixed. Her voice shrilled bloody murder. She hopped on one foot with her head inside the door and kicked wildly outside, but the rat's front teeth had hooked through the fabric of the sock, and no matter how hard she kicked, the body flapped with her. The other servants awoke to Mrs. Littleton's screams. Molly purred in contentment from the azaleas—revenge was truly a dish best served cold . . . and wet . . . and sticky . . . like a rat carcass.

But while Molly relished Mrs. Littleton's dance, she feared the overall meaning of her message may have been lost. Mrs. Littleton eventually ripped off her sock and ran inside the house screaming—which was great—but she slammed the door, leaving Molly still locked outside. *The nerve!*

Clearly, the chambermaid had not gotten the point. And to make matters worse, Mr. Littleton tried to explain the entire message away. "This is a good thing," he told Mrs. Littleton, as he dropped the dead rat into the garbage. "It means Molly is trying to provide for us. She thinks we're the leaders of her clowder. That's what they call a pack of cats. I read all about it online."

"Leader of my—As if!" Mrs. Molly huffed. *"My great, great grandfather was a bobcat. If anyone is the leader of this clowder it's me."* And that's when Molly decided it was time for a new message, a better message. *"This time, I'll get a snake."*

And so, on the night of the Littleton's broccoli argument, Molly prowled down the driveway in search of prey. It should have been a perfect night for it, but something felt off. A light breeze from the blueberry fields carried an unfamiliar scent. It smelled like berries, but also like humans.

"*Enemies.*" Molly's eyes narrowed. She ducked her head closer to the ground and stuck her butt high into the air: her kitty-cat ninja pose. All would cower before her might.

A metallic crash rang in the carport. Molly charged to meet her enemy head on, but then stopped just outside the carport door to listen. Someone was talking. The sound was barely audible, even with her keen kitty-cat ears, but she was sure she heard voices. She edged closer. Yes, definitely voices. *Perhaps a midnight snack.* She crouched deeper into her kitty-cat ninja pose, flared her hackles to appear extra fierce, and wiggled her butt high in the air.

"*On the count of three: one, two, THREE!*" Molly sprang into the carport with her claws out and paws flailing. She stabbed and hissed, swatted and swiped—she even threw in a karate chop for extra measure—but when she landed on the concrete floor, Molly was alone.

Embarrassed and confused, Molly licked her paws and casually scanned the room. *Maybe they're hiding in front of the truck? Yesss, that's it.* Molly snuck to the side of the Littletons' rusted-out Chevy. She didn't count down this time: *Jump! Kick! Hiss! Scratch! Karate Chop!* But again, she was alone. Molly stuck a paw in her ear and jiggled it around. *My ears must be playing tricks on me. Probably coming down with something. It's all my servant's fault, locking poor Molly outside. I probably caught some common alley cat disease. Poor Molly, me.*

As Molly turned to leave, a knapsack dropped over her head.

"Hey! Why, you dirty, rotten no-good-for-nothings, I'll get you! I'll smother you in your sleep! I'll eat your" — THWACK!

Everything went dark.

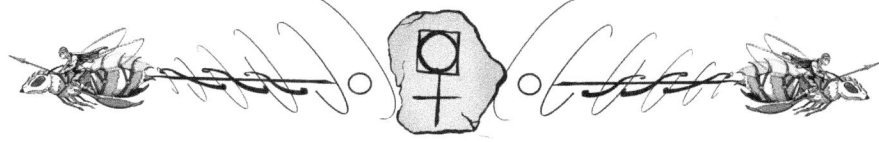

CHAPTER 5

OPERATION: RESCUE COLD CHICKEN

Timp lay in bed staring at the ceiling and replaying the argument from dinner in his mind. *The jerks.* He understood what was happening; anyone could figure that out: His parents were evil slave drivers. They probably hoped he'd drop dead from exhaustion so they could collect on some insurance policy or a government program that pays parents suffering from loss. That's what they were up to. Timp knew it.

Slowly, Timp's anger dwindled into boredom, which then dissolved into loneliness, and finally stabbed at his stomach in hunger. He thought about the leftover chicken sitting cold and alone in the fridge. *Poor chicken. Someone should rescue it.* He got up, pressed his ear to the door, and listened for movement. Nothing. Operation: Rescue Cold Chicken was underway.

Timp tiptoed down the hall, avoiding the floorboards that creaked. He prided himself on his mastery of the Jedi skills necessary to slink down the hall in absolute silence. He'd learned long ago which boards required a slide, which required a jump, and which could be stepped on like normal (provided you were wearing 100% cotton socks and it was at least 90% humidity outside—which in Louisiana was always).

Timp peeked around the corner to make sure his parents weren't lingering in the kitchen. The lights were off, but the oven clock blinked a bright glow that allowed Timp to see. The kitchen was cleaned and dinner had been put away. On the counters, several bowls were piled high with blueberries ready for packaging the following morning. The coast was clear.

Timp skated across the slick tile floor toward the fridge filled with his mission's objective: cold chicken, when something in his peripheral moved. Timp froze. A blueberry tumbled from a bowl and plopped onto the counter with a roll. Timp's shoulders relaxed. *Only a berry.*

Gravity had a way of catching up with precarious berries. They tumbled to the counters and floors at all hours of the night. Timp joked that it was his grandfather's ghost throwing out the bad berries. But then something occurred that—ghost or no ghost —had never happened before. The berry hit the counter, bounced, and rolled to a stop. Nothing strange about that, happened all the time. But then the berry started rolling again in the opposite direction. *That ain't normal.* Maybe there really was a ghost.

Timp sidled to the counter, grasping for a rational explanation. Maybe it wasn't a berry at all, but some kind of insect—a beetle, perhaps. That made sense, a beetle. Then, Timp heard the voices. At least he thought he heard voices: tiny, quiet, just-under-a-whisper voices. Timp ducked to the counter until his nose pressed against the cold linoleum edge.

The oven clock blinked off and on, as did Timp's comprehension. His brain refused to accept what his eyes saw before him. It had to be some trick of the light, or maybe he was dreaming. Yes, that was it, dreaming. He probably fell asleep while lying in bed, and now he was dreaming. He could almost laugh at his own silliness. Any moment now he'd wake up and the world would make sense again. Timp pinched himself to hurry the process. Nothing happened. He pinched himself again, harder this time. *Any. Moment. Now.*

Timp did not wake up. He wasn't dreaming. This was real. He pressed his nose against the counter until it hurt. Inches away, a man no bigger than an ant rolled a blueberry across the kitchen counter.

Each blink of light allowed Timp to study the man in greater detail. His size wasn't the only strange thing about him. He had long grayish hair that shot wildly from a leather helmet and then braided into a knotted beard below. He wore a blue tunic, leather pants, and heavy boots, all of it strapped tight with leather belts that crisscrossed over his body. A double-edged battle-axe covered his back. The axe was almost as large as the man, but the weight seemed to cause no discomfort.

27

Timp had learned about Vikings in school, and—other than the fact that he was no larger than an ant—the man looked just like one. But then Timp noticed something else strange. At first, he thought it was just the blue light from the oven, but no. As the man rolled his berry across a moonbeam that sliced through the kitchen window, Timp saw that the man's skin was blue, but not only blue, blue with dark lines of purple that weaved in tattooed designs down the Viking's arms and face. Timp thought about grabbing a mason jar to catch the tiny blue Viking, but before he could move, another Viking appeared over the edge of the berry bowl. This one was fatter than the one below. He stuffed his cheeks with berry innards.

"Is we done, yet?" the fat Viking said, shoving another handful of berry into his mouth.

The Viking rolling the berry below did not look up, but answered, "Ye'd be wise to eat in silence, O'dul, lest ye wake yon giants."

"Yipe! Did someone say 'giant'?" a third Viking said.

This one was smaller than the other two, and Timp could swear he wore glasses.

"Quiet, Fen. Ye'll wake yon giants," the Viking who'd been talking said. He pointed his thumb at Fen and added, "Can ye believe this Viking?"

The grey-bearded Viking groaned.

28

They scanned the room but failed to notice Timp despite looking right at him. Timp figured he must be so large by comparison that the Vikings didn't realize he was a person at all. He stifled a laugh as the Vikings tiptoed around the counter, inches from his nose.

"Hey-o, I's found me one!" a fourth Viking shouted from several bowls away.

This was turning into a Viking invasion.

This Viking had a long red beard, which he tossed over his shoulder before spitting on his hands and working to dislodge a berry from the bottom of the pile. Timp began to suggest that it might be easier to take a berry from the top of the pile, when a fifth Viking marched around to help—At least Timp *thought* she came to help.

The newest Viking was a woman—a whole lot of woman. She stood taller than the others. If they'd been regular size, she'd have stood at least seven feet tall and all of it corded muscle. She wore a skirt over leather breeches, but if you expected a curtsy, forget it. More likely the skirt was for wiping away her enemy's blood. A golden braid of hair weaved its way down her muscular back. If it moved out of place, she tossed it back with her spear.

The red-bearded Viking worked to dislodge the blueberry with such concentration that he didn't notice the Viking woman slip behind him. He didn't even notice as she leaned back and took aim with her spear. But he *definitely* noticed when she stabbed him square in the backside.

"Yehow!" The Viking leapt into the air and scrambled to the top of the berry pile with his hands cupped securely over his buttocks. "What'd ye do that for?" he whined, rubbing his bum.

"Bjorn said be silent, fool." The Viking woman smirked.

"Why, you lousy—"

Before he could finish, she plucked the berry from the bottom of the pile, releasing an avalanche of purple and grey. Red tried to run on top of the berries as long as he could, but soon he was rolling next to them, and then under them as he and the berries tumbled to the kitchen counter. The other Vikings roared with laughter. Red did not. He jumped to his feet and started hopping up and down. He slapped himself, huffed, and grunted. His blue skin reddened until it matched his beard. He rammed his head against the side of the berry bowl, slapped his bottom, and stomped his feet.

"What's he doing?" Timp asked.

"Never you mind him," Fen answered. "He's just going berserk." The other Vikings stood wide-eyed with mouths agape. Slowly, Fen realized he'd just spoken to a "Gi-gi-gi-gi-gi-Giant!"

The Vikings screamed and ran in circles. The ones in bowls tumbled to the counter and joined the others. They pulled at their belts, trying to draw their weapons. Axes, maces, swords, and spears fell to the ground, and then were picked up and dusted off. Eventually the Vikings organized themselves into something resembling a battle formation, but Timp also wouldn't have been surprised if they broke into the Electro Shuffle.

They waved their weapons in the air. "Back, foul beast!" one shouted then retreated to the back of the line. "We fear you not, horrible monster!" Another added and ran away. "Be gone, great stinky one!"

The Vikings paused. "Great stinky one?"

Timp sniffed himself.

"Twas all I could think," Fen stammered as he pushed up his glasses and ducked into the crowd.

The woman recovered first. She charged with her spear held high and stopped short of the counter's edge and Timp's nose. "Be gone, evil giant! Torment us no more! Return to the ice cave from whence ye came!"

She threw her spear with a grunt, and it wobbled back and forth in the end of Timp's nose. It surprised Timp more than it hurt. His head jerked back, and his hands flailed. The Vikings cheered in triumph. Their foe was defeated . . . or was he?

After Timp over came the shock of the being stabbed in the nose by a tiny blue Viking—which was a pretty surprising turn of events that evening—he pulled the spear out and handed it back to the woman. The Vikings fell silent.

"I'm not a giant," he said, rubbing his nose. "I'm a kid. And I don't live in an ice cave. I live in a house." The words felt feeble even as he said them, but Timp had argued enough for one evening.

The Vikings muttered amongst themselves, then one said, "What mean you by 'kid', Giant?"

"I mean that I'm a kid, a boy."

The Vikings stared blankly.

Timp rolled his eyes. "I'm a child, young, not an adult. Not. Fully. Grown."

The Vikings huddled. After a moment, the thin Viking with glasses popped his head out. "You claim there be giants even more giant than you, Giant?"

"I just told you, I'm not a giant. I'm a kid," Timp said. "But yes, many people are bigger than me. I'm not even big for my age. Thanks for bringing it up."

The Vikings whispered some more in a hiss. Fen pushed up his glasses, took out a book, and made some notes. Finally, they'd reached a decision. "We have decided that, despite what ye say, ye're quite giant, Giant. And while there may be those among your'n kind who think ye small, to *us* ye are giant."

Timp had never thought of himself as giant before. He smiled a toothy grin, and the tiny blue men took a big step back. The woman warrior stood her ground with her spear ready.

"And you, Giant, do thee swear upon the heads of your'n fathers not to eat us?" The grey haired Viking asked.

"Eat you? Gross!"

The Vikings ran Timp through the gamut of vows, pleas, negotiations, and litigations—complete with indemnification clauses and pinky promises. Timp swore he'd never *intentionally* eat one of the Vikings; though, he conceded that they were so small it was possible he might do it by accident, but he hoped not. The Vikings seemed satisfied; though, Timp noticed the woman warrior kept her spear ready.

Timp introduced himself, and the Vikings doubled over at his last name.

"A giant named 'little,'" they laughed.

Timp didn't see the humor.

"Little-ton," another corrected, wiping away tears.

"Aye, he's mighty little, but he weighs a ton." The Vikings rolled around and banged their fists against the counter.

Timp waited.

When they calmed down, the Vikings introduced themselves. The man with the peppered beard was the first to step forward. "I be Bjorn, named after my father before me," he said, and then added, "the bear."

Having recovered from his slapping fit earlier, the redheaded Viking stepped forward. "I be Gunnar the Red, head berserker and mighty warlord. You'd be wise to stay on me good side, Giant, lest I berserk thee!"

Timp started to ask what a berserker was when Gunnar began hopping up and down and slapping himself. Timp got the general idea.

The warrior groaned with impatience and elbowed Gunnar aside. "Ye couldn't berserk yer ma'ma," she said and Gunnar fell silent. "I be Erika the Nordis, named for the Northern warrior and eternal ruler. You, Giant, have suffered my spear, but ye've not yet felt my wrath. I trust ye not. I fear ye not. Do not cross me, Jötunn. You will lose."

Timp swallowed. He didn't know who Jötunn was, but he hoped never to cross Erika.

The plump Viking stepped up next. "I'm O'dul, named after. . ." He scratched his head in thought, and then finished, "O'dul." The other Vikings slapped their foreheads. Timp sensed this was a common reaction when O'dul spoke. "I collect rocks."

"Yer's head be's a rock," Gunnar muttered.

The skinny one with glasses jumped forward, holding up a notebook as though it were a weapon. "I'm Fenrisúlfur, learned skald, giantologist, pacifist, and swamp wolf of Hel! Fear me, Giant!" He dropped his book, held up his hands like claws, and growled himself into a coughing fit. The other Vikings stifled laughter. Fenrisúlfur blew his nose. "Um, but ye may call me Fen." He blushed, picked up his book, and fell back among the others.

Five Vikings in all: Bjorn, Gunnar, Erika, O'dul, and Fen. Timp noticed they all gave grand speeches in their introductions, speeches that included some form of threat. Maybe this was a Viking custom. He decided to reintroduce himself properly. "I'm Timp Littleton, giant to some, kid to others. Do not cross me or I'll squish you all with my mighty fist and swallow you whole." Timp laughed. The Vikings also laughed (as they backed to the opposite end of the counter).

The Vikings were easier to talk to after that. . . somewhat. Timp explained that he lived in a house, not an ice cave in the side of a mountain, and that the air was cooler because of a modern marvel called "air–conditioning," not because they were under ground. The Vikings wouldn't hear it. Timp eventually gave up and told them just to call it a house, which they did: "Giant, we have traveled to House Mountain in search of our'n homes."

"Your homes are missing?"

"Nay, not missing," Erika corrected. "Stolen by flea infested ice-giants like your'n self."

The Vikings sneered.

Timp cocked his head. "Why would giants steal your homes?"

The Vikings stared at Timp. That question had clearly not occurred to them.

"Twere nice homes," O'dul said, "roomy 'n comfy: cool in the summer, warm in the winter. . . hardwood floors, and faux finishing throughout. Them homes be outright. . . homey."

"Okay, fine." Timp rolled his eyes. "How do you know giants took them?"

"Because we saw 'em!" the Vikings shouted, shaking their weapons in the air.

"You saw giants take your houses?" Moments before, they'd asked if there were giants bigger than Timp. Clearly, they hadn't seen many.

"Well, we saw they's hands," O'dul said. "Their'n nasty *giant* hands!" Gunnar added. "Shoved 'em right into our'n village and took our'n houses, they did."

What on earth were these little blue ant-people going on about? It didn't make sense. If any giant—or rather a person— had come across a tiny Viking village, Timp would have heard about it on the news. "Tiny Blue Viking Warriors Discovered in Louisiana" was the kind of headline you remembered. There must be more to this story.

"Okay," Timp said, taking a breath. "What do your houses look like?"

"Got us one right here," O'dul said as he butted the blueberry next to him with the handle of his mace. It was the same berry that Bjorn had rolled across the counter earlier.

36

"And there be another yonder," Gunnar said, pointing to the berry Erika had pulled from the bottom of the stack.

Now Timp understood everything. The Vikings were insane.

Timp spoke slowly so they could understand, "That's not a house. That's a blueberry."

The Vikings eyed Timp with raised eyebrows. "Nay," Bjorn said, returning Timp's slow speech. "Yonder be a blueberry." He pointed to a berry across the counter, then back to another nearby. "This be a house."

Timp was beginning to get annoyed with these little know-it-alls. Clearly, their brains were too small for rational thought. "Nooo. That's a berry."

To prove it, Timp picked up the berry and tossed it into his mouth.

"What madness is this?" Bjorn shouted.

For three long seconds, Timp held the berry between his right molars, eyeing the Vikings in defiance. They were crazy. They thought he lived in an ice cave. They didn't even believe in air conditioning. Someone had to teach these Neanderthals a lesson. He'd been picking berries his whole life. He knew a berry when he saw one, and this was a berry, just a regular, every day blueberry. "Giant—"

Timp bit down.

It wasn't a berry. Dear God, it wasn't a berry at all.

Timp's mouth ran dry as wood splinters exploded onto his tongue. It was like eating a box of toothpicks (with just a hint of faux finishing). Timp wanted to spit it out, but he'd committed himself now. He chewed on. Wood snapped and broke in his mouth. Finally, he managed to choke it down.

The Vikings stared with their mouths agape.
"Ye ate me house," Bjorn said.

"Why'd ye do that? Ye promised." Fen sounded hurt.

"I promised I wouldn't eat any of *you*." Timp said, trying to hide his embarrassment. "I didn't say anything about your houses."

He forced a smile and held his chin up with false pride.

This was a bad move.

Gunnar jumped up and down and slapped himself. He shuffled his feet, babbled incoherently, and shook his head back and forth with his tongue out and slobber filling the air. Timp recognized this behavior as going berserk. He still didn't get it.

The other Vikings were no better. They screamed and cursed. Erika stabbed at Timp with her spear, and arrows bounced off of his cheek and disappeared to the kitchen floor. Timp needed to make this right, but before he could explain, yellow light poured from his parent's bedroom, filling the kitchen.

Timp's father stepped into the hall, but his mother must have asked a question, because he turned around and stuck his head back into the bedroom. Timp couldn't hear what they said, but it didn't matter. It bought him the time he needed.

He grabbed the matchbox next to the oven and dumped the matches into the trash. The Vikings shrugged at each other, wondering why their enemy refused to meet them in battle. Timp placed the box under the counter's edge, swiped the Vikings inside, and shut the lid over Viking curses.

He dashed out of the kitchen, through the dining room, and around the corner. He'd just turned into the hall when he heard his father flip on the kitchen light and open the refrigerator door.

Distracted, Timp forgot to dodge the loose floorboards scattered throughout the hall—a Padawan mistake. He was no Jedi master. He missed the first three hazards by sheer luck, but as Timp reached his bedroom door, his luck ran out.

Timp felt the board buckle under his weight, and he froze. He knew this board well. It didn't make a sound when you stepped down, but it was the loudest in the entire house when you stepped off. Timp closed his eyes in shame. How could he be so stupid? He was no Jedi knight. He was a soldier standing on a landmine.

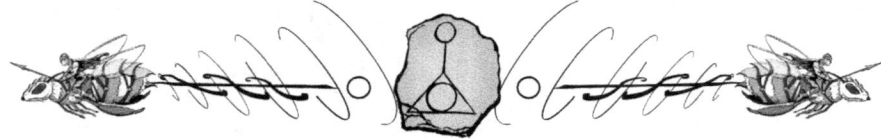

CHAPTER 6
YOU SCREAM, I SCREAM, WE ALL SCREAM FOR VIKINGS

Timp stood on the hardwood landmine awaiting his fate. He knew he couldn't stand there forever, but he thought maybe he'd try. After all, how long could forever really be? Timp waited. . . ugh, forever was taking forever. Maybe if he lifted his foot slowly. . . deep down, Timp knew better, but what choice did he have? He cringed, resigned himself to his fate, and lifted. At first, nothing happened, not a sound. He'd done it! Then the treacherous board popped up with a groan that shook the entire planet—at least, in Timp's mind it shook the entire planet. In reality, it probably only shook half the planet. He heard his father stop digging in the fridge, and Timp knew that he'd been caught. He dove into his bedroom and shut the door.

Timp's room was exactly as he'd left it. Clothes and comic books littered the floor. Broken little-league-participation trophies collected dust on the shelves. A model of the Millennium Falcon hung from the ceiling with a Spider-Man toy tethered below, and crooked posters of the Marvel Universe hung yellowed and dog-eared on the walls. His muted television soundlessly played the same show as when he'd first ventured out for leftover chicken, but that seemed so long ago. So much had happened. Timp wondered whether he'd imagined it all. He pulled the matchbox from his pocket and sat it on the nightstand. He took out his magnifying glass and slowly pulled open the box.

"A Cyclops!" the Vikings screamed. Timp had not imagined it; the Vikings were real. He pulled away the magnifying glass so they'd recognize him. "A giant!" The Vikings screamed.

Yep, real and definitely still crazy.

"I told you I'm not a giant. I'm a kid."

"Aye, a giant kid," Gunnar scoffed.

"One who eats houses," Fen added in a tone of disappointment.

Timp could see the Vikings better through the magnifying glass. They seemed somehow both plain and ornate. Their tunics and leather breeches were simple colors of browns and greys but trimmed with stitching that swirled around in knotted ringlets. These designs continued throughout their leather sheathes, their gold and steel chainmail, and even their tattoos. They all had purple tattoos covering their arms, necks, and faces. Even Fen was so heavily inked that sections of the Viking's skin were entirely purple instead of the underlying blue. Timp started to ask what the tattoos meant when—

"Back! Back, cruel giant. Back, I say. Release us from this prison, or suffer my wrath!" Again, Erika threw her spear into Timp's nose.

"Yeow! What's up with you and noses?"

Bjorn rolled his eyes and sighed, "Ye left Uncle Dene."

"Who?" It hadn't occurred to Timp that there might be *more* Vikings wandering the kitchen. He heard the hallway creak under his father's footsteps. He snapped the matchbox shut and hid it behind his back. The Vikings cursed and vowed.

As the door opened, Timp crossed his eyes and realized Erika's spear still wobbled at the tip of his nose. He yanked it out and hid it behind his back just as his father's head poked in with a knock.

"I thought you might be up," Mr. Littleton said with a wink.

The Vikings shouted muffled curses at Timp's back. He gave the box a shake, but that only made the Vikings curse louder. His father didn't seem to notice.

"Brought you some ice cream."

Mr. Littleton held up a plastic bowl shaped like an upside down baseball hat. Timp's family collected these bowls whenever they saw the Shreveport Crawbats play. Mr. Littleton took them out only for special occasions. That, along with Timp's ravenous hunger, caused him to forget about the Vikings and focus solely on the chocolate-chunk ice cream before him. He thanked his father with a mouth full of chunk and a matchbox filled with Vikings still cursing at his back.

"How you doing, kiddo?"

At first, Timp didn't know what his father was talking about. So much had happened since dinner that he'd almost forgotten about their argument or that he was supposed to be angry. Timp tried to scrounge up some residual fury about child labor laws, vacation hours, and summer heat, but his mind went back to the giant bowl of chocolate-chunk, dripping with fudge syrup—his father fought dirty. Then again, compared to the Viking brigade trapped in Timp's matchbox, his friends in Colorado suddenly seemed boring. For the first time in his life, Timp *wanted* to stay on the family farm, if only to learn more about his new friends . . . or enemies . . . Timp wasn't sure which they were yet. Curses rose from the matchbox. *Enemies* seemed the most accurate at the moment.

Mr. Littleton sat on the bed next to Timp and the room leaned. The matchbox threatened to slide from hiding, so Timp twisted his back to hold it in place.

"I know you're upset about this summer, but I promise I'll make it up to you," Mr. Littleton began.

"I don't mind, really," Timp said as he contorted his body some more to keep the matchbox hidden. "I was mad, but now

I'm okay." He hoped a quick response would hurry his father out of the room. The sound of an axe chopping against cardboard was making him nervous. The last thing he wanted was a bunch of angry Vikings getting loose and throwing spears at his father's nose.

Mr. Littleton stretched and made himself comfortable. This conversation wasn't over. "The thing is, Timp. We *all* have to work really hard this summer."

"Why? Are we in trouble?"

"Trouble? No. No. No. No." Timp felt that was too many 'no's to be true. "Just that ol' drought. Gotta catch up, that's all. But the berries are in now, and we've got our workers."

Timp's father was a terrible liar, a trait Timp had inherited and easily recognized. When they lied, their voices went falsetto, and their hairlines crawled so far back that they twitched. Being a terrible liar would make life tough for anyone, but for a boy living alone on a farm with his parents, it was misery.

"Does this have anything to do with the man in the limousine?" Timp asked.

"Him? Oh, no. No. No. No. That was no one, er, that is, just someone I know. He stopped to visit and buy some berries. He's helping us with some business."

"What kind of business? Are we selling the farm?" Timp tried to hide his excitement. He'd wanted to leave the farm for as long as he could remember. He hated getting up at five every

44

morning to work in the hot sun all day. He hated not having any other kids for at least 10 miles. He'd always dreamed of living in the city with kids all around (maybe even one next door). And a gas station nearby with Dr. Pepper Icees. *Yeah, that'd be living.* But what about the Vikings? Timp still knew nothing about them, but he was sure this farm was the only place they existed. Maybe he could take them along. Yeah, that'd work. Even Timp had to admit that didn't sound right.

"Sell the farm? No. No. Don't worry. We're not selling the farm." Mr. Littleton laughed, misinterpreting Timp's excitement for fear. "Mr. DeLaney—erm—that is, the man you saw in the limo today—"

Timp explained that he hadn't actually *seen* the man in the limo, but only smelled him—rotten cigars, like a port-a-potty—

"Anyway," his father jumped back in. "Mr. DeLaney had some business near here and decided to stop by. He's helping us out. Like I said, I know him."

"And mom isn't going shopping?"

"No," his father answered, awaking from his thoughts. He peered over his glasses at Timp. "No one is going shopping, not for a long time. You should apologize to her. You can't just accuse people of things when you don't know what's happening, and you shouldn't eavesdrop."

Timp's cheeks flushed and he hoped to change the subject.

"But everything is okay?"

"Of course. Everything's fine. Just grownup stuff."

Timp groaned, and Mr. Littleton smiled as he collected Timp's empty ice cream bowl and stood. "You said it, kid."

Kid? Humph! Timp was a giant—at least, according to the Vikings. *The Vikings!* Timp checked for the matchbox behind his back. Still there. Mr. Littleton paused at the door and turned. Timp threw his hands onto his lap and sat up straight.

"There aren't any matches in that box are there, son?"

How did he know? He always knew! Mr. Littleton smiled.

"Nope," Timp said, bringing the box around. "No matches."

He wasn't lying. There weren't *matches* inside. His father hadn't asked if the box held a raging group of tiny blue Vikings hellbent on slaying ice giants. He hadn't ask *that*.

Mr. Littleton held out his hand to receive the matchbox, and Timp's heart leapt into his throat. The jig was up. Timp didn't know why he wanted to keep the Vikings a secret; he just felt he should. But all that was over now. Timp placed the matchbox in his father's hand and waited. Mr. Littleton would open the box, see the Vikings—probably get a spear in the nose— and that'd be it. Maybe he'd faint. Maybe he'd yell. Maybe he'd scream, throw the box down, and stomp on it until the box oozed purple. Timp swallowed. This could get messy.

But Mr. Littleton didn't open the matchbox. Instead, he held it to his ear and shook it. Hard. Even from several feet away,

Timp heard the Vikings scream words that he was forbidden to say (or even think). He blushed and prepared to explain, but Mr. Littleton wasn't listening for Viking oaths. He was listening for matches. Satisfied there were none, he handed the box back to Timp, and turned his attention to the TV. "You should probably turn that off for the night," he said. "It doesn't sound like a show meant for children's ears."

Timp couldn't believe his luck. His father didn't know the TV was on mute! He jumped up and switched it off. Satisfied, his father said goodnight and left Timp alone with his matchbox full of murderous Vikings. *Lucky day!* Timp sat the box on the nightstand and was sliding it open when his father stuck his head back through the door.

"One more thing," Mr. Littleton said. Timp almost jumped out of his skin. "I've got to run to the bank tomorrow. Get along with your mother while I'm gone, okay?" He gave Timp a wink and shut the door.

Timp collapsed onto his bed with the box of Vikings still on the nightstand. How could something so small cause so much trouble?

But Timp's troubles had just begun . . .

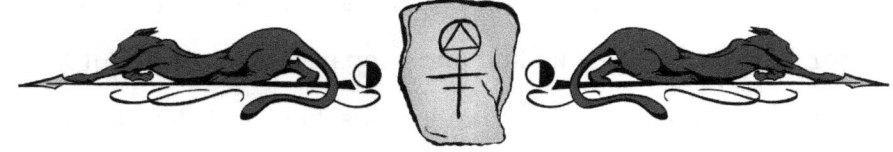

CHAPTER 7
MRS. MOLLY'S BIG BAD INCIDENT

Before the Vikings arrived, the only excitement in the Littleton household was Mrs. Molly's Big Bad Incident. Mrs. Molly was an indoor/outdoor cat, which is to say she still had her front claws and could come and go as she pleased. And that was exactly how Molly liked things: as she pleased.

On hot days, she stayed inside and watched the nature channel. When it was cool out, she ventured into the yard to hunt. Oh sure, Queen Molly enjoyed being spoon fed catnip-covered delicacies as well as any cat, but occasionally it was necessary for a queen to demonstrate dominance over the creatures in her realm . . . by killing them.

Most of Molly's hunting centered around Mrs. Littleton's bird feeder. Molly would crouch into her kitty-cat ninja pose (instantly becoming invisible to all prey).

"It's cat magic. Don't question it. Who am I talking to?"

Then she'd wait for a plump, well-fed bird to land in the grass. Molly learned long ago that fat birds take off slower than skinny ones and are therefore easier to catch. It never occurred to the ferocious feline that hunting slow, chubby birds near their feeder might be unsportsmanlike. She just fancied herself an outstanding huntress.

She'd remain hidden until a bird was distracted by a beak full of birdseed.

"*On the count of three: One.*" She'd wiggle her butt.

"*Two.*" Her back legs would shake with excitement, and her hackles would rise.

"*And Thr—*" Bang!

Mrs. Littleton would slap the kitchen window and the birds would all fly away, leaving Molly grasping in futility at empty air.

"*Stupid, rotten, no good, clumsy chambermaid!*" Molly cursed.

"You know better than that," Mrs. Littleton would shout through the kitchen window.

"*I?—Wha!—How dare you disturb my royal games! I am a huntress, wild and free, queen of all I survey. You are a . . . a stupid chambermaid! Go clean my box, chambermaid!*" But as usual, all Mrs. Littleton heard was "Meow. Meow," and of course, "Meow."

It was infuriating living with humans.

It happened the same way every time. If Mrs. Littleton was home, the best thing Molly could hope to catch was Zs. So, on the day of "Mrs. Molly's Big Bad Incident," Molly didn't bother going out at all. Instead, she lay inside, basking in the cool air and watching a nature documentary about that very delicious dinner topic: birds.

She had just finished watching a show called *Birds of Prey*, which Molly found wildly humorous. All birds were prey, she didn't need a show to tell her that, but this show focused on birds as *hunters*. The mere thought sent Molly into fits of giggles and purrs. She imagined the stupid, fat birds she chased around the feeder calling themselves "predators." *As if!*

Molly rolled onto her back with laughter as hawks chased rodents across the screen. She laughed harder still when the title of the next show appeared: *Whacky Birds.* What a ridiculous title. All birds were whacky too. "*Birds are whacky, stupid, fat, slow, and delicious—mmm, so delicious. Humans sure do like to point out the obvious. But then, they do have very slow brains.*"

Molly stretched into a more comfortable position and prepared to keep the laughs coming, but what Molly saw next didn't make her laugh, not at all.

Molly stared at the television in awe-struck horror. Her pupils dilated, and her hackles rose. The phantasmagoria that flashed the screen was so disturbing, so sickening, so absolutely hideously outrageous that Molly couldn't turn away. Her chambermaid, Mrs. Littleton, stood in the kitchen packing berries into salable containers, unfazed by the atrocities on the TV. Molly rolled onto the remote and turned up the volume. *This must be some kind of trick,* she thought, knowing it wasn't. *It's a lie. It has to be a lie.* But it wasn't that, either. *How can this be?* There, on the screen in ultra high-definition clarity, a grey bird sat perched on a woman's arm . . . talking.

The woman wore a safari outfit, and the bird was something called a "*Par-Rot.*" She asked the parrot questions — which did not surprise Molly at all. Humans talked to everything. Molly'd seen the Littletons talk to dogs, pigs, chickens, and even plants. *Plants!* But none of those things ever talked back, at least not in that vulgar human-speak, but this bird did! The questions were simple. Molly easily answered each in her head, but when the *parrot* responded the crowd cheered. They cheered! *It was absolutely absurd!* It was bad enough that her dinner could fly when she could not, but now it could talk to humans too? *That's crossing a line.*

Molly thought about all the times she'd growled orders to her servants only to have them ignored. Their simple servant brains couldn't understand the exquisite language of Cat's Meow. She'd order them to open the sliding glass door, and they'd stand there, threatening to close it again. Their idiot brains couldn't understand that she wanted the doors left open, and Molly's sweet kitty-cat voice was far too delicate to tell them so in that horrid human-speak. When she tried, her stupid servants never understood. They just heard meows, closed the door, and she had to start the whole process over again. It was maddening.

Molly thought about all the times Mrs. Littleton had scared away her dinner. Her dinner, which according to the TV, could talk! Molly was a cat, queen of the world, top of the food chain, master of all, servant to none. If anyone should be able to speak to her chambermaid, it should be her, not her dinner!

Molly looked to Mrs. Littleton for reassurance, but the chambermaid continued cleaning berries, humming, and bobbing her head unrhythmically. She seemed unimpressed by the discovery of talking birds. How could she be so nonchalant about this discovery, unless . . . she already knew—Molly's eyes narrowed and her lip curled. *Traitors!*

She kneaded the couch with her claws while she contemplated the ramifications of this treachery.

"No, Molly, not on the furniture. Use your scratcher," Mrs. Littleton said. She grabbed a spray bottle filled with water and fired it at Molly.

"Wha—How dare you!"

That was the last straw. Mrs. Molly House Wrecker went nuts—or, as Gunnar would say, "berserk."

She sprang from the couch, spitting and hissing with her claws flying. She gnawed and scratched at the pillows until the air filled with cotton and down.

"Molly! What's gotten into you?"

Molly wanted to scream back so many profane things, but she couldn't. She couldn't, but a bird could! *Ahhhhh!* It was enough to drive a cat mad, and it did.

Mrs. Littleton chased Molly as she jumped from couch to bookshelf, to coffee table, to china cabinet, to the couch again. The room crumbled in a shower of books, movies, vases, plates, and glassware. When Molly finally stopped to catch her breath, glass and ceramic littered the floor, a goldfish flopped on the carpet, and Mrs. Littleton scrambled to scoop it into a glass of water.

Goldfish saved, Mrs. Littleton armed herself with a broom and opened the sliding glass door. She had it in mind to sweep Molly outside, but the ferocious beast had other plans. Molly jumped onto the stand where the flat-screen TV stood precariously on its base.

"Don't you dare," Mrs. Littleton warned. She did not speak Cat's Meow, but even a simple-minded, cat-serving human could tell what Molly was thinking.

Mrs. Littleton eased toward the cat-turned-ticking-time-bomb and tried to position the broom between Molly and the TV.

"Is it the green wire or the red, maid?"

The broom had just touched Molly's fur, when the TV host announced, "And now, a singing and dancing number by that special little group of feathered friends: The Perfect Paulies."

A curtain opened to four parrots singing and dancing. The audience stood and cheered, Oohed and Ahhed.

"Nothing but garbage on TV these days, absolute filth." Molly pushed her weight against the TV.

After that, Mrs. Molly TV Smasher was demoted from indoor/outdoor cat to just plain outdoor cat, a decision that saved the last of the Littleton's fine china, but changed the course of their lives forever. After all, had Molly been *inside* on the night Timp met the Vikings, that meeting never would have taken place. But then again, had Molly *not* been *outside* to investigate the carport noise, she wouldn't have suffered such a cruel and horrible fate.

Poor Molly.

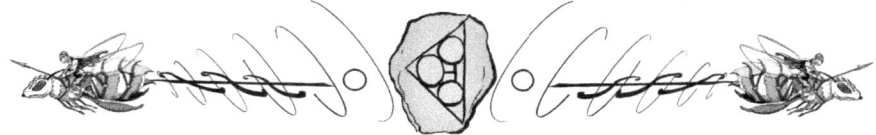

CHAPTER 8

CIRCLE CIRCLE DOT DOT,
NOW YOU HAVE YOUR VIKING SHOT

"Move it!" "Ouch!" "This be my side." "I twas here first."

"Will you guys shut up?" Timp said, as he dropped a handful of berries into a bucket strapped to his hip and reached for more. "You're driving me crazy."

Two farmhands stopped picking and watched Timp with fists full of berries and eyebrows raised. Timp moved further down the row.

It was a typical summer morning, and as usual, Timp was picking berries. But unlike other mornings, that day Timp's hair and ears were full of angry Vikings.

"I can't believe I let y'all talk me into this," he said when he was out of earshot of the other workers.

He'd spent several hours the night before pleading and promising to get the Vikings to forgive him. After eating Bjorn's house, stuffing the Vikings into a box, and shaking them like maracas, they took some convincing. Timp promised to find their houses—well not Bjorn's house, Timp had swallowed Bjorn's house, but he promised to replace that one, and find the others. And he promised to find Uncle Dene—whoever that was. He vowed on bended knee to carry the houses back to their village, which he imagined was probably a bowl of berries in the freezer or something. And as always, he swore not to eat anyone . . . on purpose—again, they were just so tiny, and accidents happen all the time. Satisfied with his promises, the Vikings agreed to a temporary truce and built camp on his nightstand. Erika stood guard with spear in hand.

That morning, Timp had rolled out of bed before the sun came up. The Vikings snored in a circle. Even Erika snoozed: propped up on her spear and probably dreaming of slaying giants. The Vikings almost passed for sweet when they were asleep. It was a shame they had to wake up. Timp dressed quietly to avoid disturbing them. He planned to do his chores, then return to fulfill his list of promises. The Vikings had other plans.

"Just where do ye think you're going, Jötunn?"

Timp suspected Erika may have been playing possum. He explained that he had chores to do. "And what of your vows to us?"

The other Vikings began to stir and arm themselves. *So much for sweet and asleep.*

"Aye, ye gave your'n word," Gunnar said as he began to hop up and down, slap himself, and make Three-Stooges noises.

56

Timp rolled his eyes. "Does he always have to do that?"

"Calm your'n self, Gunnar," Bjorn said.

"Aye, let us give him chance to explain," Fen added.

"Or better still, we kill him for a sneak and an oath breaker!" Erika pointed her spear at Timp's nose.

"Hold it. Hold it," Timp pleaded. His nose had suffered enough. "I have to pick." The Vikings stared at Timp in blank incomprehension. Erika drew back her weapon. "No! No! Listen. I, um, I have prior oaths, or vows that I am obligated to thus hither to go forth and what have you." *Speaking Viking is tough!* "Anyway, when I'm done I'll come back and help you find your uncle and your houses, okay?"

The Vikings eyed Timp suspiciously. Bjorn broke the silence. "There is honor in what ye say; though, not so in the way you say it. If you are sworn to duty, then duty you must."

"Hehe 'duty,'" O'dul giggled.

"Right. So, I'll do my chores then come right back. I mean, it's not like I can take you with me." Timp laughed at the absurdity of the notion, but stopped when he saw the Vikings' eyes light up. "Oh, no. No. That's a terrible idea. No way. I'm putting my foot down on that. Nope. Not going to happen. Absolutely not. No way. No. No. No. No!"

And that was how Timp ended up with his hair and ears full of angry, ant-sized Vikings. "Get off me foot!" "Nay, ye get off mine." They refused to get back into the matchbox. (The mere mention of it made Fen cry, Gunnar slap himself, and Erika grab her spear). They feared getting squished in his pocket. So they insisted his hair and ears were the best option. They could move his hair to hide as needed, and they were close enough that Timp could hear them speak—a feature Timp already learned to hate.

Timp groaned as he wiped sweat from his brow and checked his watch. It was only 9 a.m., yet already 95 degrees. Every breath filled his nostrils with the sweet scent of baked grass and burning skin. The heat was his torture and his salvation. In two or three more hours the berries would become too hot and soft to pick, and he'd get to break for lunch. Even his cruel child-laboring parents couldn't defy physics. A hot berry was a soft berry, and you can't pick soft berries. It was a cruel irony of the summer fruit that Timp loved, but also the reason the Littletons were so far behind that season.

Unfortunately, escaping the heat didn't mean escaping work. After lunch, the Littletons washed and sorted berries, baked pies, made jam, vinified wine, packaged berries, printed labels, stuck labels, stacked labels, labeled stacks of labels—Timp spent a lot of time with labels. Farm life was the pits.

"Yeow! Back, you." "'Tis my side of the giant's stupid head."

"Nay, twas I here first." "Nay, twas me truly." *Just three more hours,* Timp told himself. *Three long, torturous hours.*

It felt odd having Vikings wiggling around in his ears. It took all of his will not to dig them out. Erika had anticipated the temptation. She warned Timp that her spear was pointed soundly at his eardrum, ready to stab at the slightest provocation. The thought not only scared him enough to keep his fingers wax free, but he also adopted a new way of walking. Timp glided through the orchard in long even strides with his head perfectly level, as though balancing an invisible glass of water. Farmhands snickered and whispered as Timp slid by. No doubt, he looked silly, but at least his eardrum was safe . . . for now.

"Hey, Giant, what's that?" Fen shouted as the old water tower came into view.

Timp's ear rang with Fen's voice.

"A water tower. And you don't have to shout. You're in my ear. I can hear you fine." Timp had explained this several times and was beginning to suspect the Vikings enjoyed causing him pain. *Surely not.*

Fen leaned out of Timp's ear and shouted, "Oi, guys? Don't! Yell! Up! There!" Timp jumped at each word.

O'dul and Bjorn stuck their heads out of Timp's hair, "Aye?"

"I! Say! 'Don't! Yell!'"

"Oh, for Pete's sake." Timp cringed.

"Giant claims he hears us fine!" Fen continued.

Gunnar, who was in Timp's opposite ear, shouted back, "What? Forget me not! Why must I be over here all by mine's lonesome?"

"Because ye stink!" Erika shouted back.

Timp knew Gunnar was about to go berserk, and he didn't even want to imagine how loud that'd be. "Stop it! Y'all stop it!"

The Vikings giggled with delight.

"I were only trying to help," Fen mumbled.

"I bet."

"Steady on, Giant!" Erika shouted as Timp stumbled over a loose rock.

He regained his footing only to stumble again. The Vikings shouted a mélange of threats.

"Take care, you!"

"Aye, Bjorn, grab yer horn. Summon a swarm of killer bees upon this Jötunn," Erika barked.

But Bjorn didn't blow a horn. Instead, he reasoned. "Twas a slip, friends, an honest mistake. Be easy."

Erika grumbled.

Timp was grateful to Bjorn for saving his hearing; though, he doubted that a bunch of Vikings who could barely draw their weapons without dropping them could summon bees with a horn. Timp hated that they'd piqued his interest. "What's this about bees?"

"Killer Bees," Gunnar corrected from his other ear.

"Okay, what's this about *killer* bees?" Timp repeated, making sure to stress the word "killer" while shaking his hands in the air.

"Mess with uses and finds out, Jötunn."

Timp sighed. He was learning to expect this kind of response from the Vikings.

"Who ya talking to?" This voice didn't come from inside of Timp's ears.

He turned around to find his mother standing behind him. How long had she been there? What had she heard?

"Speak of us and suffer mine spear," Erika warned.

Timp could almost feel the blade poking into his eardrum. He cringed and wobbled his head to the side while his mother watched him with raised eyebrows. He tried to relax.

"Uh, no one. I wasn't talking to anyone," he said, and then added, "I was attacked by a bee."

"A *killer* bee," O'dul corrected.

"Shut up," Timp whispered, hoping his mother didn't hear.

She was too distracted to notice. "Oh. I thought maybe you were talking to Molly. Have you seen her around?"

"No, I haven't seen her all day," Timp said, realizing it was true.

Every morning since Mrs. Molly's Big Bad Incident, the determined cat met Timp on the porch to battle her way inside.

Sometimes she dove for his legs; sometimes she waited next to the door to sneak in as soon as it opened; once, Timp was almost certain she'd swung down from the ceiling. Usually, Timp was ready for her with shin guards, a helmet, and a broom, but that morning he'd been so distracted by the tiny blue tenants taking up residence in his ears that he didn't even notice Molly was missing. *Weird.*

Timp's mother frowned. He could tell she was thinking of places the cat might be so he tried to come up with places too. *The stable? Underneath the house? The carport?* He concentrated so hard that he didn't notice the Vikings snickering in his ears.

"Well, let me know if you see her," Mrs. Littleton said as she checked under the bushes one more time and turned away.

When she was gone, the Vikings' snickers erupted into laughter.

"What's so funny?" Timp asked.

"Aw, is your'n poor li'l guard-beast missing?" Gunnar said.

"Guard-beast? What are you talking about?"

"Ye know well what we mean, Giant," Erika said. "As ye stole our'n houses, ye put out yon beast to guard your'n ice cave. All part of yer plan to protect your'n giant's treasure, no doubt."

"That's ridiculous," Timp said.

"May not we all just get along," Fen pleaded.

"Nay, not with this Jötunn! Do ye think it a coincidence, Fen? Guard-beast 'tis put out and village plundered? I like it not."

There was that word was again, "Jötunn." Timp knew by Erika's tone that it wasn't something nice. He'd have to ask what it meant when she wasn't so angry—or at least, when she wasn't holding her spear.

"Be at peace, Erika. The giant hath given us truce."

"Truce? Bjorn, he ate your'n house!"

Timp could tell he wasn't going to win Erika over with his winning smile, but he couldn't argue her point either. He had eaten Bjorn's house.

"The hilmir would spit if he learned of this truce. I say we have our'n vengeance here and now!"

"Aye!" Gunnar agreed and began barking like a dog in Timp's other ear.

Timp was starting to feel dizzy from all the shouting, and he was pretty sure he could feel Erika's spear pressing against his eardrum. "Okay. Okay. Everyone just calm down." The Vikings settled and Timp took a deep breath. "Now, let's back up. What 'guard-beast'?"

"Aye, 'what guard-beast?'" Gunnar mocked. "What giant, vicious, drooling beasts with teeth that could impale mine's house, and claws long enough to tear through villages? Aye, what guard-beast set outside to protect House Mountain, indeed."

"Molly?" Timp laughed. "That's our pet cat—"

"Pet? Humph! Just the type of foul beast a disgusting giant would claim as a pet!"

"Be calm, Erika."

"Besides, yon beast won't be bothering us no more," O'dul chuckled.

"Shut it, O'dul!" the Vikings shouted at once.

"No. No. No. Don't shut it, O'dul. What do you mean? Why won't Molly be bothering you?" The Vikings chortled. A frightening realization began to form in the back of Timp's mind. "What did you do to my cat?" No answer. "Now, you listen here, you little—"

"Timp? Are you all right?"

Timp turned to find his father standing behind him, first his mom, now his dad. This farm was getting way too crowded. "What's a kid gotta do to get some privacy around this joint? Geez!"

Timp's eyes went wide. Had he said that out loud?

Mr. Littleton looked up at the hot sun beaming down and then back at Timp. "Maybe you should go inside and get a hat," he said, then added, "and some water. Timp, get a lot of water."

The Vikings oohed the way kids in class do when an evil teacher sends some one to stand in the corner. Timp guessed some things were cross-cultural.

"Oi, yon giant be even more gianter than ye, Giant," O'dul said of Timp's father.

"Thank thee, iViking Captain Obvious," Erika said.

Her tone was so heavily laden with sardonic loathing that Timp had to laugh when O'dul responded in earnest, "Ye're most welcome. Hear that, Bjorn? I been promoted to captain."

The Vikings groaned. It comforted Timp that they were as cruel to each other as they were to him.

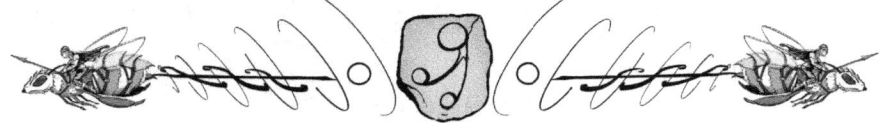

CHAPTER 9

HOUSE HUNTING? IN THIS MARKET?

Timp went into the house to get a hat and some water—okay, a lot of water. With everyone working outside, the kitchen was empty.

"Now be our chance," Gunnar whispered in Timp's ear.

"Our chance for what?" Timp whispered back. (He had no idea why they were whispering).

Erika didn't whisper. "To fulfill your'n promise, Jötunn!" She leaned out and stabbed Timp's earlobe.

"Yeow! Erika, I swear, if you stab me one more time, I'll—"

"Ye shall what, Giant? Ye shall what?"

"Ouch! Ouch! Ouch!" Timp flailed his arms as Erika stabbed his earlobe again and again.

"Erika, please," Bjorn said as the other Vikings fought to contain their mirth.

Erika stopped and muttered curses under her breath. Timp was glad Bjorn was there. He seemed to be the only person Erika would listen to.

"But they speak true, Giant," Bjorn said. "With the other giants away from House Mountain, now be the time to seek our'n homes, aye, but more importantly, to seek Uncle Dene."

Timp had forgotten about their uncle. He'd seen enough crime shows to know that the first 24 hours were crucial for tracking a missing person. He checked the oven clock. He could probably hole-up in the house for 30 minutes before his parents noticed him missing from the orchard, but 30 minutes wasn't much time to find a blue needle in blueberry haystack. They had to move fast.

"Okay," he said, "you find your uncle. I'll find the houses." The Vikings cheered their approval, and Timp smiled. It felt good to have them working with him, instead of against him. Timp soon learned the two were oddly similar.

The Vikings had tried to be discreet the night before. They went about the kitchen without disturbing anything or making any noise. They no longer felt that level of care was necessary.

As soon as Timp placed them on the counter, the Vikings ran, screaming war cries and waving their weapons as if raiding a small village. They jumped onto spoons that sent berries flying and bowls tipping over. They leapt onto the curtains, stabbed their knives through the fabric, and slid down the way pirates descend sails in movies.

If Uncle Dene was nearby, this search party would sooner kill him than save him. Gunnar slapped himself, shook his head back and fourth, and ran around in circles while spouting a string of gibberish. Timp still didn't see the benefit of going berserk, but it seemed to make Gunnar happy. Erika unscrewed the caps from the salt and pepper shakers and stabbed her spear deep inside. When she didn't hear Uncle Dene cry out, she knocked the shakers over, and search on. O'dul ripped open a packet of sweetener, shoved his head inside, and called Uncle Dene's name. When no one replied, he threw the packet to the side, grabbed another from the tray, and started again. Fen stood on the counter, sneezing from the pepper kicked into his nose by Erika, and Bjorn spun around and around on the spice rack, flinging spices across the kitchen. Timp wasn't sure if Bjorn was searching for Uncle Dene or just having fun. It did look fun.

"Come, Giant, the day grows shorter," Bjorn shouted.

The Vikings' excitement was infectious, but there was something Timp needed before he could join the hunt. He ran to his bedroom while the Vikings busied themselves with destroying the kitchen and grabbed his magnifying glass from his nightstand. Now he could distinguish house from berry. He started back when it occurred to him that he could search faster if he used both hands.

He found a scratched up pair of sunglasses buried deep in his closet and pulled some wire from the back of an old picture frame. He popped the right lens out of the glasses and wired the magnifying glass to the frame. He looked like a mad scientist, but it worked—magnification monocle. *Awesome.*

Timp fumbled into the kitchen and was met by Viking screams. "Ah, a Cyclops!"

"Not this again."

The Vikings ran and hid. Well, not Erika. She charged to the edge of the counter with her spear held high and her smile bright with battle lust. Timp lifted his glasses. "It's me."

"Oh. *You.*" Erika lowered her spear in disappointment.

The Vikings resumed destroying the kitchen while Timp buried his head in a pile of berries. They all looked alike. How would he know which were berries and which were houses? They *tasted* different, he knew that, but did they *look* different? He imagined the houses at least had doors and windows, so he searched for those features.

Through his homemade magnifying monocle, Timp analyzed each berry as though it was his first time seeing one. He made two piles on the counter: one for berries that were really berries and one for berries that were actually houses. So far, the pile for berries that were actually houses was marked by a blank spot on the floor (by then, the only clean space in the entire kitchen).

The peripheral world blurred as Timp focused on each magnified berry. Sounds faded to a steady hum of Viking destruction: berries flew into the air and bounced off the walls;

the ice machine gurgled and spit frozen cubes onto the floor; the faucet fired a steady stream of water until the sink overflowed; the blender wobbled in circles while the Vikings rode it across the counter like an enormous bull; and the radio blared music from a hundred different stations as Vikings ran on the tuner like hamsters on wheel; but Timp heard none these things. Engrossed in his search for berry Viking houses, he didn't even hear the backdoor swing open and close.

Timp held up fistfuls of berries and scanned them with his magnifying monocle. If a hand came up house free, he threw the berries over his shoulder and grabbed another batch. Then he saw something—a berry slightly larger than average with several holes hollowed into the side. He singled out that berry and threw away the rest. Somewhere, in the distant fog of Timp's mind, he heard the water faucet shut off, the ice machine stop gurgling, the radio crackle to silence, and the blender stop spinning. As he pored over the berry and wondered if the holes might just be bug bites. Two dark, blurry blobs formed at the top of his vision. He adjusted his magnification monocle and . . . Yes! He could see it. The holes were windows, and there, a door!

"I found one!" Timp shouted with his excitement magnified 30 times in his right eye. He held the blueberry high for all to see, but where he expected cheers, he found silence.

Timp scanned the kitchen with his enormous eye wobbling in circles. The world was a blur beyond a few inches.

Two black blocks moved. From the floor, they almost resembled two angry giants—those Vikings were really getting into his head. He twisted his magnifying glass.

"Did you hear me? I found one." Where were they? (It never occurred to Timp to open his left eye. That'd be too easy).

Then an angry blur spoke, "Timp, what the devil—"

"Ah!" Timp screamed as he sprang to his feet, sending berries and an enormous, magnified eye flying toward his parents.

"Ah!" Timp's mother screamed as she jumped back, slipped on some ice, and grabbed Mr. Littleton's sleeve for balance.

"Ah!" Mr. Littleton screamed as he and Mrs. Littleton splashed onto the cold, wet floor.

"Ah!" The Vikings screamed, partly because they felt left out, but also because it was terrifying to see so many clumsy giants screaming and falling all over the place. (Thankfully, Timp's parents were too busy flopping on the floor to hear).

Timp yanked off his magnification monocle and scanned the room. His parents sat on the kitchen floor. For a moment, he saw the situation through their eyes: the kitchen in ruins, the sink overflowing, the floor soaked, the counter covered with salt and pepper, spices, sweetener, and berries, and their son with a magnifying glass wired to his head and holding up a blueberry and shouting like he'd just won first prize at the state fair. Timp couldn't explain himself so he said the only thing that came to mind, "What's a kid gotta do to get some privacy around this joint? Geez!"

Mr. and Mrs. Littleton stared at him with their mouths agape and berries squished to the seat of their pants.

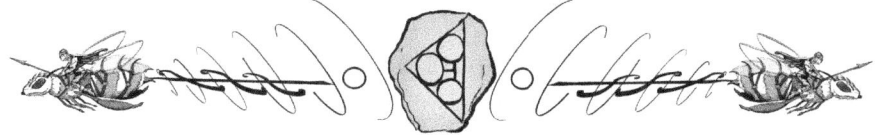

CHAPTER 10
THE MAN WITH A REALLY LONG NAME

Timp spent the next several hours cleaning the demolition zone that had once been a kitchen. *How could such tiny creatures make such a big mess?* His parents had been remarkably calm about the ordeal, but parents are always calm when you expect them to explode, and they always explode when you expect them to be calm. Parents are annoying like that.

After changing into dry clothes and cooling off, Timp's mother ventured outside to resume her search for Molly. Timp's father showered and dressed for his trip to the bank. He stepped out of his bedroom wearing his best suit, an ill-fitting JC Penny with a frayed collar. The Vikings had taken their places in Timp's hair and ears, and whistled catcalls.

"You about got it?" Mr. Littleton asked, checking his tie in the reflection of the microwave door.

"Yeah." Timp rang out a sponge of soapy water into a bucket.

He was too embarrassed to meet his father's eyes. He hoped things might return to normal now that the kitchen was clean, but he needed to be on his best behavior for the rest of the day . . . if not the rest of the year . . . or rest of his life. No sooner had this thought crossed Timp's mind, than a berry-shattering scream tore across the backyard. Timp and his father scrambled to the kitchen window to look outside. What they saw struck terror into the hearts of father and son alike: Timp's mother charged the house, shaking her fist over her head and gritting her teeth. Her face was red with fury. "Timp John Paul George Ringo Matheson Jr Esquire, you get out here this instant!"

"'Tis one angry giant," Fen said, and Timp heard him writing notes in his pad.

"Aye, she's gone berserk, that one," Gunnar said.

Even Timp's father had nothing helpful to say. "That was one long name."

"I know," Timp replied.

"She went through all of the Beatles."

"I know."

"And then some."

"I know."

"You must be in big trouble."

"I know."

"Like really big trouble. Huge."

"I know!"

Timp's stomach lurched and his legs felt weak. The last time his mother invented a name that long was three years before. Timp remembered it well. It was an honest mistake, could have happened to anyone, really. He still didn't see the problem, to be honest. What was the big deal? So he released a few venomous snakes into the house. Okay, a few hundred, but he did it with the best intentions. . . . He wanted to be a snake charmer. It made perfect sense. You don't just up and become a snake charmer on a whim—You have to practice. It takes practice. So, practice he did. His parents found him standing on the couch, playing a plastic recorder amidst a floor covered with copperheads, rattle snakes, and water moccasins. Timp had been collecting the snakes in buckets under the house for weeks. For the first time in Blueberry Springs history, there were more snakes *inside* than there were *outside*.

It took three pest-control workers five days and two ambulance rides to catch every snake. The Littletons camped in tents on the lawn, sweating through the hot summer nights until they finally cleared the house. Even then, Timp's mother didn't look as mad as she did now, her face not as red, her voice not as shrill.

Timp and his father swallowed the lumps in their throats. "What'd you do?" Mr. Littleton whispered.

"Aye, Giant, what'd ye do?"

"I don't know," Timp answered in earnest. He didn't know who was more frightened: him, his father, or the Vikings.

Mrs. Littleton kicked the door open with such force that Timp was sure it would fly off the hinges. He wanted to run, but his legs wouldn't move.

"What's wrong with you?" she shouted as she grabbed Timp by the collar.

"Brace your'n selves," the Vikings screamed. "Wild giant on the loose!"

Timp couldn't answer. His mother had not struck him since he could remember, but he was sure she was about to.

Timp's father stepped in and grabbed Mrs. Littleton just in time. "What's going on, sweetheart? What's wrong, angel?" He pleaded with pet names as if calling her these things would make her so, but the devil was an angel too.

"You!" She reached for Timp again. "Are you crazy or something?"

"Me?" Timp shook his head in baffled desperation. What'd he do?

"Oh, my God," she gasped, as if struck by a sudden realization. "You *are* crazy. This is how it starts. I saw it on Oprah."

"What?" Timp's father begged. "How what starts? Wha'd you see on Oprah? What'd Oprah tell you, baby! What'd she say?"

"Come see what your son did!" Then she glared into Timp's eyes and gritted her teeth. "Both of you."

His mother stormed out of the house.

"Follow not, Giant. 'Tis a trap."

Timp didn't want to go—

"Come on!"

—but he had no choice.

Mrs. Littleton stomped across the lawn with brisk determination. She didn't look back, didn't slow down, and didn't speak. Timp and his father almost had to jog to keep up.

Meanwhile, the Vikings prattled out theories about what Timp might have done. "I'll wager he's left his sword in the rain and allowed it to rust," one said. "Nay, he's gone and lost him's helm, to a certain. Ye see he don't wear one," another said. "Nay, He's sunk their battleship." "Or burned their'n crops." "Or ate him's neighbors." "Or perhaps he's forgot the Hokey Pokey—"

The Vikings paused. "O'dul, what in Thor's name are you on about?"

"The Hokey Pokey," O'dul said. "The giant's music box in yon kitchen claimed the Hokey Pokey be what 'tis all about."

"What what's about?" Fen asked, jotting the discovery into his notebook.

"Everything," O'dul said with complete confidence. "'Tis all about yon Hokey Pokey."

"O'dul, ye be dumber than a bag o' rocks."

"Thanks," O'dul smiled. He liked rocks and had quite the collection . . . or so he told Timp every chance he got.

Timp's mother stopped when she reached the barn. "That! That's what he's done."

Her finger pointed into the open barn door. Timp and his father saw nothing out of the ordinary. They shrugged at each other in puzzlement.

But the Vikings weren't puzzled.

"Oh, that's all this be about?" Gunnar said, sitting back down and relaxing in Timp's ear. "Here I thought twas something serious."

"Aye, like yon Hokey Pokey," O'dul added.

"Shut it, O'dummy."

The other Vikings snickered, and Timp suspected that they knew something he did not.

"What is it?" Timp's father asked, peaking through the barn door. He hesitated to go inside. He probably thought the barn was filled with venomous snakes, ready for charming. Timp knew he'd never live that one down.

"Go in," Timp's mother urged as she pushed Timp and his father through the door. "Go see what *your* son did."

Man, Timp *was* in trouble. Not only had she given him the longest made-up name in the history of made-up names, but now, she'd completely disowned him. Timp couldn't remember the last time she'd given his father the "*your* son" line. He didn't like where this was going. Not one bit.

Timp and his father stood in the center of the barn. The tractor was parked in the back among the other tools of the trade: pitchforks, axes, mauls, chicken wire, splints, wedges, buckets, crates, and boxes. Everything seemed in order. Timp's mother huffed, stomped her foot, and pointed up. They followed her finger to the ceiling. It took a moment for their eyes to adjust and even longer for their brains to comprehend exactly what it was they were seeing, but there, strung up by her paws and hanging from the rafters with a bag over her head was—
"Molly?"

"*Who's that? Who's there? Get this bag off my head. I demand you release me at once,*" Mrs. Molly cried from above. "*I'm far too pretty to be cat-bagged and burgled. I've been cat burgled. Ugh! That's my job. I'm the cat! Me!*" But, as usual, all the Littletons heard was a pleading "Meow. Meow," and of course, "Meow."

Molly wiggled with a bag over her head and her ample bottom up in the air and legs sticking up like a roasted turkey. She was uncomfortable but otherwise unharmed. The rope that bound her paws wrapped under and around her body in such a way that her weight was distributed as though she were resting in a makeshift hammock. It was a cruel and terrible thing to do to a cat, absolutely, but Mr. Littleton was a dog person. He stifled a laugh.

"Don't laugh! I found her up there like that!" Mrs. Littleton stomped. "Who knows how long she's been there!"

"I know," Gunnar said, and the other Vikings snickered.

"Why didn't you let her down?" Timp's father asked as he climbed the ladder to the hayloft.

Mrs. Littleton's jaw dropped. "Me?" She'd been so focused on her stomping tirade up the lawn that it hadn't occurred to her to let Molly down. She pointed to Timp. "Your son did this, not me!"

Timp's father stopped climbing to the hayloft and looked down. Timp wanted to deny everything. He wanted to explain that he hadn't made the mess in the kitchen. He hadn't put a bag over the cat's head, and he most certainly hadn't tied the cat to the barn rafters. No. It was a group of tiny blue men—and one vicious blue woman who liked to stab, stab, stab people in their noses. Yes, the tiny blue Vikings did this, not him. And that was where Timp's explanation fell apart. Every kid knows you just can't go around blaming things on tiny blue people who live inside your ears. That's a surefire way to spend the rest of your days bouncing around a padded cell in a straight jacket. So, Timp did the only thing he could; he took the blame.

"I, uh, I tied Molly up there like a piñata because I'm a . . . a real crazy person . . . who enjoys tying things to ceilings because it's . . . fun. Yep, I'm real nuts, just, you know, straight up insane. I probably need a hobby."

Timp was the worst liar in the history of liars, even worse than his father, but he didn't want to get locked away for good, and everyone knows that the best way to sound completely sane is to admit when you're acting crazy. At least then, it shows you're capable of recognizing crazy. Admitting you're insane is the sanest thing a crazy person can do. Therefore, calling himself crazy was proof positive that he wasn't. Timp searched for holes in his logic and found none. *Foolproof.*

"But why, Timp? Why would you do this?" his mother asked.

Timp had no answer. He was a good kid, not the sort of horrible, nasty kid who would string a cat up in the barn. He went to school with some of *those* kids, and he gave them wide berth when passing in the hall. Timp wondered what one of *those* kids might say now.

He grasped for a rational explanation of why someone might do this but found none. Luckily, the Vikings were there to help. "Tell her ye tamed the beast and freed your'n lands from the guard-beast's tyranny at long last."

"Shut up," Timp whispered.

Mrs. Littleton's jaw dropped and her eyes burned red with fury. "What did you just say to me?"

Maybe it was *unlucky* that the Vikings were there to help.

81

"Watch out below," Mr. Littleton called, lowering Molly between Timp and his mother.

Timp's mother clasped Molly as soon as the cat reached arm's length. She removed the bag from Molly's head and kissed her all over, stopping only to untangle Molly from the rest of the ropes and spit out cat hair.

"Poor, Mrs. Molly. Did that bad boy hurt you?" Timp's mother asked as she checked the cat all over for bruises and scratches. There were none.

"*Boy? No, it wasn't the stupid servant boy. It was somebody else. I didn't see who did it, but I heard them, the pests,*" Mrs. Molly growled. "*I'll get them, believe that. I know what they smell like. I'll hunt them down, and tear their hearts out. I'll—*"

"I know, baby. I know. He's a horrible, wicked boy, but you're safe now," Mrs. Littleton said, coddling Molly in her arms. Mrs. Littleton glowered at Timp in disgust, "You."

"*Yeah, you,*" Mrs. Molly repeated. "*You're fired. You're all fired. This never would have happened if you hadn't locked me out of my palace. I'll have your heads for this. I'll smother you in your sleep. I'll . . . I'll . . .*" But as usual, all the Littletons heard was "Meow, Meow," and of course, "Meow."

"I know. I know, Molly. Let's get you back inside. You've earned it."

Timp's mother left the barn and headed for the house.

"*Yeah, I earned it,*" Molly purred. "*I think I feel faint. I may have earned a delicious kitty-feast too, not that nasty dry food, but the fancy canned stuff. Yes, and maybe some catnip. Oh, and ice cream. Yes, catnip flavored ice cream. Bring this to me, chambermaid!*"

Timp's father rested his arm on Timp's shoulder as they watched Mrs. Littleton march up the lawn with Molly cradled in her arms. "You'd better come to the bank with me," he sighed. "It may not be safe for you here."

Timp thought he caught a glimpse of a smile on his father's face before Mr. Littleton turned away, but Timp wasn't off the hook yet.

"We going on an adventure, Giant?" Bjorn asked.

"I guess so," Timp said, and all of the Vikings cheered.

Well, almost all. "Hokey pokey? What'd I miss?" O'dul yawned, waking from a nap.

"Aye, fulls of rocks."

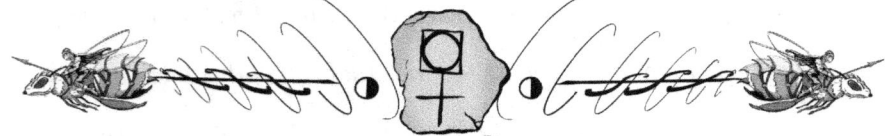

CHAPTER 11
TIMP AND THE VIKINGS GO TO HEL.

Mr. Littleton filled the 45-minute drive to Shreveport with lectures about animal rights and the importance of being humane. Timp limited his replies to a series of "yes sirs" and "no sirs," and tried to ignore the tittering Vikings in his ears. Considering what they'd done to the kitchen, Timp dreaded seeing what the Vikings might do in public, but so far they'd been shy around other giants. Maybe that would hold true at the bank as well. Surely the Vikings appreciated Timp taking the blame for Molly. Maybe they'd be friends from now on—Timp was blindly optimistic.

As the truck rattled into the city, the Vikings grew more and more excited. They shouted their amazement at skyscrapers that—by New Orleans standards—were small, but to the Vikings were towers that reached through the heavens to the Bifröst bridge of Asgard.

The Vikings stayed out of Mr. Littleton's sightline, but they didn't contain their excitement. Timp understood. In summers past, his family explored the city every weekend. They watched movies, saw live theatre, visited museums, and ate sushi. Timp's mother said it was important that Timp learn city smarts, as well as country smarts. She said the more he knew, the more he could do. And so, for Timp, the city meant opportunity and adventure. He often dreamed they'd move there. It pleased him that the Vikings felt the same.

As they watched buildings roll by, Timp wondered aloud why cities built out when they could so easily build up, up, up. He imagined it was due to laziness or fear of heights—Timp understood that well. But his father said it was cheaper to build out than up and then sighed. "But one day we'll stop measuring decisions in dollars and cents and start measuring them by right and wrong."

Sometimes Mr. Littleton sounded like he was reading from a fortune cookie.

Everything with adults revolved around money. His parents fought over money. He couldn't go to Colorado because of money and therefore had no friends because of money. Timp was beginning to hate money, and he told his father so.

"You and me both, kid," Mr. Littleton agreed as they pulled next to the tallest and darkest glass building on Louisiana Avenue: the Shreveport Bank and Trust.

Their footsteps echoed across the lobby's marble floor. The room was cold and quiet. The people, like the bank itself, were dressed in shades of gray. Timp checked his shirt to make sure he hadn't stepped into a black-and-white movie. No one smiled or spoke above a whisper. Even the Vikings were silent. It was as though the world's joy had been drained from this place. "Sit on that bench over there. I'll be there in a minute."

Timp did as he was told while his father walked to a squat faced receptionist pounding documents with a stamp. The Vikings leaned out of Timp's hair and ears to get a better view. "Oi, Giant. Be this Hel?"

"What?" Timp was sure he'd misheard. "Are you asking if this is Hell as in H-E-L-L—fire, brimstone, and Satan—that Hell?"

"Stupid giant can't even spell Hel," O'dul chided. "Dumber than a bag o' me rocks, that one."

"Aye, they truly be as stupid as legend," Erika agreed.

"For fact," Fen said, "Hel in giant culture be spelled with two Ls."

"Actually, my name's Fen, and I know everything about everything about giants 'cause I loves them so much. I wanna have big ol' giant babies," Gunnar mocked with a high-pitched voice.

"Shut it, Gunnar," Erika snapped.

It struck Timp as odd that Erika the heartless nose stabber of Asgard would stand up for Fen the sniveling giantologist, but before he could think much about it, Fen continued: "Understand, Giant, Hel—as in H-E-L, with but one L—is a place

86

where Vikings who've lived but ordinary lives go when they die. 'Tis a cold, dark place, empty of color and joy, where the spirit is trapped in a dreamlike trance devoid of feelings or adventures. 'Tis an empty hole for empty souls who lived empty lives, for all eternity."

Timp shook away a chill as he scanned the cold, gray lobby. "In that case, I believe this is Hel."

"What the Hel ye Vikings talking about?" O'dul asked.

"But do you have an appointment?" Timp overheard the receptionist ask his father.

"Well, no, but it's like I told you, DeLaney said—"

The receptionist scoffed. "Mr. DeLaney is the vice president of this bank. He is a very busy man. I will put your name down for Ms. Laurent. She'll call you whenever she's available. Wait on that bench over there." She stamped a document, and her words were final.

Mr. Littleton walked over and sat next to Timp with a groan. "Not the friendliest receptionist in the world," he said and then grunted as he adjusted his seat. "Not the most comfortable bench in the world either. Is it?" Timp didn't reply. The coldness impeded his speech. "It'll be a few minutes before they can see me. You're welcome to come with me, but it's going to be a lot of boring grown-up talk. You might want to wait here, but it's up to you."

"I'll wait here," Timp said. The last thing he wanted to do was listen to a bunch of boring talk.

"Okay, but you'll need to behave yourself. People around here have work to do, all right?"

"All right."

"Promise?"

"Promise."

Timp's father smiled and rested his arm on Timp's shoulders. He was about to say something else when a pale woman in a business suit appeared next to the bench. "Mr. Littleton?"

"Yes, that's me," Timp's father said as he stood up and straightened his slacks.

"Right this way."

She led Mr. Littleton to a nearby cubicle maze where the walls reached above eye-level, just high enough to block the sun from the pasty, despondent employees within. Florescent lights hung from the ceiling, but instead of providing illumination, they supplied the workers with a constant and annoying buzzing sound. Timp was beginning to think this really was Hel and wondered if the devil ran it.

Before Mr. Littleton disappeared into the maze, he leaned back and mouthed the word, "BEHAVE."

"I will," Timp mouthed back and rolled his eyes.

He really wanted to keep that promise too, but the Vikings had other plans.

"I cannot recall having been to Hel before," Bjorn said as soon as Mr. Littleton was gone.

Timp nodded absentmindedly, not yet realizing what Bjorn was driving at.

"Aye, and we do not wish to end up here permanently," Fen added, picking up some hidden cue.

"Aye, we must seek adventure in our'n lives so's when we die, we shall eat at the tables of our'n fathers in Valhöll, instead of dwelling in this most wretched Hel," Gunnar said.

"Oh, no you don't." Timp was beginning to catch their meaning.

"Shall we explore?" Erika asked.

The other Vikings cheered their support.

"No. No. No. *No. No!*" Timp cupped his hands over his hair and ears to hold the Vikings in place. A passing group of executives quickened their pace. One dropped a piece of paper, but took one look at Timp and decided it wasn't worth the risk of stopping to pick it up before chasing after the herd. Timp lowered his hands. "Y'all just won't be happy until they lock me away."

For once, the Vikings had no smart-aleck replies. This made Timp nervous.

"Hello?" He checked his hair and ears. They were gone! He dropped to his knees and searched the floor around the bench. "Bjorn? Erika? Please don't do this to me. Not here." He checked, double checked, and rechecked his hair. Then he saw them, bouncing like fleas several yards away. Timp was amazed at how high they could jump. It would have been like someone jumping over a five-story building. They hopped and laughed, making there way straight for the receptionist—

The receptionist!

"No!" Timp shouted in a strained whisper. "Come back here!"

He dove after the Vikings, but a passing line of bankers stymied his path. He dodged left and right through a forest of black and gray pinstripes as the Vikings reached the reception desk.

The receptionist pounded her rubber stamp against documents: "*Denied,*" "*Denied,*" "*Denied!*" With each stamp, she slammed her fist down as if crushing some imaginary insect. Timp ducked to avoid her gaze and crawled to the side of the desk.

The Vikings huddled around the corner, watching the receptionist and muttering plans. Timp reached down to scoop them up, but they moved from behind the desk's protective cover and into plain sight. Timp shook his fist in anger but could say nothing for fear of being heard. He had to admire how quickly the Vikings had overcome their timidity before giants. They were fearless beneath a hideous, fist-pounding receptionist, who was 100-times their size, when that same giant terrified Timp.

They jumped onto her purse and sprang to the counter at her back, where several sheets of paper rested atop a laser printer. The Vikings grabbed the top sheet and began folding it into a shape familiar to Timp—and to any one who has experienced countless hours of classroom boredom. They were making a paper airplane.

"Don't. You. Dare," Timp mouthed silently.

"Got you!" the reception said as she slammed her fist on the desk. Timp flinched, but she wasn't talking to him. "Pesky little vermin."

Timp counted Vikings. They were all there. Who was she —The receptionist brushed a dead fly off her desk and onto Timp's lap. Timp's eyes widened, imagining imagining what she'd do to the Vikings.

"COME. HERE," he mouthed, but the Vikings ignored him.

A large stainless steel fan sat on the counter under a coat of dust. The blades hung like a bowed head. It was so cold in the lobby that the fan served little use, but the Vikings had a use for it. Fen jumped onto the base and began pulling the "On" switch.

"No. Stop it!" Timp hissed, but then ducked back when the receptionist paused her rhythmic stamping. She searched the area, but after several heart stopping moments, she wiggled her finger in her ear and resumed her mind-numbing task.

Erika and Bjorn put the finishing touches on their paper Barksdale B-52 Bomber, while Gunnar helped Fen tie a string to the fan's stubborn switch. O'dul sat at the tip of the plane with a wide grin. He was ready for liftoff.

Timp signaled the Vikings to come back with a series of curt hand gestures and mouthed silent curses and vows. The Vikings persisted.

Gunnar and Fen finished tying their string around the power switch and jumped onto the paper plane with the other Vikings. They all grabbed the string, giggling with excitement, and pulled. The fan's head shot up, alive with purpose, and the blades powered on full blast.

"No!"

The plane took off like a bottle rocket.

Timp leapt to his feet to catch it as papers, envelopes, stickers, slips, and checks filled the air. The receptionist squealed and flailed her arms as the office shrapnel bombarded her back. Bankers dropped their briefcases and spilled their lattes. A security guard thought they were being robbed, threw his gun in the trash, and hid behind a plastic ficus with his eyes closed.

"Why, you little—!"

The receptionist chased Timp; Timp chased the plane; the plane chased the wind; And everyone chased out of the lobby and into the hall. The Vikings giggled, banked left, and then right. Every time the plane started down, they pulled a corner, and caught an updraft, gliding just beyond Timp's reach.

At the end of the hall, elevator doors rang open and a businessman stepped out to find a paper kamikaze preparing to crash-land into his face. He shrieked and ducked behind his briefcase while the plane barrel-rolled around him and flew into the elevator with Timp chasing in its wake.

"Oh no you don't," the receptionist said as she caught him by the collar and pulled him back.

"Stop! I have to get on that elevator! Let go of me!" But it was too late. The doors closed with a thud, and the elevator started its climb without him.

CHAPTER 12

IT'S A SMALL WORLD, A VERY SMALL WORLD.

The receptionist waddled down the hall, dragging Timp by his collar.

"Where are you taking me?" Timp demanded as they passed the door to the stairwell.

"You're coming with me." Soporific adults love answering the obvious.

Timp didn't have time for this. He needed to get back to the Vikings. They didn't stand a chance without him. His father's mouth appeared before his eyes. "Behave." He'd promised he would, but he'd also promised to return the Vikings safely to their village. When vows collide, Timp decided, the first vow reigns supreme. Besides, this was life or death; he couldn't let the Vikings die. They were the most infernal creatures in the universe, but they didn't deserve to die. Well, maybe Erika. But the not the rest! He had to do something!

As if reading his thoughts, the receptionist's sausage fingers tightened around the back of his neck. There was only one thing to do, and he did it. He did something he'd seen Gunnar do several times and never understood. Timp went berserk.

He hopped up and down, slapped himself, and rolled his eyes.

"What's this?" The receptionist asked. "Are you having some sort of a fit? What's going on here?"

Timp spun around in circles, alternating between robot noises and Three Stooges sounds, "Boop. Beep. Boop. Bop Bop. Wha. Wha Wha. Whappy, Whappy, Whappy." He was going berserk like a real pro. Gunnar would've been so proud.

"Oh, lawsuit. Oh, dear. Oh, my. Help!" The receptionist released Timp and backed away.

"Chugga Chugga Chugga, Toot Toot. Vroom Vroom."

"Don't worry. Oh, my. I didn't do this. I'm not responsible. I'll get help. Help! Help!"

She waddled away as fast as her hams could carry her under the constraint of her rigorously tight skirt and exceptionally high heels—which is to say not very fast at all. She made it five feet before she face-planted onto the marble floor.

That was Timp's cue. He checked the elevator marquee. The Vikings had reached the fourth floor.

Must be a slow elevator. Lucky me. Timp thought, but he wouldn't feel so lucky soon.

He darted through the stairwell door and up the staircase, skipping steps three at a time. When he reached the fourth floor, he checked the marquee again. The elevator had reached the seventh floor. Timp sighed. He wasn't gaining much ground.

On the fifth floor, he passed a nervous accountant, smoking and muttering numbers. On the sixth, a frightened rat ran into the wall. On the seventh floor, a man cried in the corner. Timp didn't stop. He ran to the eighth and then the ninth. He was winded now and stopped to catch his breath as he peaked through the stairwell door. The marquee showed the Vikings were on the tenth floor, pushing to eleven. Were they trying to ride all the way to Asgard? It'd be impossible to catch up if he used another elevator, though he dearly wanted to. He ran on.

Timp was tired when he reached the fifteenth floor. He was exhausted when he reached the twentieth. His shirt sagged, heavy with sweat that felt cold against his back when he leaned against the stairwell door to push it open. The elevator had stopped, and the doors had retracted. The paper plane lay on the floor, and Timp collapsed next to it.

He unfolded the plane and checked the paper on both sides, as if the Vikings might be stuck to one side and not the other. They weren't. Timp groaned and peeled himself off the floor. He crawled on hands and knees, first searching the elevator floor, and then the hallway. He continued down the hall, calling their names. He appeared to have the floor to himself but didn't dare speak above a whisper.

Several yards from the elevator, a set of double doors opened into a large conference room. Timp peeked inside to make sure it was clear to pass. It was. He started to scoot by when he noticed an architectural model sitting on the long oak table in the center of the room. The model interested Timp for three reasons: First, models are cool. Second, if the Vikings saw the model, they'd definitely check it out. But the third and final reason the model caught Timp's attention was because he recognized the highest feature. It was his water tower.

Timp climbed to his feet and slinked into the conference room for a closer look. Blueberry Springs Farm was pieced together in meticulous detail: the water tower, the hills, the pond, and the stables. It even had their sign with the words "Welcome to Blueberry Springs Farm" painted in tiny blue letters against a white background. Timp's entire world had been carved out of balsa wood, miniaturized, and painted for display, but why? Timp pondered this question as the front door of his tiny blue house opened and Gunnar stuck his head out.

"Get off me lawn, ya smelly giant!" he yelled and then slammed the door.

The other Vikings betrayed their hiding places with laughter. Miniature plastic bushes shook and shimmied, small plastic cars rolled back and forth, tiny shuttered windows slammed open and shut against the house. Timp ran a quick tally in his head. All were accounted for.

"What's the big idea, running off like that?" he said, but the Vikings ignored the question.

"Feast your'n eyes upon this beauty," Bjorn said, patting the model of Timp's house. "'Tis a proper size shrunk-ature of your'n House Mountain, aye?"

"Yes, it's a model of my moun—er, that is, my house," Timp said, "but what does it mean?"

"Means Bjorn shall have his house back," Fen said in an unusual boost of confidence. Everyone stared at the four-eyed Viking, and Fen sighed. "Yon stupid giant ate Bjorn's house. Now, we shall replace it with the giant's mountain shrunk-ature. 'Tis perfect."

The Vikings cheered their agreement. Timp did not. "We can't take it. It doesn't belong to us."

"What mean thee, Giant?" Bjorn asked. "You say your'n self, 'tis a model of *your'n* House Mountain."

"Yeah, my family owns the house, but we don't own the model."

The Vikings stroked their mustaches and scratched their heads. Timp rolled his eyes and left them to puzzle it out while he walked toward a peculiar table hidden beneath a stark white cloth. Four steel legs stuck out from under the cloth and ended in thick rubber wheels at the floor. All manner of cranks and levers ran up the legs and disappeared into the shadows. The 4ft x 5ft top stood at an angle like a drafting table, with the tall side rising

as high as Timp's chest and the low side at his waist. Whatever
lay under the cloth seemed ominous. It reminded Timp of
Frankenstein's monster: cloth-covered and laying on a steel
gurney, ready for Dr. Frankenstein to lift him into the air, shoot
him full of electricity, and yell, "*It's Alive!*"

Timp knew a monster wasn't hiding under the sheet—the
object was totally the wrong shape—but he also knew nothing
good ever came out from under cloth-covered carts—except
room service. Still, he had to see. Timp reached for the cloth. Just
as his fingers touched the soft linen, the elevator doors down the
hall ground open with a resounding "*Ding!*"

"Quick, hide!" Timp whispered to the Vikings.

They dove back into their model houses, plastic bushes,
and tiny metal cars. Timp ducked under the large oak table and
pulled the chairs close so that any busybody-bankers passing the
conference room wouldn't notice him. Unfortunately for Timp,
the busybodies didn't pass the conference room. They walked
right in.

Two men and a woman walked inside.

"Cover that model," the man in front snapped.

Timp couldn't see his face, but his voice was nasally and
cold in a way that sent chills crawling down Timp's spine. He
stopped next to the table, and Timp leaned back. He stood close
enough that Timp glimpsed his own reflection in the man's
shiny, black leather shoes. The stench of musty cigars filled the

cramped space beneath the table. Timp knew that smell. He knew this man's name—

"Mr. DeLaney, should we leave the other model covered as well?" the other, much younger, man asked.

"Yes, leave it, but stay on hand to reveal it to the board."

Other model? So, that's what was under the cloth. But why would they need two models? Timp's stomach lurched with an understanding that his brain didn't yet comprehend.

"Hurry. They'll be here any minute. Get me some water, pull down that screen, warm the projector, cue the presentation. Now! Move people!"

DeLaney's assistants scrambled around the room in a blur. Timp thought about making a run for it. He bet he could get through the doors before anyone gave chase, and if he made it to the stairs, he'd be set. But what about the Vikings? He couldn't leave them—no matter how much trouble they caused. Maybe DeLaney and his assistants would step out for a minute, then Timp could grab the Vikings and get out of there. No sooner had he thought this than someone coughed at the door—not a real cough like normal people do, but the silly sort of bark that grown-ups do when they want attention.

"Mayor Wagglesback, how good of you to arrive *sooo early*." DeLaney masked his sour voice with a thin layer of phlegm to create a warmer friendlier tone, but Timp heard the malice beneath, and apparently so did the mayor.

The mayor shuffled his feet nervously. "Um, yes. Ahem. Terribly sorry to be early, you know. I was worried, you see. Worried I may be late again. That is, I didn't want to upset you like last time. And again, I'm terribly sorry about that, terribly. I left extra early this time so it wouldn't happen again, you see. I trust I'm not too early though. I could leave. I could come back, wait in the lobby, hotdog across the street. I can wait in the hallway, if you prefer. That is, if you want." The mayor stuttered and stammered so fast that Timp thought he might be going berserk.

"No, Mayor. I want you to . . ." DeLaney trailed off, allowing awkward silence to devour the room. The mayor rubbed his sweaty hands together and shoved them into his pockets. His discomfort was palatable. Timp imagined DeLaney was enjoying this. ". . . sit. Stay. The other members should arrive shortly."

The mayor obeyed; though, he chose a seat at the far end of the table—the farthest away from DeLaney. Slowly, others trickled into the room, introduced with their occupations: contractors, accountants, attorneys, entrepreneurs, investors, real-estate moguls, and a congresswoman.

"I see Big Oil is late as usual." A contractor complained.

"Now, what'd make ya go and say a hurtful thing like that?" the oilman said with a belly-shaking laugh.

No one answered. It was apparent, even to Timp from under the table, that the question was intended to announce his presence rather than to seek an answer.

The oilman stood in the doorway, a true giant. His tight round belly pressed against his silver and gold belt-buckle until it threatened to pop off and fly across the room. His boots were a hairy cowhide with brown and white spots. It looked like he'd shoved his feet into the mouths of two fat cows and then walked around with them mooing at his feet. But what they lacked in class, his boots made up for double in cleanliness. They'd never known mud. He held the type of cowboy hat that Timp's mother called a "ten-gallon hat"—though, Timp had recently proven that these hats could hold only three quarts of orange juice . . . Timp's father still hadn't forgiven him for that one. But the oilman's hat was much bigger. Timp thought it might actually hold ten gallons. If only he had some orange juice.

The room clamored with the gossip of Louisiana's wealthiest and most influential: men and women Timp had heard of but never met, people who lived on high hills in big houses with heated toilet seats in every bathroom. *Lucky Devils*. They were people whose great grandparents had built Louisiana, and therefore believed the entire state belonged to them. Truth be told, most of it probably did. Any one of them could brush away the Littleton's financial problems with a swipe of a hand, but at the moment, they seemed more in the mood for kicking.

They stepped on Timp's hands, stomped on his fingers, and kicked his ribs, all without realizing he was there. He maneuvered to the middle of the table to get out of range of vicious stilettos and flyby spats. He hoped to go unnoticed there until the meeting ended, and he hoped the Vikings did the same within their model hideouts above. He trusted Bjorn and Fen to have enough common sense to stay quiet, but the others . . . well, they were another story. O'dul had a tendency toward general stupidity, Gunnar went berserk at the slightest provocation, and Erika had a penchant for using people's noses for target practice. This meeting had disaster written all over it.

Timp crawled down the table hoping to put more distance between his ribs and the relentless horde of kicking feet, when an enormous pair of hairy cowhide boots plopped onto his back. The oilman had mistaken Timp for the table's support beam. His heels dug deep into Timp's spine, locking him in place. Timp was stuck. Really stuck. He couldn't move; he could barely breathe. He hoped it'd be a short meeting.

"Okay, we've got a long presentation ahead of us, so let's get started."

Son of a—

The presentation dragged on in an endless collection of charts and graphs that left Timp shaking on his hands and knees under the oilman's heavy cowhide boots. So far, DeLaney hadn't said anything important. He prattled on about market shares, job revenues, and property values, but none of it had anything to do with the model of the Littletons' farm. Had Timp not been so focused on breathing without moving his back, he'd have lost his mind from boredom. Why would anyone come to this meeting voluntarily?

"And now for the moment you've all been waiting for," DeLaney said.

Timp doubted that. The moment he'd been waiting for was the moment this gargantuan oilman would take his stinking rot-hide, hairy boots off his blasted back so he could breathe again. That was the moment Timp waited for, but he listened all the same . . . it wasn't like he had a choice.

The assistant DeLaney called Stephon flipped on the lights while DeLaney stood before the table, tapping his right foot. Stephon twirled around and stopped next to DeLaney with the dramatic pose of a magician's assistant. He owned it.

"What I'm about to show you is a set of two models," DeLaney said, "before-and-after models, if you will."

In the protective darkness under the table, Timp swallowed the lump lodged in his throat. He already knew which model his house was, and it wasn't the "after" model. DeLaney snapped his fingers, and Stephon pulled away the linen cloth with a swooping scoop.

"What you see before you is a model of Blueberry Springs Farm. Quaint, isn't it?" Everyone around the table laughed. Timp did not. "As you can see, the blue house—"

The room fell silent, save a few murmurs and giggles. DeLaney's assistants shuffled their feet nervously. Everyone had noticed something not visible to Timp from under the table. He prayed that whatever it was, it had nothing to do with the Vikings. But deep down, he knew better.

"Stephon! Where is it? What did you do with it?" DeLaney demanded of his assistant.

"Becca! Where is it?" Stephon demanded of DeLaney's other assistant.

"Me?" she replied. "Stephon, you're the one who—"

"Find it," DeLaney gritted through his teeth. His assistants were already scouring the room.

Timp tried to ignore the heavy boots cutting into his back and focused on being invisible in case their search brought DeLaney's assistants his way. Then, the tiny blue model of his house plopped onto the floor near the table's edge and began walking his way. The house wobbled left and right. Every now and then, it paused and turned, as if to look around. Finally, the house stopped in front of Timp and settled to the floor.

"My apologies," DeLaney said to the board members above. "The model of the house was merely there to illustrate how quaint and useless this land is, but with the house gone, it's even more quaint and useless, which I have to confess, I didn't think possible."

Everyone around the table laughed. Timp did not. He hated his house as much as anyone, but he preferred to be the one to complain about it.

DeLaney's assistants searched through boxes, messenger bags, and brief cases. Stephon dropped to his hands and knees and checked under a nearby food cart. Timp knew it was a matter of seconds before he turned to look under the table. Timp's heart climbed into his throat.

The Vikings peeked their heads out of the tiny blue house and waved at Timp with proud new-homeowner smiles. Timp made sure they were all accounted for, then stuffed the house— Vikings and all—into his pocket. They yelled in protest, but Timp had no time to explain.

"Moving right along," DeLaney continued. "I'd now like to present you with the second, and I dare say greatly improved model." DeLaney snapped his fingers, but his assistants didn't respond.

Becca flipped through folders in a filing cabinet on the other side of the room while Stephon finished searching under the food cart and began crawling toward the table. He focused on the floor as he crawled, his eyes panned left and right, but when he reached the edge of the table, he slowly lifted his head. Timp's heart pounded. He wanted to back up, but the oilman's boots pinned him in place. It wouldn't have done any good anyway. It was too late. Stephon stared into Timp's terrified, saucer-like eyes.

CHAPTER 13
MEANWHILE, BACK AT THE FARM

Mrs. Molly Barn Bobber stretched out on the couch, reaching her paws as far as they'd go. It felt good to be back in the air-conditioned house; so good, in fact, she rolled onto her back and allowed Mrs. Littleton the distinct honor of petting the royal belly.

"Poor, abused Molly," Mrs. Littleton said as she rubbed.

"*Yeah, poor abused me,*" Molly agreed.

"You want a treat?"

"*Yes, servant. Fetch me a treat. It's about time you got your act together, chambermaid. I'm your queen, after all.*" But as usual, all Mrs. Littleton heard was, "Meow. Meow," and of course, "Meow."

Molly ate her treat, performed some light afternoon grooming, and then stretched and contorted in kitty-cat yoga exercises. The day was shaping out splendidly.

"Well, Molly, we better make some pies," Mrs. Littleton said, getting up from the couch.

She walked into the kitchen, pre-heated the oven to 375 degrees, and flipped on the fan. The blades panned back and forth, filling the house with the scent of blueberries, piecrust, and . . . something else. Molly stuck her nose in the air and sniffed. The smell was faint, barely detectable even with her keen kitty-cat nose, but she recognized the scent. It was the same scent she'd been chasing when some rotten scoundrels threw a bag over her head and strung her up in the barn.

"*Enemies.*" Her eyes narrowed, her ears pulled back, and her hackles rose. They were here, in her palace. She sniffed the air as she climbed to her feet.

Molly was on the prowl, and though she didn't know it yet, she was hunting Vikings.

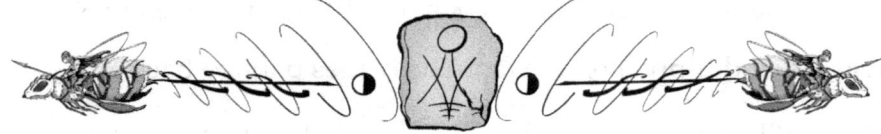

CHAPTER 14
THA THA THA THAT'S ALL, VIKINGS.

Stephon stared back at Timp with a blank expression. His eyes had not yet adjusted to the darkness under the table, and for five long seconds, Timp could tell Stephon's brain didn't register what his eyes were seeing. Timp wanted to jump and run, but the oilman's heavy boots pressed down on his back even harder than before. Stephon blinked twice, shook his head, and looked again.

Timp tried not to move. Maybe if he remained perfectly still, he'd disappear.

Timp did not disappear.

Stephon's glazed expression found focus in Timp's eyes. "Yiiaelp!" He squealed slammed his head into the bottom of the table.

Everyone jumped.

"What's wrong with you?" DeLaney demanded as he grabbed Stephon by the arm and pulled him to his feet.

Stephon tried to respond, "but-but— "

But was cutoff by DeLaney, "I'm trying to give a presentation. Do you understand that?"

"Ye-yes, sir, I ju—"

"Get over there and prepare to reveal the other model."

Stephon started to protest, but DeLaney stomped his foot and growled, "Now!"

Stephon walked to the second model and stopped. Timp could tell what he was thinking: maybe he could rat the boy out quickly. Once it was out, surely DeLaney would forgive the interruption. It was a matter of corporate security, after all. Maybe he'd even get a promotion.

DeLaney stomped his foot again.

Stephon shook himself from his daydream, took up the cloth, and stood ready to unveil the second model at DeLaney's command.

"My apologies for yet another interruption. I assure you, it will be the last." DeLaney glared, and Stephon shrank three sizes.

Timp would have felt sorry for Stephon, but he knew it was just a matter of time before he ratted Timp out to DeLaney. Timp dreaded the thought.

"And now, I present to you the new and improved Blueberry Springs Shopping Center: The mall of the future!"

The Mall of the what now? Timp didn't understand. His father had said they had nothing to worry about. Shopping. He lied! They both lied! His parents knew. That's what they whispered about in the hall. His mother wasn't going shopping. Timp's father had just told her that Blueberry Springs Farm was about to be destroyed and replaced with a strip mall. "*Grown-up stuff*." Timp was so mad he could spit.

DeLaney snapped his fingers impatiently, and Stephon unveiled the second model (though with noticeably less enthusiasm than before). The model must have been quite a sight. The board members gasped and clapped their approval as Delaney described each section in gory detail:

"The facility will be comprised of three sectors. Sector one will include all of the standard fast-food drive-thrus: McFrugals, Burger Buns, Chicka-Doodles, and Chicka-Damnation (for when Chicka-Doodles is closed on Sunday, because you know that's always when you crave Chicka-Doodles)."

The board members laughed. Timp did not.

"Sector two will showcase the specialty stores: Sheets and Shanks, Bargain Buys, World Exploits, Pet Clonez. . ."

With each new store, Timp felt as though something was squeezing the breath out of him — that is, something other than a pair of size 17 cowboy boots.

"Sector three includes the super stores: Will-Fart's, Bullseyed — which let's face it is just a fancier and more expensive Will-Fart's, and of course, Home De'Same.

Gas stations will be here, here, and here, and will keep drivers going from store to store without feeling obligated to walk anywhere."

Everyone clapped emphatically. *They must really hate walking.*

Timp felt sick. A million times he'd hoped his parents would sell the farm. A million times he'd wished they lived in a neighborhood with other kids, where he could have friends in the summer. He'd imagined the farm burning, getting hit by a tornado, crumbling under an earthquake, beamed up by aliens, vacuumed into the 9th dimension, and even sold for millions of dollars to an eccentric billionaire whose prize dog, Peaches, needed a puppy mansion. Timp had imagined a hundred ways his family could lose their farm, but he never imagined losing it to laziness and greed. And he certainly had never imagined the applause.

The board clapped on. The stores they'd mentioned already filled shopping centers 10 miles down the I-49 extension. Why build more of the same? Timp remembered his father's words. These men and women measured the world in dollars and cents, not right and wrong. But was it wrong? Timp's mind whirled. Could they really take the farm? And if so, would that be such a bad thing? He hated himself for asking, but he hated working his summers away too. He hated being alone all the time. Hadn't he wanted this all along? Maybe it was all his fault. He'd wished hard enough, and his wish had come true.

But Timp didn't feel like he thought he would. He thought he'd feel happy, even relieved. Instead, he felt dirty. Timp wanted to jump up and run away, but the oilman adjusted his legs and pushed down harder. *Come on!*

"Reckon *all* them farmers done sold you their property?" the oilman asked.

"All except one," DeLaney answered coldly. "We've acquired the surrounding properties, here, here, and here, but we're still waiting on Blueberry Springs Farm."

Mom and Dad will never sale, Timp thought.

"Now, if I know anything 'bout anything, it's you ain't supposed to count yer chickens 'fore they hatch. How can you guarantee them blueberry folks gonna sell?"

Timp didn't like being referred to as "them blueberry folks," but he was glad to hear someone talk as though they still had options. Maybe his parents would come out of this rich. They could buy a mansion in the city with a pool and a Dr. Pepper Icee machine.

A knock at the door interrupted Timp's daydream.

"Mr. DeLaney, I am sorry to interrupt. May I have a quick word, please?"

Timp recognized the pale figure standing in the doorway as the woman his father had met downstairs. He hoped their meeting wasn't already over. If his father was searching for him, Timp was in trouble.

DeLaney started toward the woman, but Stephon grabbed his arm. Stephon still hadn't given up on telling DeLaney about Timp. DeLaney shrugged his hand away, shushed him into silence, and walked to the woman.

There was a series of short whispers back and forth. The woman appeared to be pleading, but DeLaney cut her off, "Because, Ms. Laurent, that's how I want it. When you become vice president of this bank, you can do whatever you like, but until that day, if you want to keep your job, you will do as I say. Now, get back down there and deal with him."

Ms. Laurent clinched her jaw, said she understood, and left the room.

With a wide smile, DeLaney returned his attention to the oilman. "What fortuitous timing. In answer to your question, Bronson, we don't need 'them Blueberry Folks' to sell. We need them to fail."

So much for a Dr. Pepper Icee machine.

This bank holds their loan and the owners trust me implicitly. The woman you just saw is on her way to hammer out the details now. So, if—no, excuse me—*when* they fail to pay, the bank will simply take back what is already ours and begin building a much more profitable tomorrow."

The board members clapped, but because the oilman's boots didn't shake, Timp could tell that Bronson didn't join in.

"But . . . but what if they *do* pay?" Mayor Wagglesback asked nervously, speaking for the first time since he'd sat down.

"Impossible," DeLaney said. "They have two months' notes to go. If they miss or are late on either payment, the farm is ours. It's as simple as that. And let's just say that I have it on good authority that this will be a bad summer for blueberries."

DeLaney spoke with a silky confidence that made Timp's blood run cold. There was no doubt in his voice; the farm was as good as his.

"You can count me in," someone at the table said.

"Me too," another agreed.

"DeLaney's never steered us wrong before," the congresswoman added with a slight, and—Timp suspected— quite practiced British inflection.

More and more board members began to speak excitedly about this plan. Timp's world was slated for demolition, and everyone rejoiced.

"Well," Bronson said, "I reckon you ladies and gents have a lot to discuss, but, beg'n your pardon, this here just ain't my kind of investment. And here I come thinking I was gonna get to buy me some cattle."

Bronson released a boisterous laugh that was met with silence from the rest of the board. He cleared his throat and lifted his feet. Timp stifled a cry of relief as he rubbed his aching back. He doubted he'd ever stand up straight again.

Bronson rose from the table and bid his goodbyes. DeLaney returned the nicety with a tone of thinly veiled disgust, then immediately addressed the remaining members as though the oilman was already gone. "Where was I?"

Bronson left, whistling a tune Timp didn't recognize.

Stephon seized the break in conversation to get DeLaney's attention. He was nothing, if not tenacious, but DeLaney shushed him again.

"Oh, yes. I almost forgot the pond," DeLaney said. "That's the best part. As you can see, the land already has a natural spring-fed pond—" Timp didn't need to see the model to picture his pond. He swam in it every summer and swatted mosquitoes from it every day. But he had a notion swimming and swatting wasn't what DeLaney had in mind. "—The pond will cut our costs by providing water for our vast utility needs: sprinklers, fountains, toilets—"

Toilets? Toilets? My pond for toilets? Timp's knuckles turned white as he clinched his fist. It was one thing to promise him a mansion and a Dr. Pepper Icee machine, but using his pond for toilets? That was too far. The blood-thirsty Vikings shimmied with excitement at the impending battle. They'd worked their way out of Timp's pocket and back into his hair and ears, and where they whispered battle strategies: "Tear the bloke apart, lad!" "Berserker! Berserker!" "Toilets?"

Toilets! Timp took a breath to calm his nerves.

The Vikings had other plans.

They sprang from Timp's ear and landed on the ground with weapons drawn. "Odin owns ye all!" "Týr and toilets!" "Toilets!" "Toilets?"

The Vikings had a strange new battle cry. Without the oilman's heavy boots holding him down, Timp scrambled after them. Until he reached the edge of the table. By then they'd landed on DeLaney's shoes and started hacking away with their axes and swords. DeLaney started to look down. Timp sprang out from under the table like a wildcat with rabies and latched onto DeLaney's foot.

DeLaney shrieked in terror and fell to the floor kicking his legs as if they were on fire. The Vikings screamed threats that only Timp could hear. Timp thrashed and clawed at DeLaney's legs, trying to grab the Vikings. "Toilets!" Why did he have to say toilets, clearly that was a declaration of war to Vikings. He feared that he might truly be going berserk. Fen stood nearby and catalogued the event in his notebook. "A giant be a most unstable creature, prone to wild flights of violence."

"Shut it!" Timp said. He threw Fen and two others in his pocket, and dove at DeLaney's legs for the others.

The room erupted into chaos. Some board members mistook Timp for a wild animal and stood on their chairs, dancing from one foot to the next. Others abandoned ship, pushing, shoving, and elbowing one another to get out the door. Mayor Wagglesback fainted from shock and slid off his chair and landed in a heap under the table. An accountant cried in the corner, muttering something about HR and hostile work environments. No one saw the Vikings.

Stephon recovered his wits first, but only because he already knew that Timp was a boy and not a rabid, mange-ridden billy goat. He grabbed Timp by the feet and pulled, but Timp clung to DeLaney's calf with such vigor that he remained fixed.

"They don't belong to you!" Timp clawed. "They're mine!"

"No we's not. We's our'n's." Gunnar said as he fell from DeLaney's pants into the model of Timp's house, which had fallen out of Timp's pocket in the kerfuffle. The other Vikings soon followed.

Timp picked up the model of the house and held it up to DeLaney. "Mine!"

DeLaney looked at the model in confusion. "The—the—farm?"

"What?" And then Timp realized the confusion. DeLaney hadn't seen the Vikings. He thought all of this was about the farm. *Grownups are so stupid!*

Stephon and several others yanked Timp away from DeLaney. Timp growled his aggravation. Timp pulled himself free and climbed to his feet panting.

Stephon helped DeLaney to his feet and then tried to adjust his crooked tie, but DeLaney slapped Stephon's hands away.

"Get off of me!" DeLaney shook his head to recover his bearings and flushed red.

The board members who remained stood in a half circle around Timp, keeping their distance in case the wildling lashed out again. That satisfied Timp just fine. He puffed himself up for one final roar.

"Toilets!" The war cry didn't seem as scary when he yelled it.

He scanned the room full of grownups, and suddenly he didn't feel quite so tough. Their stunned expressions melted into anger, and Timp knew he'd exhausted their patience. He had one more option: He ran.

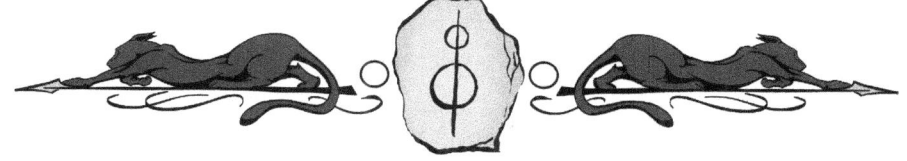

CHAPTER 15
A KEEN KITTY-CAT DETECTIVE

Mrs. Molly Enemy Stalker prowled the house with her head low and her butt high in the air. She dutifully rubbed her cheeks on corners, plants, and bookshelves as she moved through the house, marking her hunting territory with her own (and she would say much more pleasant) scent. Occasionally, Molly stood on her tiptoes and strutted diagonally across a room—a classic kitty-cat ninja technique she'd perfected after years of training.

Molly tracked the peculiar scent to the filthy servant boy's sleeping quarters. There, she found many curious and horrid smells—as one might expect to find in a servant boy's room, but she also found something that boggled her kitty-cat mind. A small matchbox lay open on the nightstand, filled with the scent of her enemies. A smell this strong meant they'd held the item for a while. *Probably torturing the boy with matches, trying to get secrets about his queen.* Molly almost felt bad for her servant, but when she sniffed the air for the faintest hint of blood and found none, she decided the boy had not been tortured. And if not tortured, then . . . Molly's eyes narrowed. The boy could be in league with her foes. *No, surely not. I'd never tolerate betrayal from in my kingdom. Maybe they bagged his head too.* She had to confess, she'd thought about doing just that to the boy several times.

Her enemy was tougher than she thought.

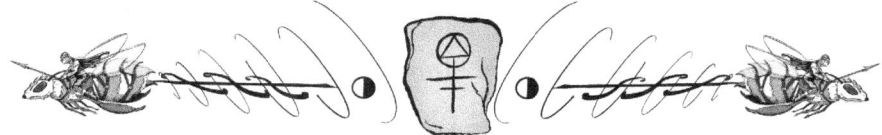

CHAPTER 16
LET'S GET THE HEL OUT OF HERE

Timp sprinted down the hall. He made it halfway to the elevator before he heard DeLaney shout, "Get him!"

DeLaney lead a pack of suits in chase, huffing and puffing. They were not accustomed to chasing children and having to do so now fueled their anger and determination. Timp didn't know what they planned to do with him if they caught him, but he wasn't going to stick around and find out. He quickened his gait and set his eyes on the elevator at the end of the hall. The doors were open, but wait, no. They were closing! He wouldn't make it. The horde was gaining on him, a pack of hungry wolves, foaming at the mouths and snarling.

"Faster, Giant. Faster! " "Be that as fast as ye can go?" "They are gaining upon us, Giant!" "Move yer giant lumbering legs, Giant!"

"How 'bout a little support, here?" Timp panted.

"If you're talking, then ya ain't running, Giant. Now, run!"

Timp gritted his teeth and pushed himself as hard as he could. The elevator doors were almost closed. They were just wide enough to . . . He might make it if he . . . Yes, he had to—"JUMP!"

Timp dove head first into the elevator and face-planted onto the floor with the doors dinging shut at his heels. He could hear the pack of wolves barking and biting on the other side.

"The button. Hit the button!" DeLaney's muffled voice said, but he was too late. The elevator was going down. "The other elevator. The other elevator!" The race wasn't over, but Timp welcomed the hiatus to catch his breath. He rested his forehead against the floor and released a deep and well-earned sigh of relief.

"And here I thought DeLaney hated *me*," a voice said from above.

Timp flipped over to find the oilman, Mr. Bronson, standing above him with a wide grin.

"What are *you* doing here?" Timp asked, not impolitely. He hadn't noticed the man standing in the elevator before, but then, he had been a little preoccupied with running for his life.

"Well, I reckon someone had to hold the elevator for ya. You don't reckon these things start down on their own, do ya?"

Timp hadn't considered why the elevator doors were still open, nor had he wondered how the elevator began down on its own once he was inside.

The oilman helped him to his feet, brushed off his shoulders with a few rough sweeps, and then slapped him on the back. "There ya go. Good as new."

"But how did you know I'd need the elevator held for me?" Timp asked.

"You can tell a peculiar lot about the temperament of your footrest by how much it wiggles under your boots."

"You knew I was under the table?" Timp gave the oilman a shove with both his hands and all of his weight, but Bronson didn't move an inch. Instead, he studied the ceiling and whistled innocently. Timp rubbed his aching back. "Your boots are heavy. You know that, buster?"

Timp didn't normally speak to adults this way, but he felt emboldened by his confrontation with DeLaney. Luckily, the oilman was a good-natured fellow and laughed. "I *am* sorry about that," Bronson said in earnest, "but I recognized you from the lobby as Pam Littleton's boy, and figured apples don't fall too far from them trees. I knew if I didn't hold you down, you'd up and do something silly like attack somebody, which, I surmise, is exactly what you gone and done after I left. Am I right?"

Timp furrowed his brow. Pam was short for Pamela. Only close friends called his mother Pam. It made Timp uncomfortable to hear a stranger say it. And why would having Pam Littleton as his mother make him more likely to attack someone? Also, he didn't attack anyone. He was trying to prevent the Vikings from killing a giant. Technically, he saved a life.

Bronson mistook Timp's confusion for shame. "Oh now, don't be ashamed. I reckon I'd a'done the same thing in your boots, but this is grownup stuff, ya understand? You just gotta let the grownups work it out."

Timp groaned. He was sick of hearing that kind of talk and decided to say so: "I'm about sick of hearing that kind of talk."

This started Bronson chuckling anew. Timp decided the oilman was too happy to be sane, and decided to say that too.

"I think you're a loony." Somehow Timp knew Bronson wouldn't take it as an insult.

"Me? Nah, when you're as rich as I am, you ain't crazy, you're eccentric. And believe me, sometimes that's the best way to be."

"What do you mean?"

Bronson met Timp's eyes. "When people want something from you, they treat you different. Oh, it's nice, at first. They're sweet and try to get you to give it willingly, but when they see they can't have it, that's when their true nature shows its ugly, little head. Some give up. Some beg. Some con. Others take. Everyone wants a piece."

Timp realized the Bronson's southern accent had dropped to a slight drawl. He wondered if the oilman might be faking the rest of the time.

"So you find ways to protect yourself, to keep them away." Bronson's voice trailed off, and he stood there, deep in a memory too personal to share.

"Is that why you dress like that?" Timp asked.

The oilman shook himself out of his thoughts and smiled widely. "What's wrong with the way I dress? Are cowboys not in this year?"

Timp looked up at the oilman's yellow, ten-gallon hat, then down at his brown and white spotted cowhide boots. "I don't know if that look was *ever* in."

"So I dress funny, is that it?" Bronson said with a wink, his humor and accent returned to their former glory. "Reckon next you'll be saying I talk funny too, you rotten little whipper-snap."

Timp laughed.

"But, you're a sharp whipper-snap, I'll grant you. Hit the nail right on the head. I started acting like this a long time ago to keep vultures like DeLaney from taking me seriously, but let's keep that between you and me."

Timp didn't understand. No one ever took him seriously, and he hated it. Here was a grown man trying *not* to be taken seriously. He lifted his shoulders in resignation. "I don't get it."

"Well, you can buy a host of things with money, kid, but you can't buy friends. I'd venture you can't buy anything *worth* buying, at all. So might as well let'em underestimate you and see who your real friends are verses who's just after your money."

Timp agreed that friends and family were all fine and dandy, as was happiness, and a world of other things, but there were definitely things *worth* buying: his family farm, for one, if for no other reason than to protect his family and the Vikings from DeLaney. Also, food was definitely worth buying. Oh, and toilet paper. Timp was a big fan of toilet paper. A faster elevator would be nice too.

"Yeah, I'm not sure I can totally agree with that," Timp said, thinking back to toilet paper. *So important, toilet paper.* "There's gotta be a middle ground."

"I tell you what, kid, you ever find anything worth buying, you let me know. But for now, you better run."

"What?"

The elevator doors opened. The receptionist stood at the end of the hall, staring at the ground and muttering. Her hair shot out in a misshapen mess, and light dirt patches besmirched her once pristine black dress. She must have been pacing the lobby in fury ever since Timp escaped. Beyond her, the sun burst through the revolving glass doors. The receptionist was all that stood between Timp and freedom.

"Well, I reckon DeLaney and his gang gonna be along, shortly. Do me a favor, kid. Keep your distance from DeLaney. You've humiliated him in front his peers. He won't soon forget that. I do business with him because I have to, but that doesn't mean I like the man, and it certainly don't mean I trust him. If DeLaney wants something, he takes it. And he always, *always* gets what he wants." Bronson's haunted stare returned but he quickly shook it away with a smile. He held the elevator doors and slapped Timp on the back. "Y'all come back now, ya hear?"

Timp wanted to explain that DeLaney had nothing to fear from him. He didn't even mean to humiliate him. He was just trying to get the Vikings, that's all. The Vikings were to blame, not him. But the elevator doors began to shut. Time was up. Timp thanked Bronson and started down the hall.

"What a strange giant," Fen said, and Timp agreed.

Timp crept down the hall with slow, deliberate steps as the receptionist bit her nails and muttered. "Little brat. Stupid, little, punk kid."

Timp stopped. He felt invisible when standing still, but he knew he couldn't stay that way forever. DeLaney and his rabid pack of suits would charge from the other elevator any second. Timp searched the walls for a cranny to hide in, but there was none.

"What's amiss, Giant?" Erika hissed in Timp's ear. "Charge her!"

Timp did not move.

"Tell me ye be not afraid of her, Giant?" Gunnar mocked.

"I'm afraid of her," Fen said

"Ye get afraid when O'dul breaks wind," Gunnar said, and all of the Vikings got quiet.

"I believe we *all* be afraid of *that*," Bjorn said, and the Vikings laughed their agreement. Even O'dul laughed, for he feared his own wind.

Ding! The elevator rang at Timp's back. The death-toll echoed down the marble hall. The receptionist ceased her mutterings and locked eyes with Timp. "You."

"There he is!" DeLaney's voice shot from the elevator like a bullet straight into Timp's back.

Time was up. He was trapped between a receptionist and a hard face: DeLaney's hard face. Timp had to choose: move forward and face the receptionist from Hel, or retreat and face a hungry pack of wolves led by DeLaney.

Timp chose the receptionist.

He ducked his head like a ramming bull and charged full speed.

"Charge!" Erika cheered.

The receptionist widened her stance and braced for impact. Her skirt stretched to its limits around Greek pillar legs built into the marble floor. She seemed so much a part of the building that Timp knew she would not move, not for Timp, not for the mob behind him, not for 2000 years of wear and tear. Timp had only one option—

"DIVE!" the Vikings screamed.

Just as Timp was about to plow into the receptionist, she leaned forward to take the hit, she leaned just low enough for Timp to swan dive over her head. The Vikings cheered in exuberance as Timp soared over her, landed on the other side with a roll, and got back to his feet like a real deal, full caliber, Jedi knight. Timp felt he'd earned some bragging rights, so he turned around and stuck his tongue out at the angry horde fighting to untangle themselves from the pile-up on the receptionist. He'd done it. There was no way they could catch him now. Then, as so often happens in our greatest moments of triumph, Timp hit a wall. . . . At least, it felt like a wall.

Timp's backside smacked against hit the marble floor. His father stood over him with a furrowed brow. "Why are you running? I was looking for you. I— " Mr. Littleton looked up at the group of disheveled business men and women headed their way. His shoulders sank. "You promised me you'd behave."

His father's disappointed tone pained Timp worse than anger. "I did. I just—"

But before Timp could explain, DeLaney arrived with his plastic smile. "John! I didn't know you were here. How good of you to drop by."

"Hi, Mark," Mr. Littleton said.

Timp's jaw dropped. His father had just called DeLaney by his first name. Timp couldn't believe DeLaney *even had* a first name. Surely evil like that wasn't born, but sprung from the festering pit in a deep dark cave in Mordor—or worse yet, Alabama. Everyone in the lobby froze, equally surprised by the familiar greeting. "Just thought I'd stop by and see about getting some of that good financial advice you were talking about yesterday."

"Well, you've come to the right place, that's for sure," DeLaney glanced down at Timp and back to his father, as if piecing together a puzzle for the first time. "Does *this* belong to you?" DeLaney patted Timp on the head, then looked at his fingers with disgust, flicking away some imagined filth.

Timp frowned, checked his hair to make sure it was clean and then moved closer to his father and out of DeLaney's reach.

Mr. Littleton sighed, "Yes, I'm afraid he does. Has he caused you any trouble?"

"Oh, No. No. No, not at all," DeLaney lied, again. "I just met him near the restroom, a delightful child, so . . . spirited."

Unlike Timp and his father, DeLaney was a most adept liar. The bigger DeLaney's lies, the more his smile grew and grew. DeLaney smiled from ear to ear as he looked down on Timp, but his eyes told a story of embittered hatred. Bronson was right; Timp had humiliated DeLaney at an important meeting. DeLaney would not soon forget that, even if he hadn't really done it on purpose. But looking at DeLaney up close, he also didn't regret it.

Timp rubbed his hands on his shirt. He felt unclean, allowing a man like DeLaney to protect him with such foul, greasy lies. Timp would almost have preferred to be in trouble than to share a secret with the likes of DeLaney. He thought about telling his father the truth right then and there, but given the trouble he was already in over Molly, maybe he could let this one slide.

"Were you able to find all of the assistance you needed?" DeLaney asked.

"Not really, I— "

"Well, don't you worry," DeLaney interrupted as he took Timp's father just above the elbow and began walking them toward the revolving doors. He scanned the lobby conspiratorially and then whispered as if taking Mr. Littleton into his confidences. "It's like I told you, yesterday. There are some people around here who want to take your farm, but I'm your inside man. I'm going to make sure that doesn't happen. Trust me. I just need a little time. You'll see."

"Thanks, Mark," Mr. Littleton said as all the tension left his shoulders. "I really appreciate you looking into this for us. I think you're right. Definitely some people in here are out to get us. Ms. Laurent didn't seem to want to help me at all today. I'm glad you're going to look into it for us though. I know you're busy—"

"Think nothing of it. It's the least I could do, after," DeLaney's lips tightened, "all we've been through."

Timp's stomach churned with questions and disgust.

The two men shook hands and bid their goodbyes. Timp started to follow his father out when a firm hand grasped his shoulder. "You take care, young man," DeLaney said digging his fingers deep into Timp's shoulder. "I'll see you again, very, very soon."

Timp was certain it was a threat, but when he looked to his father, Mr. Littleton just smiled and patted Timp on his other shoulder. "Say 'Thank you,' Timp."

Timp looked at his father. He had to be joking. Thank DeLaney? For what, chasing him? For trying to steal their farm? For threatening his life? "Bollocks to *that*!" Erika the Viking said, capturing Timp's sentiment exactly.

Timp resisted in silent protest, but his father smiled expectantly, and DeLaney's fingers dug deeper into his shoulder. He relished Timp's discomfort. Timp just wanted to go home.

"Thank you," he mumbled as his face flushed red.

Timp couldn't help but feel as though he'd lost some unspoken battle. The Vikings were happy to lend their support: "Giant, ye's might be's the biggest coward I's yet seen."

Timp was beginning to rue the day he'd met these Vikings.

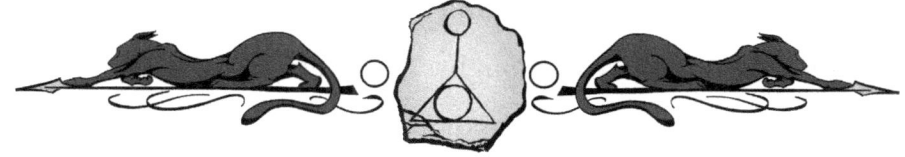

CHAPTER 17
WILD HUNTRESS OF THE KITCHEN

Molly slinked down the hall, back to the kitchen. She followed the scent trail to the counter, where her chambermaid stood preparing another pie. Molly jumped onto a nearby stool and peaked over the counter top. At first, everything seemed in order: her chambermaid kneaded dough around a pan; the radio played oldies; and there was no sign of her enemies. Then something moved. Molly focused on the movement with her keen kitty-cat peepers, and almost fell backward from the shock of what she saw. There, in a bowl overflowing with blueberries, a tiny blue man tried to free a berry from the pile.

Molly had not seen the Vikings the night before. She'd only heard and smelled them. Seeing one now transformed her anger into bewilderment. He stretched his back and groaned, unaware he was being watched, and then continued his work. Molly studied him with fascination. He looked just like a regular human, except tiny, blue, covered with strange purple markings, and oddly dressed. He cursed and swore as he pulled. He was so grumpy. *A grumpy.* Molly thought. *That's what he is.*

As he pulled on the unmoving berry, Molly decided to do what she always did with things that confused her:

She decided to eat him.

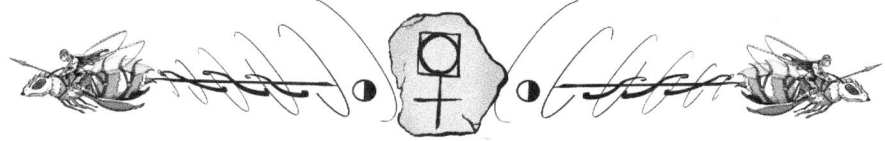

CHAPTER 18
YO, DADDIO

Timp and his father basked in the warm summer sun. The outside world with its azure skies and verdant trees was a welcome contrast to the bank's cold, colorless halls. They stretched their backs as the chill melted from their bones.

After a long groan, Timp's father scanned the area, "Oh, lunch."

Across the street, a hotdog cart shined in the sun—a metallic beacon of delicious, processed-meat goodness. Timp licked his lips and followed his father over. They each ordered hotdogs with all the fixings and sat on a nearby bench in the shade.

"What be that yer eating, Giant?" Bjorn asked. Timp heard the Vikings smacking their lips with hunger.

"A hotdog," Timp said as he held it up proudly.

The Vikings gasped in horror. "Ye're eating dog?" "Monster." "What kind of devil-giant are ye?" "You're sick, Giant.

You're a sick giant." "I want a new giant." "I think I'm gonna vomit in your'n ear!"

Timp sighed, "It's not *really* made out of *dog*."

Mr. Littleton raised one eyebrow at Timp then spoke slowly and deliberately, "No, son, it isn't *really* made out of dog."

Timp flushed and lowered his eyes. He needed to stop answering the Vikings when other people were around, but it was hard to avoid. They were battle-tested in the art of aggravation.

After the Vikings knew that hotdogs were not actually made out of dogs, they decided to investigate. They climbed down Timp's shoulder and arms and stood on his hand, examining the feast. They poked the side quizzically, stabbed at it, tasted a bit on the tip of their tongues, and then attacked it with ravenous veracity. Timp left the Vikings to their deep moans of culinary delight and turned to tell his father about DeLaney. "You don't really believe him, do you, Dad?"

"What do you mean? Believe who?"

"DeLaney. You don't really believe he's trying to help you, do you?"

"Of course I do. Why wouldn't I?"

"Because he's lying."

"That's a pretty bold accusation, Son."

Timp couldn't believe what he was hearing. His father wasn't a genius—he was a notoriously bad speller, for one—but he wasn't an idiot, either. How could he not see through DeLaney's lies?

"It's not bold; it's true. And you lied too. We're not fine. They want to build a shopping center on top of our farm."

"Who told you that?"

"I, uh." Timp didn't want to lie, not while he was lecturing his father on the merits of honesty, but he couldn't very well tell him that he'd followed a gang of purple and blue Vikings to a conference room upstairs and then hidden under the table to eavesdrop on a business meeting. He knew his father well enough to know that story wouldn't fly. So, he settled on the simplified truth: "I overheard it."

"Oh, I see. You overheard it."

"You know I'm right."

"Yes, Timp. I know. But it's a little more complicated than that. When you're older, you'll understand."

"Don't tell me that! I'm tired everyone telling me that. This is my world too. I want to understand now."

Timp's father sighed and threw the rest of his hotdog in the trash-bin next to their bench. "Okay, a group of investors want to buy our farm so they can build a shopping center, but they don't want to pay near what we owe. If we took their bid, we'd be broke and homeless, instead of just broke, so your mother and I told them 'no.' Mr. DeLaney is an old . . . Look, he knows about this sort of thing. So he's helping us out. But the shopping center has nothing to do with DeLaney. It—"

"It has everything to do with DeLaney!" Timp interrupted. "He's the one behind everything."

"And how did you come by that nonsense?" Timp's father asked.

Timp tightened his lips. He couldn't just keep saying that he'd overheard things. That'd only lead to more questions, but maybe more questions wouldn't be so bad. He thought about telling his father everything: about the Vikings, about hiding under the table, about the mind numbingly dull presentation, toilet water, and about the oilman's warning. But, Erika resolved his dilemma, "Think not upon it, Giant." She'd returned from her hotdog feast and resumed her position in Timp's ear. He felt the sharp point of her spear poke against his ear canal.

"I-I—"

"Killer Bees," Gunnar warned.

"—I just know," Timp said.

"Just know, huh? Same way you *just knew* that your mom wanted to go shopping after eavesdropping on her?"

His father had him there. Timp studied the cracks in the sidewalk.

Mr. Littleton sighed, "Timp, you've developed a bad habit of hearing part of a story and drawing your own conclusions. You need to make sure you have all the facts."

"But this time—"

"—is just like last time," his father jumped in. "You need to gather all of the facts before you spout your mouth off. Do you understand? Mr. DeLaney wouldn't do anything to hurt our farm. I know that for a fact."

Timp gasped to choke back his disbelief. It was almost laughable. And the funniest part was, Timp didn't care if they sold the farm. Not really. At least then he'd have friends and summers off. He seriously doubted that they'd end up homeless. Grown-ups were so dramatic. The question that nagged him was why did his father trust DeLaney? This merited investigation.

"Who is he?" Timp asked suspiciously. "How do you know him?"

"Don't worry about it," his father said. "I just know that we can trust him."

Timp shook his head and let the subject drop. He'd let the grown-ups sink themselves. That'd show them. Then they'd have to admit he was right, and probably buy him a Dr. Pepper Icee too.

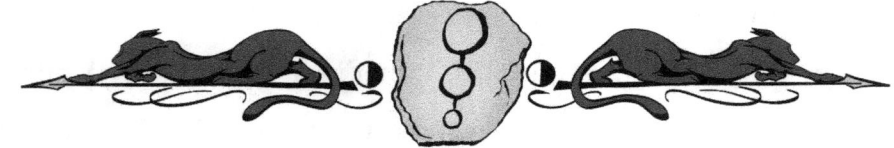

CHAPTER 19
A VERY BERRY VIKING SNACK

The night before, Uncle Dene had been knocked unconscious and covered in a berry-lanche. It all happened so quickly. He didn't even cry out before being swallowed by the mountain of blueberries. Not the best way to spend the night, but he'd slept worse. He awoke that morning, found his house among the berries, and now worked to dislodge it from the bottom of the pile. He grunted and pulled as sweat poured from his brow. It was the scent of that sweat that Molly stalked, the scent of fatigue, of weakness, of desperation. It was the scent of prey.

Molly had stalked that delightful scent to the kitchen counter, where she now prepared to eat her just deserts—or at least, a Dene dessert.

Mrs. Molly Viking Slayer crouched on a stool in her kitty-cat ninja attack pose. Her tail flicked back and forth in the air. Her eyes narrowed to the counter and bore into the tiny blue man with intense concentration. Her hackles rose, and her pupils dilated.

What a tasty treat you'll make, she thought. Her smile revealed a row of sharp, pointy teeth. Her whiskers twitched. Her bottom waggled. She lifted one foot and settled into a comfortable jumping position. Then she waggled her bottom some more. You really can't have too much bottom waggling when you're a cat. Two more waggles and she was ready to strike.

Her prey paused from pulling the berry. He seemed to sense that he was being watched. Molly shivered with anticipation and choked back her mirth. He turned to find two giant, and Molly would say purrfectly gorgeous green eyes glaring down at him. In that instant, three things happened: First, Mrs. Molly licked her chops. Second, Uncle Dene broke wind. And third, a giant hand reached from the heavens and grabbed the Viking, his tiny house, and a pile of berries.

"Shoo, Molly, get away from those berries," Mrs. Littleton said. "Shoo!"

Queen Molly's fur sizzled. *"Give that back, you stupid, silly servant. That's my snack!"* she hissed.

"Odin's Raven, I'm saved! Saved!" the man cried as he soared through the air in the safety of the chambermaid's grip.

"I saw it first. He's mine," Molly demanded. *"I'm your queen. You will obey me. I'll smother you in your sleep, I'll—"* But as

usual, all Mrs. Littleton heard was, "Meow. Meow," and of course, "Meow."

"Saved, I say! Eat this yon stupid guard-beast." The man slapped his rump, danced his happiness, and fell back in a sigh of relief, "Thank thee, Odin, for thine generosity. I's saved—"

Then, Mrs. Littleton dropped the berries into a pie, shoved the pie into the oven, and shut the door.

"—or not."

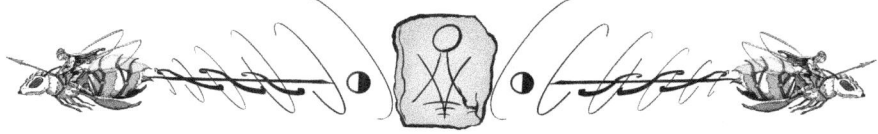

CHAPTER 20
THERE AND BACK AGAIN, A VIKING TALE

Wind whipped around Timp's head, and the Vikings screamed into his ears as the truck rattled up I-49. Timp had told his father it was cooler in the bed, which was true. Their truck had no air conditioning (As old as it was, Timp considered it lucky that the truck had an engine). He could tell his father didn't believe his reason for wanting to ride in the back, but allowed it, probably thinking Timp wanted some time alone after their argument. He wasn't entirely wrong. Timp did want time alone, but *not* because of their argument. He planned to lecture the Vikings on self-control.

"Okay, Quiet!" Timp began. "I don't know how it is in Vikingland, but here in the real world, you can't just go running off and acting a fool."

"Real world? Humph! Our'n world may be small, Giant, but 'tis as real as your'n."

"And we know nothing of this 'Vikingland.' Tell us the location, and we shall wage war upon their peoples for stealing our namesake."

"I was being sarcastic," Timp whined as he threw his hands into the air. He remembered himself and turned around.

Inside the truck, his father talked on his cell. Their eyes met in the rearview mirror and they both quickly looked away.

Timp continued his lecture. "The point is, you're not back home; you're in the land of the giants, and when you're in the land of the giants, you have to act civilized."

"Civilized me Asgard! Never heard of a civilized giant in all mine life!" Erika said.

"I'm civilized," Timp said defensively.

"Ye call eating Bjorn's house civilized? And abandoning Uncle Dene to the wilderness, be that civilized? What of locking us within your'n torture box? Oh aye, most civilized, that. And running through Hel with an army of giants in pursuit, my how civilized ye giants be."

Timp watched the trees blur past. He had done those things.

"Now, Erika, be fair," Bjorn began.

At least Bjorn had Timp's back . . . "The giant be large, but his brain be quite slow." ...or not. "He knew not of Uncle Dene, and—"

"And if he should fail to fulfill his vow to locate Uncle Dene and our'n houses, I shall summon the fury of all our'n killer bees upon him!"

Timp threw his hands up in the air. "There you go again with your bee talk."

"Killer bees," Gunnar corrected.

"Ye doubt me, Giant?" Erika asked. The other Vikings grew silent. "Ye think I jest? Imagine a swarm of bees falling upon thee like a plague—"

"Killer Bees," Timp corrected.

"Interrupt me not, Giant! This be not a joke. Imagine you a swarm of *killer* bees descending upon thee, their stingers driving into every inch of your'n soft, boy-giant flesh. You scream, aye, and attempt to swat them away with your'n clumsy, giant hands, but their'n armor protects them. Bees fill yer mouth and your'n lungs, eyes, and ears. They sting and they sting, again and again until your weak, giant body resigns itself to shock and fails thee as ye suffocate on the crawling, scraping of bees. Think on that, Giant, for that be what awaits thee if ye don't find our'n homes. That be what shall happen if'n Uncle Dene be not safe."

Timp swallowed. Had he known that Uncle Dene was baking until golden brown in a 375-degree oven, he might have thrown himself from the moving truck for a quicker death. *Bees.* The thought was too terrifying to imagine.

Timp tried to poke holes in their story to put his mind at ease. "How'd the bees know to attack me? Why wouldn't they just fly off?"

O'dul started to answer, but the others shushed him into silence. They muttered and debated amongst themselves. Timp rolled his eyes. Everything was a secret with these Vikings. Finally, Bjorn answered, "'Tis because of the Vaskrél, Giant."

"The Vass—what-now?" Timp asked.

"Thor's hammer, Giant, be there no end to your questions? Fen? Where be Fen? Fen?" Erika called. "Fen, ye be the Giantologist. Explain to this idjit giant so his idjit brain may understand. . . . Idjit."

Fen cleared his throat ceremoniously—he loved explaining things. "The Vaskrél art the brave rulers of the sky. It is for their'n bravery we name our'n warriors of flight."

"I thought brave warriors lived in Valhalla, not Louisiana."

"Nay, Giant. You speak of Valhöll, the great hall where you go when you die. And by 'you' I really mean 'us,' as in we Vikings, because they certainly shan't allow a Jötunn into Valhöll —I'll tell you that for nothing." Fen snorted and laughed. Timp did not. "Sorry. 'Tis only that, well, Valhöll be for—"

"Valhöll be for warriors," Gunnar interrupted. "Which be why you'll not enter their neither, nerd."

"Oh, aye?" Fen said, "Valhöll 'tis reserved for *heroes*, and a hero can be anything, anyone."

"As long as they be Viking," O'dull added.

"And not filthy, dirty, no-good, nutcase berserkers!" Erika said.

"Filthy? Dirty? Why you— "

Erika and Gunnar fought and rolled around Timp's ear. It tickled and itched and took all of his will not to scratch. He tried to distract himself by thinking of something else, like how Erika had just butted in to defend Fen again. What was up with that?

"At peace, ye two. This be no way for either of ye find Odin's halls," Bjorn said and the itching stopped.

Timp continued, "So, let me get this straight. Vaskrél control bees?"

"What? Giant, be your'n brain smaller than our'n's, or be it just so big that it should run at snail's pace? None may control a bee. Riders may only hope to join their'n vígbýs."

"Vígbýs?"

"Aye, a vígbý be a proper battle-bee."

"*Killer bee*," Timp corrected with a smirk.

"Indeed."

"Few Vikings be granted the distinct honor of flying among yon bees. Thus are they the Kindred Kind. Chosen. Of them, even fewer become one with their'n vígbý. Only then are they so named 'Vaskrél' in honor of their bravery to conquer the skies, for they are the brave storm that defends our'n lands."

"Ohhhhhh," Timp said, not getting it at all.

"All who achieve singularity with their'n vígbý carry the name Vaskrél."

"Oh. Yeah, I don't get it at all."

"When we speak of the Vaskrél, we oft mean the rider, we oft mean yon vígbý, but in truth a Vaskrél be both, rider and vígbý as one."

"Be it really all so difficult for thine simple non-Viking brain to understand, Giant?" Gunnar whined.

Timp had grown used to this kind of remark. "Are *you* a Vaskrél?"

"Me? Gods no, Giant. Think I have a death wish, do ye? I've told ye, I be Berserker. I require no mite-ridden killer bee to help me in a fight. Nay, my brethren and I summon the power of the bear to slay all who stand in our'n path."

"You sound like a nut to me," Timp said.

"I'll second that," Fen said, and then they were at it, pushing and fighting.

"Peace, friends. Peace." When everyone calmed, Bjorn returned his attention to Timp, "Giant, 'tis difficult to understand the Vaskrél without seeing them with thine own eyes. They are calmed with inner peace, brave, and strong. They forge the path between two worlds: the air and the earth. 'Tis an honor awarded few, but make no mistake, Giant; though brash, Erika doth not jest. The Vaskrél be deadly. Even to one so large as your'n self. They have killed many giants, some even more giant than your'n self, Giant. If ye cross us, if ye do not hold to your'n word, or if Uncle Dene is at all harmed, ye shall meet the Vaskrél's wrath; ye shall suffer their sting, and ye shall meet a death of untold horrors."

"Are you a Vaskrél?" Timp asked just above a whisper. He didn't know if Bjorn could hear him in the windy truck bed, but he had.

"Nay."

Timp and the Vikings did not speak the rest of the ride home. He thought about how amazing it'd be to ride in a swarm of bees, but how terrible it'd be to get attacked by one. He didn't wish to suffer the sting of 1,000 Vaskrél. He decided to find Uncle Dene as soon as he got home.

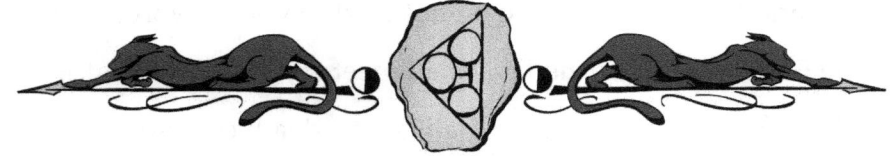

CHAPTER 21
THE MIGHTY MRS. MOLLY

Mrs. Molly Fit Thrower perched on the stool next to the kitchen counter, shouting curses at Mrs. Littleton, "*How dare you, ridiculous human. How dare you steal my dinner. You think delicious little blue pests grow on trees? . . . Well, they might. I don't know where they come from, but I do know that I'm hungry. Do you know there are cats starving in this world? True, most of them are dirty, rotten, alley cats who deserve it, but that's not the point. I'm your queen! You'll do as I command, servant! Now, open that oven, and get me my dinner!*"

Mrs. Littleton ignored Molly and busied herself with preparing another delicious pie. Molly sank back in her seat, and swished her tail in annoyance. It wasn't fair. For her entire kitty-cat life, she'd asserted her rule over these silly humans only to be continuously ignored. Now, she'd finally found a human small enough to actually rule—and better still, to eat—and what happened? The chambermaid stole him and threw him in a pie! It was enough to drive Molly mad.

Molly glared through the oven's glass window. The pies were starting to brown on top. Her delicious little blue snack was almost certainly dead by now. She yeowled in agony. She so loved to eat her dinner raw. It just wouldn't be as tasty baked and covered in fruit mush; though, she'd probably eat it anyway.

"*That pie better be for me,*" she warned. "*I'll have my snack, or you will suffer my wrath. My Big Bad Incident will be a pleasure cruise compared to what I'll do to this place if you don't give me my vengeance!*"

Mrs. Littleton didn't respond.

"*Give me my grumpy, chambermaid!*"

But as usual, all Mrs. Littleton heard was "Meow. Meow," and of course, "Meow."

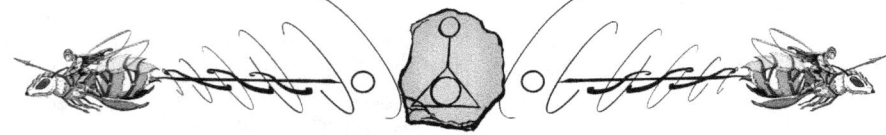

CHAPTER 22
HOME AGAIN, HOME AGAIN, JIGGITY—WHAT?

The Littleton's truck lurched into the carport and died with a gurgling pop. Timp reluctantly awoke from a daydream where he'd been riding a giant bee. The dream felt so real that it seemed almost a memory, and the best part was that he wasn't afraid. He soared through the clouds but felt no fear at all. Timp thought about his tree and swing by the water tower. His fear rushed back. So much for pleasant dreams. He hopped down from the truck bed. "Remember what I told y'all. Act civilized."

"You watch *your'n self*, Giant."

Timp rolled his eyes. Inside, he heard Molly whining her meows.

"Stupid, selfish, no good, stinky servant. Where am I going to get another grumpy as plump and as tasty as that one? Where, I ask you? Where?"

"No Molly, I already gave you a treat,"Mrs. Littleton said. "Get down."

"*Do not presume to order me, servant! Get me that pie! I demand you get me that pie, at once! I'm your queen!*"

"What's gotten into Molly?" Mr. Littleton asked, kissing his hello.

"I have no idea. She's been acting weird all—" Mrs. Littleton stopped mid-sentence. Timp stood in the kitchen, gasping for air. "Timp? Are you all right?"

"What do you think you're doing?" He cried. He scanned the counter. Bowls that had overflowed with berries the night before now sat in the sink, empty. That meant the berries must be in the . . . "The oven!" *The Houses! Uncle Dene!* "The bees! The bees! The bees!"

"Killer bees," Gunnar corrected.

Timp dove into the oven, and pulled out the pies. He stood with one in each hand, then realized the pies were still hot, very hot.

"Yeow!" He threw the pies. For a dreadful moment, they hung in the air, spinning in slow motion. Without thinking, he grabbed them again, got burned, and threw the pies again. "Yeow!" Catch. "Ouch!" Throw. Had Timp been able to think, he'd have entertained plans of joining the circus—Timp the Amazing Pie Juggling Clown. But, as is the way with all pie-jugglers, gravity got the last laugh. *Ker-splat! Splat!*

Timp wasted no time. He fell to his knees and began digging through the sticky hot pie mush. His mother and father watched in stunned silence as bits of blueberry flew into the air.

"The bees!" Timp shouted as he dug. "The bees!"

"Timp! What has gotten into you?" Mrs. Littleton asked after being slapped awake by a sticky chunk of piecrust.

"This be what ye call civilized, is it, Giant?"

"Shut it!"

"Do not speak to your mother that way," his father said, not realizing Timp had been speaking to the tiny blue people living in his ears. (Parents can be sooo oblivious).

Timp ignored his father and continued digging. The soft mush made house searching easier. He mashed his hands through the berry mush over and over until he found something hard.

"I found one!" Timp shouted, holding up a Viking house — or to his parent's eyes, a blueberry.

"You see what I mean?" Mrs. Littleton said. "That's exactly what he did earlier."

Timp held the berry to the light, and tried to look through a small opening on one end.

"Uncle Dene better be in there," Erika threatened, "or 'tis the Vaskrél for thee."

Timp tilted the berry and wiped away the slime. He shook it, and a blob of mush splattered into his palm.

"It's him! It's him! I found him!" Timp said, showing the mush to everyone and beaming with pride.

His parents nodded with smiles contorted in concern and disgust. They exchanged wide-eyed glances and shrugged. Timp picked up the glob, studied it closely, and then shoved it into his ear.

"Well, that's just gross," Mr. Littleton said.

"He didn't do *that* earlier," Mrs. Littleton agreed.

His parents muttered amongst themselves while the Vikings gathered in his ear to check on Uncle Dene. Their movements went unnoticed to his parents, but not to Molly.

"*He's infested!*" she said, eyeing Timp with her keen kitty-cat gaze. "*He's covered with those nasty, little, blue pests. He needs to be dipped, de-fleaed, and made to wear a collar. And, what's more, he's stealing my treat when he already has so many of his own! That's stingy! The servant should share.*" Molly crouched into her kitty-cat ninja attack pose.

The seconds lasted years before Fen shouted, "Uncle Dene's going to be fine."

Timp deflated with a sigh of relief. No killer bees would murder him that day. Then for the first time since he got home, Timp took notice of his surroundings. The kitchen was a mess. Gelatinous pie innards stuck to the floor, appliances, counters, and ceiling. And his parents . . . were not alone.

"Timp, you remember Dr. Housen."

Dr. Housen stood in the corner, wide-eyed with her mouth hanging open and holding a cup of tea.

"She's gonna have a little talk with you about your . . . um . . . recent behavior, okay?" His mother flicked a piece of blueberry mush from her cheek and studied the floor.

"They called the law on their'n kin," Fen said, noting the behavior in his notepad.

Timp opened his mouth to speak, but something flew across the room and latched onto his face.

"Molly!" Mrs. Littleton screamed.

Timp sprang to his feet with Vikings shouting and a cat hissing in his ears. He shook his head back and forth and tried to throw Molly from his face as she clawed and scratched to reach the Vikings.

"Molly, stop that!"

Mr. Littleton tried to help, but Timp wind-milled through the house. "Timp, stay still!" Mrs. Littleton grabbed a broom and began beating Timp over the head with it.

"Not helping!" Timp yelled.

In a panic and blinded by a mass of black fur, Timp tripped over trunks, knocked over the coat rack, and slammed into bookshelves. He ran into cabinets and heard dishes crash. He shook and gyrated, yelled, and went berserk, but Molly clung to his face like an alien in a Sigourney Weaver film.

"*Give me my treats!*" Molly demanded in an ear-shattering screech. "*You stingy, rotten, no good servant!*"

The Vikings hid deeper in Timp's hair and ears. The pain stabbed at his eardrums. They poked at Molly's claws with their spears, axes, and swords, but it did little to deter the tenacious beast. "Back, foul demon! Back!"

"Ahead, Giant, yon door!" a Viking yelled.

Timp charged toward the sliding glass door.

"No! It's not open!" Timp's mother leapt across the room and yanked open the door so that Timp could run outside unobstructed. He followed her voice, but blinded by the cat, he missed the open side and slammed into the plate-glass with a resounding *SMACK!* Molly fell to the floor in hisses and curses, and Mrs. Littleton swept her outside.

Timp slid down the door with his cheek smearing against the glass in a rubbery groan. He'd knocked himself unconscious.

The last thing he heard was Erika. "Civilized, indeed. Humph!"

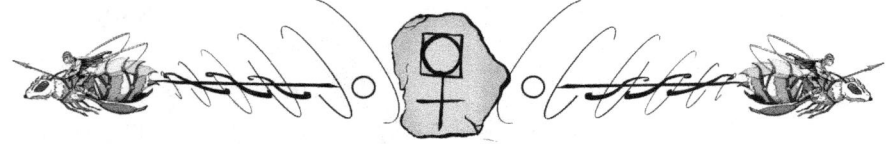

CHAPTER 23
DR. WHO?

An hour later, Timp sat in bed wrapped like a B-movie monster with white gauze covering his head and hands, and Sponge Bob Band-Aids stuck to his face in random directions. The burns on his hands were 1st degree, and the scratches on his face had barely broken the skin, but any time Timp had the slightest cut, scrape, or bruise, his parents seized the first aid kit and practiced the ancient Egyptian art of mummification.

"Okay, Timp. Now what do you see?" Dr. Housen asked.

Timp scrunched his nose. The ink splatter on this card definitely resembled a butterfly—even more so than the last ink-splatter butterfly, which Timp had to admit looked even more like a butterfly than the one on the card before *that*. Come to think of it, they *all* looked like butterflies . . . or maybe it was bees. Killer bees.

"'Tis the head of a gorkin," one Viking said. "What? T'where?" another replied. "Aye, there. See it? That be its teeth and its eyes." "That be no gorkin. 'Tis a flying newt" "Flying newt? Ye're a flying nutter!"

"I believe 'tis an image of ink, spilled upon yon card," O'dul said profoundly.

"Silence, they're testing the giant," Fen said. "This is most fascinating. I think he may be dumb even by giant standards."

"If that be true, he'd make a fine berserker," Erika said.

"I resent that," Gunnar said.

"Be quiet," Timp gritted through his teeth. His patience with the Vikings was wearing thin. He tried to speak low so Dr. Housen wouldn't hear, but she had sharp ears.

"I didn't say anything," she said.

"Oh, I wasn't talking to you," Timp said, and then realized how that might sound. "I mean, ergh, that is—"

"Do you often talk to yourself?"

"Oh no, never." Timp knew it was best not to talk to yourself.

"So, you hear voices?"

Doh! Now he wished he'd said that he talked to himself. Timp didn't know much about psychology, but he knew hearing voices was a bad thing, probably worse than just talking to yourself. Why hadn't he said he talked to himself?

"No. No. No voices. I was talking to . . . " Timp strained for an answer that wouldn't sink him deeper. " . . . to my imaginary friend. Yeah, that's it. Imaginary. Friend. . . . Oh, and I know he's imaginary. I don't think he's real. Imagin . . . ary. So, we cool?"

"You seem a little old to have an imaginary friend," Dr. Housen said.

"You know, that's exactly what I told my imaginary friend."

Dr. Housen laughed and Timp knew his answers had been satisfactory.

"I better go talk with your parents," Dr. Housen said as she stood with a grunt. "No. No. Don't get up. You stay. Rest." She patted Timp's cheek with a smile.

As soon as she left, Timp hopped out of bed and stuck his ear to the door, tracking her movements down the hall by the creaking floorboards. Silly Dr. Housen, she didn't know his Jedi secrets. He waited until she turned the corner and then followed.

"Is he all right?" Mr. and Mrs. Littleton urged in hushed voices.

Timp eavesdropped from the hall.

"He's fine," Dr. Housen said. "Just a normal boy with an active imagination. A bit lonely, perhaps, but perfectly normal."

"Lonely? What do you mean? What should we do?"

Dr. Housen laughed. "I don't know, Pam. Maybe find him a friend his own age for the summer?"

"A friend . . . that's good. That's good. But you're sure he's okay?"

"Yes, I'm sure," Dr. Housen said, and then added with a wink, "But then again, I'm a veterinarian. What do I know about psychology?"

The Littletons knew Dr. Housen was a veterinarian, of course—she was their vet—but she was also a family friend and the only doctor of *anything* the Littletons knew. So, for them, Dr. Housen wore many hats . . . as long as all of the hats said "doctor."

Mr. Littleton laughed and sighed, "Well, in that case, can you tell us what's wrong with the cat?"

Dr. Housen studied Molly through the sliding glass door. The cat stood on her hind legs, stuck to the glass like a Garfield doll suction-cupped to a rearview window. "*Stupid servants! Let me in this house! I demand you open this door, immediately! I'm your queen! Your queen! Your quueeeeeeeeeeeeennnnn!*"

"Medically speaking," Dr. Housen said, "that cat is bonkers."

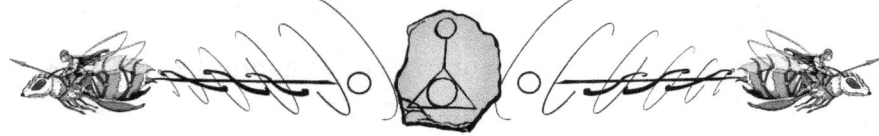

CHAPTER 24
A VERY VIKING DINNER

For the second time that week, the Littletons ate dinner in silence. They'd invited Dr. Housen to stay, but she politely declined. She had enough excitement for one evening. Timp understood. He spent the hours leading up to dinner cleaning blueberry mush and pie innards from every kitchen surface. On the bright side, he found another Viking house. On the less bright side, he was exhausted. He didn't even have enough fight left in him to protest the huge pile of broccoli lumped onto his plate. In fact, he could barely stay awake at all. His head bobbed closer and closer to his mashed potatoes; and then, just before his nose dipped into the gravy, he awoke with a start and began the process anew. Timp needed a vacation from his summer vacation.

"Hey, Timp, guess what," Mrs. Littleton said in a tone filled with such forced excitement that Timp knew whatever she was about to say would be dreadful, "Your dad and I were thinking we'd invite your cousin, Trevor, to stay with us for a while."

That woke Timp up.

"Trevor? Why? What'd I do? I'll be better, I swear."

Mr. Littleton choked back a laugh. Trevor was Timp's cousin from Dallas and quite possibly the worst human on earth. It was bad enough to see him at Christmas, but now summer too? His parents must really be mad at him.

"This isn't a punishment, Timp," Mrs. Littleton said defensively—Trevor was her nephew. "It'll be fun."

Timp doubted that very much, but before he could say so, an olive stood up and began walking across the table.

"Oi! Oi! Lookie what I found," a voice echoed from inside of the olive.

"What'd you say, Timp?"

"Oh, nothing," he answered, scooping up the olive and tossing it into his shirt pocket.

His parents exchanged glances, but continued eating while the other Vikings crawled out of his hair and ears to investigate the pickled pocket treasure. "This be even better than a berry house. 'Tis already hollowed." "Aye, I even favor the color." "Smells a might funny though." "That'll wash out . . . I hope."

Timp sighed and ate a piece of broccoli. "Trevor," he muttered. His mood soured with every bite. The Vikings were ruining his life.

Timp asked if he could be excused and started for his room.

"Wait! Wait! What of our'n dinner?" a Viking yelled.

Timp dropped his shoulders and rolled his eyes. He turned around, with his elbows locked in annoyance, grabbed a chicken thigh off of his plate, and walked away.

Mr. and Mrs. Littleton shrugged. "Teenagers," Mr. Littleton said, and Mrs. Littleton nodded in agreement. That explained everything. Timp wanted to remind them that he was only twelve, but then again, he felt like the Vikings had aged him a hundred years.

He walked into his room and dropped the chicken thigh on his nightstand. The Vikings hopped down and inspected the chunk of meat while Timp fell into his bed.

O'dul tried a bite. "Tastes like gorkin."

"You think everything tastes like gorkin."

"That's 'cause everything *do* taste like gorkin."

Part of Timp wanted to ask about gorkins, but so much more of him no longer cared. His hands were burned, his face scratched, and now his cousin Trevor was going to invade his mountain—er, that is, his house. Timp rolled away from the lamp on his nightstand and away from the Vikings. With the olive from dinner, the model they'd stolen from DeLaney, and the four berries, Timp had collected all of the Viking houses—replaced the one he ate, and he'd found Uncle Dene. Alive. Thank gorkin-chicken for that. Tomorrow he'd bring the Vikings back to their village—wherever that was—and the healing process could begin.

The Vikings chatted with Uncle Dene. They regaled him with exaggerated tales of their adventures through Hel, and Uncle Dene told them what it was like to be baked in a blueberry pie. "'Tis like a sauna in there." (It was a short story.)

Of course, had Uncle Dene been in the oven a minute more, he most certainly would have died, and then the Vaskrél would have attacked Timp on their killer bees, and he'd be dead too. Timp tried to tuck away the thought.

"Giant?" Uncle Dene said with a mouthful of chicken.

Timp pretended to be asleep.

"Morose sort of giant, ain't he? Oi, Giant?" Uncle Dene called again.

When Timp still didn't respond, Uncle Dene took out his leather sling out and loaded it with a stone shot, which is to say an almost microscopic pebble. Timp heard a strange whirling sound at his back and rolled over to investigate. He opened his eyes just in time to see Uncle Dene launch the pebble straight into his cornea.

"Yeow!" Timp jumped up, rubbing his eye. "What's wrong with you?"

"Oh, nothing," Uncle Dene said gladly. "I'm feeling quite well. Got a little berry goo stuck in me drawers, but other than that—"

"No, I mean what do you want?"

"Oh, I simply wished to thank thee."

"Well you sure have a funny way of saying it," Timp said as he dug the dirt out of his eye. *Scratches, burns, nose stabs, and now dirt in the eye. These Vikings are going to kill me.*

Uncle Dene silently mouthed the words "thank thee" to himself. He asked the other Vikings if they felt he'd said the words funny and they all agreed he had not. "Tell me, Giant, how say you the words 'thank' and 'thee?'"

Timp groaned, "Not by shooting a rock in someone's eye!"

"Oh!" Uncle Dene said, understanding. "The stone was merely to get your'n attention so I could thank thee." He smiled and slapped his belly, glad that the confusion was resolved.

Timp buried his head in his pillow and in a muffled yell cried out, "You Vikings are driving me crazy!"

"Where's crazy?" "Be we driving there?" "When?" "Ye promised ye'd take us to our'n village, Giant!" "We hardly have time to visit this land of Crazy."

"I *am* taking you to your village. First thing in the morning, I'm taking you, your houses, and your Uncle Dene all to your village, and I'm leaving you there, forever!"

There was a moment of silence, and then all at once the Vikings cheered: "Yayah!" "Wonderful!" "We knew we could count on thee, Giant." "Thou honor be as large as thine head."

Timp covered his face with the pillow and beat the other side with his fist. He truly was in the land of Crazy.

"Ye will love our'n village, Giant," Uncle Dene continued. "A bit small for one so large as your'n self, but you'll love it all the same."

Timp took a deep breath and collapsed with his pillow still covering his face. All he wanted was sleep. He needed to heal and forget.

"The villagers may not like thee at first, being as yer large in brain yet slow in wit, but we shall tell them how ye helped us." "Aye, then perhaps they won't kill thee," O'dul said cheerfully.

"Aye, *perhaps* so," the other Vikings agreed.

"Perhap—what now?"

"Oh, aye. Giants be our'n sworn enemies. Surely ye knows this, being's you is a giant, Giant. But if'n they do kill thee, at least ye'll have carried our'n houses back home fer us."

"Here! Here!" the Vikings cheered.

Timp pulled his quilt over his head. He'd get no sleep that night.

"Any poor souls who trespass against us,

Whether it be beast or man,

Will suffer the bite or be stung dead on sight

By those who inhabit this land.

For theirs is the power and this is the kingdom,

As sure as the sun does burn,

So enter this path, but heed these four words:

You shall never return."

the Raconteurs

Brendan Benson and Jack White

PART II

The Realm of Vikings

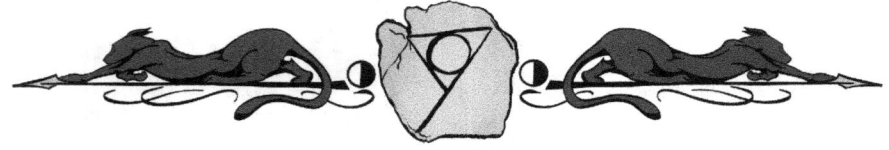

CHAPTER 25
MOLLY REMEMBERSSSSSSS

Molly spent the night cursing, hissing and spitting in kitty-cat growls as she paced back and forth across the porch.

"Infested! This whole place is infested! Oh, I detest infest. I detest infest and little blue pests. And now, I'm rhyming! Oh, I hate rhyme. It's a complete waste of time. Aarrrrrrrgh!"

Molly stopped her grumbling and watched her chambermaid work on the porch.

Mrs. Littleton organized buckets and straps for the workers to pick up as they arrived that day, then she strapped two buckets to her hips, looked over the orchard, and started down the steps. Today was her day to pick berries while Molly's manservant stayed inside to make blueberry jam and wine. But inside or out, the servants never complained. They worked. *"As they should!"*

Molly sniffed the air. It'd be another scorching hot day.

Molly's kitty-cat ears flicked as she listened for movement within the house. If the manservant was staying inside today, her only hope of entry was the boy. He'd be up soon. Molly would be ready.

Molly slinked onto the bench next to the door. When the boy came out, she would leap onto him, tear him to ribbons, and leave his carcass in her wake as she entered the cool, air-conditioned palace.

"What are you up to, Molly?" Mrs. Littleton asked.

Molly had forgotten her chambermaid was still there. This required clever and decisive action. Molly sat down, batted her eyes with the utmost dignity, and licked her bottom.

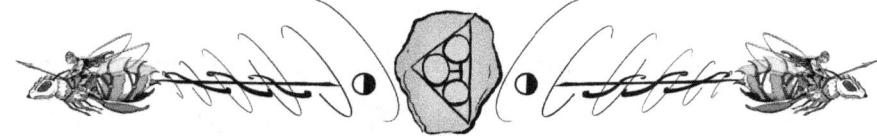

CHAPTER 26
SHORT TRIP HOME, LOOOONNNNG TRIP BACK

Timp opened bloodshot eyes to the dawn. He'd spent the night tossing and turning with anxiety. *"Perhaps they won't kill thee." Perhaps.* What did that even mean? The Vikings' words spun through his mind on a torturous carousel. By morning, Timp found himself worse off than he'd been the night before. Not only was he still scratched, bruised, burned, and battered, but now he had an exhaustion headache as well. He wanted to stay in bed, but light sliced through the blinds without mercy or apology. Timp's head buzzed. The Louisiana sun had pity for none. *Wait, the sun? I should've been up hours ago!* Timp groaned. His headache felt even worse with a layer of guilt.

The Vikings were ready. They had awoken before dawn, gathered their belongings, and packed some leftover gorkin-chicken. They waited on the nightstand next to their houses—which is to say: four renovated and shellacked blueberries (with faux finishing), one stolen model, and a pickled olive. "Up with ye, Giant. Up with ye," they urged.

Timp groaned and was hit in the head with a small rock in response. Patience was not a Viking virtue.

"I'm up. I'm up." He climbed to his feet before another rock flew his way. Soon he'd be on his own again. He was ready. Wounds and strained family relations aside, Timp could use a Viking break.

He stumbled down the hall and into the living room. His father threw pots and pans around the kitchen and muttered like the Muppet chef. In an hour, the kitchen would be in ruins akin to a Viking raid (Timp now knew from experience). Timp coughed. His father stopped digging through the cabinets, rested his fists on the counter, and sighed. "Have you seen my bazooka?"

Timp rolled his eyes. It was a joke he'd heard a million times. Last week, his father explored the depths of their kitchen for The Ark of the Covenant, the lightening of Zeus, and Davey Jone's locker. It made Timp smile even when he knew the joke was coming, but especially now. Things were already returning to normal.

"Nope. Sorry, I haven't seen it. I believe we keep the heavy artillery on the top shelf."

"The top shelf you say? I'll check." Mr. Littleton dove back into the cabinet and pulled out several bowls.

"You store weaponry in your'n kitchen, Giant?" Fen asked. Timp didn't have to see him to know that Fen was writing this detail down in his tiny notebook. "Most strange Giant. Most strange."

"What be wrong with that?" Gunnar asked. "I keep my's crossbow under me bed."

"Aye, we know. Twas I who pulled the arrow that shot through your'n mattress and stuck ye in the Asgard," Erika said and the other Vikings snickered.

Timp stepped onto the porch and took in a deep breath of damp morning air. The constant talking in his ears would soon be over. He might be dead, but even so, the talking would be over. Molly sprang from the bench and attacked his ankle in a blur of teeth and claws.

"They're mine! Mine! Mine! Give me! Give me my little blue pests! Give me my treats!"

Timp screamed and shook his leg, dancing his way to the end of the porch, where he kicked out and sent Mrs. Molly Kick Ball flying into the tall grass.

"She really hates you," Timp's mother said.

"I'll say," Timp agreed, baffled by the insanity of the animal.

"But, that's what you get for tying her up in the barn."

Timp started to protest but his mother had already turned back toward the orchard.

When she was out of earshot, he sighed. "Okay, where do I go?"

Bjorn peeked out of Timp's hair and climbed on top of his ear for a better view. "Ye go, um, that is . . . ye go . . ."

"You don't know where you live?"

"Aye, let's see ye find your'n way in a world where ye be no bigger than a ya find a fair-sized ant, stupid," Gunnar answered.

"Well, how did you find your way to my house to begin with?"

"We followed the mountain," Bjorn said. "But when ye stand upon the mountain, what shall ye follow to return, eh Giant?"

That was a fair point. "Okay, fine. What about those bees you kept talking about?"

"Do we look like we have bees, Giant?"

"Aye, if we'd bees, we'd not need thee, Giant," Erika added.

"I thought you said you had a horn that could summon the wrath of the Vaskrél."

The Vikings hesitated before one coughed, "Eh, we might'n of exaggerated a wee bit there, Giant. Only Vaskrél scouts carry blast horns."

"Great. Just great. You made me look like an idiot in front of my parents."

"Me thinks ye do a fine job of that on yer own, Giant."

177

"I shall explain the workings soon enough, but for now, pray give me a moment to think." Bjorn studied the layout of the farm in so far as he could see. "Well, the mountain is here, and . . . um, we're here."

Timp rolled his eyes. These idiots had convinced him that they could control bees. He couldn't believe he'd fallen for their lies. He was past ready to get rid of these Vikings. "How about I just walk around until something looks familiar?"

"Grand idea, Giant."

Timp knew the Vikings lived inside berries so he headed for the orchard. They walked for what seemed like hours. Timp would stop in front of one bush, then another, but the Vikings dismissed each as nothing more than a regular ol' berry bush. To avoid suspicion from his mother and the other workers, Timp dropped a handful of berries into his bucket before moving to the next bush. In this way, Timp and the Vikings worked their way through half the farm.

"I've an idea might help," Fen said as they curved to a finish around yet another row of berry bushes. "Our'n village is near the sea. If we go there, mayhap we can find our way."

"The sea?"

"Aye, the sea. Where might we find it?"

"The nearest sea is the Gulf of Mexico," Timp said, "but that's clear across Louisiana." Of course, the Vikings had no idea how far "clear across Louisiana" was. They probably didn't even know they were in Louisiana. They probably thought they lived in the black forest of Cajun-gard.

"This gulf you speak of, be it large?" Bjorn asked.

"Heck yeah it's large. It's *the* Gulf. You can't even see across it."

"Aye, that be it! Take us to your'n gulf, Giant!"

Timp was flabbergasted. He had no idea the Vikings had traveled so far. The Gulf was at least five hours down I-49, and Timp didn't own a car—well, not one of his own—and there was no way his parents would give him a ride: "Hey dad, can you take me and my ear-Vikings to the beach?" Yeah, right. Timp didn't need the Vikings cleared out of his ears to know how that sounded.

"I can't take you there. It's too far. There's just no way. The Gulf of Mex—" Timp stopped. The Vikings thrived on confusion. "Describe this 'sea' of yours."

"'Tis large, even bigger than your'n self, Giant."

"And filled with horrible sea monsters," Uncle Dene said.

"And water," O'dul added.

The other Vikings groaned. "Aye, O'dul. He knows the sea be filled with water. He be dumb and giant, but even him's stupid brain knows that."

"Are the sea monsters bigger than me?" Timp asked, still digging.

"Nay, Giant. Never have mine eyes seen any that are, but who can know what lay at the bottom of the sea?" Bjorn answered.

"Some can jump as high as thee, I'll wager," another added.

"Sea monsters that jump? What do those look like?"

"They have sickly wet yellow eyes and the tongue of a gorkin."

"Aye, and their skin be slimy and green."

"And the sound they make—Oh, Thor's hammer, the sound." The Vikings agreed.

"They sing a croaking battle cry, like this—" Gunnar croaked. The Vikings joined him, croaking over and over in Timp's ear.

"Okay. Okay. I get it," Timp said. "And this sea of yours, is the water salty?"

"Nay, Giant. There be no salt in this sea. 'Tis black and still —"

"Dead still and endless deep."

"Aye, deep as the depths of Hel," Uncle Dene said.

"Oh, deeper than Hel," O'dul said. "We been there. Hel was only 22 floors—" "Shut it, O'dul," Erika said.

Timp had the whole picture now.

"Okay, y'all listen up. That isn't a sea. It's a pond. And those aren't sea monsters. They're frogs."

"Oh yeah? And what of the other monsters?" Gunnar asked. "Scaly beasts who spring to the surface from the deepest depths and swallow ships whole."

"Fish," Timp answered.

"And giant serpents with neither arms nor legs, whose teeth spit acid into the eyes of its enemies?

"Snakes," Timp yawned.

"And the gorkin, what about the gorkin?—"

"And dragons!"

"Look, we could do this all day," Timp said, "but none of those are monsters. They're fish, frogs, and snakes. And the pond is just over here." Timp pointed down the hill and started toward the pond.

"You see the world in a most boring way, Giant."

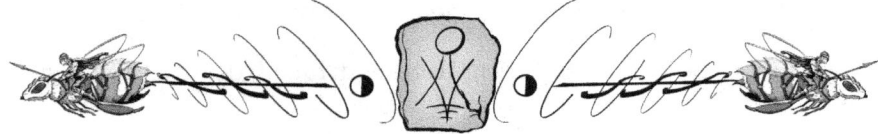

CHAPTER 27
THE VIKING VILLAGE

Timp walked until he reached the bottom of the hill where the blueberry fields met the pond's edge. He searched the bank for something resembling a small settlement or village but saw nothing unusual. "Okay, where is it?"

"Ye must go in," Bjorn said.

"You have got to be kidding me."

This side of the pond was murky at best. Diaphanous slime snaked in the shallows and disappeared into the muddy shore while a green sheet of duckweed undulated on the water's surface, hiding the still blackness below.

"What's the matter, Giant? 'Fraid of monsters?"

It did seem the kind of place for monsters, but Timp would never admit that to Gunnar. He peeled off his shoes and socks, and waded into the pond, praying the water moccasins were sunning on the shore. "I can't believe I'm doing this."

It wasn't that Timp never swam in this pond. He swam in it often, but always on the other side, where the water was much more open and way less freaky. The duckweed, trees, and bushes on this side of the pond made it an ideal place for water moccasins. Timp knew because this was where he'd collected them years before to study snake charming.

While Timp wasn't afraid of snakes on land, something about the way they moved in water—specifically the speed with which they moved—made him uneasy. He also didn't like traipsing through duckweed where he couldn't see them. That saying that snakes can only bite on dry land: . . . a lie, and Timp knew it, a lie to make swimmers feel safe. He supposed it was better than a more truthful saying, "Have fun swimming. Hope you don't die." So, when Timp swam, he jumped into the deep end from a small dock that his family had built. Entering this way avoided a snaky death and—bonus—skipped the slippery green algae that now slimed its way between his toes. *Gross.*

"Okay, now what?" Timp asked, knee deep in muck and slime.

"Our village lay on the other side of yon massive tree."

Timp walked toward a blueberry bush that jutted over the water's edge. "You mean to tell me someone came all the way in to the pond just to pick berries, er, I mean to steal your houses?"

"Oh, no," Bjorn said, "The giant who stole our'n houses did so from the land side of the bush, where 'tis dry."

Timp stopped. He watched the muddy water rise up his thigh as his toes sunk deeper into the slimy silt of the pond floor. "You're a real piece of work. You know that?"

"What's amiss, Giant?"

"The dry side? You're telling me that you can reach your village from the dry side, and you had me walk all the way in here?"

"Aye, ye wished to see the village," Bjorn said. "I thought I'd treat thee to a special view. 'Tis a beautiful village, especially from the sea."

"A special? . . . Treat me?" Slime squished between his toes. "It's a pond!"

"Mayhap, but we Vikings been working day and night to fortify the land side against another giant attack. This way be much easier. and as I say, more beauteous. 'Tis but a bit further, Giant. Ye shall see."

Timp crouched low and walked deeper into the shadowy bushes hanging over the water. "Fine. Where is it?"

"Before you."

And there it was. Beautiful. Clusters of blueberries reached down, barely touching the water's surface. No, not berries, houses. Timp saw that now. Tiny blue houses with silver decks and railings that glowed in the shadows. The Vikings attended every detail in craftsmanship. Each house connected to another by bridges and staircases that spiraled seamlessly throughout the village. Golden lights burned in open windows and doors, spreading a warm glow that made the village feel peaceful and inviting. Now that Timp saw it, the word "village" felt weak. It was a city, a living, breathing work of art, houses growing upon more houses until they met in the middle to form a town square. Silver arches served as aqua ducts, delivering water to a fountain in the center of town. A metal statue of a man rose from the water. He had a wing-tipped helmet and a steel hammer that glowed like a beacon. Timp recognized the figure at once: Thor. Power and grace permeated every facet of these extraordinary little people.

Despite the comparatively enormous size of the city, no part of the Viking's world appeared mass-produced. They handcrafted everything. Every inch was planned, designed, and decorated with a masterful skill and compassion that was almost entirely absent from Timp's world of aluminum shopping centers and temporary buildings. If the Viking world mirrored their souls, Timp wondered what his world said about giants. But of course, unlike the blueberry Vikings, human houses didn't grow on trees. Timp wished they did. Boy, that'd solve some problems. Then they could get a house in the city and keep the farm.

Timp shook away his daydream. Something struck him as odd—that is, something other than the fact that he was standing knee deep in muck, staring at a village built out of blueberries. At first, Timp couldn't quite place what troubled him, and then he realized: there were no people.

"Where are the villagers?" he asked, but before Bjorn or any of the Vikings could reply, Timp got his answer.

"For Týr!" The battle cry echoed across the water, and a barrage of flaming rocks catapulted from the shadows. *So much for peaceful and inviting.*

"Yipe!" *Thwack!* "Ouch!" *Bang!* "Ow!" *Swoosh!* "Hey!" *Zip!*

The rocks left stinging whelps where ever they made contact. Then came the arrows, some of them flaming and not all of them tiny. Two arrows the size of half-sharpened no.2 pencils shot past Timp's head and stuck into a low hanging limb. A chain ran from the arrows back to the village and blue specks with axes, spears, and bows charged up the links to get a better shot at Timp's nose. Why did they always go for the nose? Timp stumbled backwards, but regained his footing.

"Fire! Fire! Fire!" Curtains of flaming arrows flew threw the air with orange comet tails dragging in their wake. Timp blocked his face. Most arrows bounced away, but many stuck into his forearms in pinpricks. Fen and Bjorn the yelled for the villagers to stop, but their screams were lost in the cacophony of battle cries emanating from the city below.

"Kill the Jötunn!" "Down the beast!" "Summon the warships!" "Týr!" "Sòkn!" "Odin owns ye all!"

A marina floated on the water's surface at the base of the city. Several ship fleets lined the wooden docks in perfect rows. Each ship had a series of small holes on the sides for ores and a single mast in the middle for a sail. Ornately carved figures decorated the bows and sterns, making the fronts and backs identical. Timp learned under fire that this design's chief benefit was maneuverability. In a matter of seconds, the ships undocked, and circled into attack formations. To change directions, the oarsmen needed only to paddle in the opposite direction. They seemed to hold no immediate threat, but Timp didn't like the way they circled. He reached down to splash them away, and flames shot from the bows.

"Yeow!" Timp yanked his hand back and sucked his burned thumb.

"Get him! Kill the Jötunn," Erika cheered.

"Really?" Timp demanded.

Erika laughed and retreated behind his ear.

For some reason, he thought she'd be on his side. At least the other Vikings in his hair and ears tried to stop the madness. They yelled, called for peace, and begged for calm but they were too far away for the villagers to hear.

Flames shot from the ships' bows with each push forward. The oarsmen grunted in rhythm to drums as the line moved closer. Timp backed away. Each fire-ship was no larger than his pinky, but like the Vikings themselves, they were tiny in size but massive in intimidation. Arrows, spears, rocks, and flames, the Vikings threw everything they had at Timp—well, almost everything.

"Call the Vaskrél!"

Horns blew.

"NO!"

Was that Erika? Did Erika the fearless giant slayer just cry 'No'? Timp's mind fired in an electric blitzkrieg. The horns echoed as all chaos stopped. The air was still and silent.

"Run, Giant. Run," Bjorn said, not in a yell, but a whisper.

But Timp's legs wouldn't move. His hands shook and his throat felt dry. He knew what was coming; he heard it—the buzz of the Vaskrél . It was faint at first, then louder and louder. It came from nowhere and everywhere all at once. "Bees."

"Killer Bees," Gunnar cried. The normally brave and battle ready berserker sounded ready to run to his berserker mommy. The thought would have made Timp laugh . . . under normal circumstances.

The swarm dropped from the branches like a fleet of World War II Mustang fighter planes. The fire-ships moved steadily closer to Timp's shins while the bees swirled his head. Buzzing filled his ears. The Vaskrél moved fast, almost too fast for Timp to see. He could barely make out the tiny blue riders atop the bees' backs, but he heard their yells: "Kill the giant!" "Down the Jötunn!"

Timp swatted and stumbled. Rocks smacked his head, and a bee stung his neck. He slapped in defense, but as he did, a fire-ship shot a burst of flames into his shin. Timp jumped back. How could he fight back when they attacked from so many directions at once? Timp retreated further and further still. Another sting. Another flame. Another rock, but this one hit Timp right between the eyes. His heel caught a broken limb under the water.

"He's going down!"

"Timpber!"

Timp hit the water with a splash that sent fire-ships and Vikings flying into the air and a wave roaring toward the village. The marina exploded under the wave's might. Villagers scrambled like ants floating in the ocean.

When the waves settled, ships lay scattered and flipped. The docks were twisted and shattered. Vikings paddled through the duckweed and debris. Timp lay in the water with only his face sticking above the surface. Bjorn and the other Vikings had either tumbled out of his ears as he fell or been yanked out when he hit the water. They scrambled to find hold upon the dry ground of Timp's face, and then climbed to the highest possible point—his nose. *Always with the nose!*

"Giant? Be you alive?" Bjorn asked, peering down into Timp's eyes.

"I think I'm just going to lay here for a bit," Timp said.

He was unhurt . . . for the most part, but he didn't move. He reasoned that more of him under water meant less of him available to sting. It made sense. The swarm of Vaskrél hovered over his face, daring him to move. The riders glared down at him, their lances, swords, axes, and bows drawn and ready. Bjorn looked up and agreed it was best if Timp made no sudden movements.

Timp sank deeper into the mud. Algae, slime, and silt soaked through his pants, while a stick poked uncomfortably at his side. He wondered how long he'd be stuck there. *Forever.* Timp knew it'd be forever.

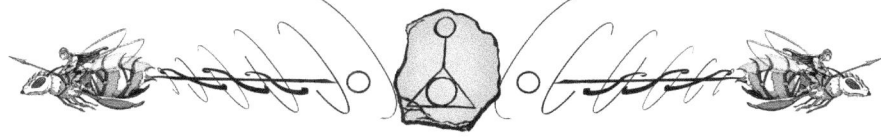

CHAPTER 28
A MEETING OF MINDS

Timp sat waist deep in the murky, snake-infested water with his knees bent and hands bound in his lap. Vaskrél circled his head while mud and slime oozed into his drawers. It wasn't the worst day he'd ever had, but then again, it was still early.

After a heated debate, the villagers had decided Timp could sit upright, provided he allowed them to bind his hands. Timp had agreed. After all, any rope tiny Vikings had would surely snap with ease.

The rope was strong. Timp pulled, twisted, yanked, and flexed, but his hands stayed stuck. For the second time in two days, he was trapped.

The Vikings emptied Timp's pockets in search of "giant, top-secret weaponry." What they got was two Skittles, three Bazooka Joe cartoons (one wrapped around a pink wad of chewed bubble gum), half of a pencil, a compass with permanent condensation cloud stuck under the plastic bubble, six Viking homes (well, four homes, one model of *his* home, and one pickled olive), and his magnifying glass—Timp had salvaged the magnifying glass from his makeshift monocle the night before. The villagers laid the treasures in the square, studying Bjorn's model and Uncle Dene's olive with fascination. In a city where every house was fashioned from blueberries, a square house made of balsa wood and a pickled olive caused quite a stir. Uncle Dene kept a close eye on his olive house to deter the more adventurous viewers from trying a bite. "'Tis a good way to lose thine window treatments."

The villagers let Timp keep his magnifying glass, but only after rigorous testing to ensure it was in no way magical. (For the Vikings, "rigorous testing" meant stabbing the glass with spears and taking turns yelling at it.)

Timp held the magnifying glass precariously between his fingers and bent his head down to peer through. The villagers crammed into the far side of the square. Nervous glances avoided Timp's magnified gaze. Only Bjorn, the other five Vikings who Timp knew well, and the Vaskrél ventured near the giant eye.

"Dene? Dene?" an old woman called from the crowd. "Where you, Dene?" She was blind, and Uncle Dene limped over to meet her. When they met, she touched his face all over until she found his lips and then kissed him repeatedly. "Did yonder giant hurt thee?"

"Nay, dear. Nay. Yon giant *saved* me," Uncle Dene told her, and then proceeded to spin her a tale of his adventures in the culinary arts—literally *in* the culinary . . .

"Who's that?" Timp whispered to Bjorn.

"That be Uncle Dene's wife."

"What's her name?"

Bjorn peered back. "Aunt Dene."

"Giant, ye's be's dumber than a bags of axes," Gunnar laughed.

The Vikings had a real gift for making Timp feel like an idiot.

Aunt Dene hobbled to the platform's edge. "Be this true, Giant?" she asked in the general direction of Timp's face. Her boldness surprised Timp. Unlike other villagers, she seemed unafraid of him. "Did ye save my Dene?"

"Um, yes, ma'am. I suppose so," Timp answered. He left out that he saved Uncle Dene under threat of death by killer bees. She didn't need to know that part.

"Then ye be a friend of mine," Aunt Dene said, "and I take care of mine own. I shall concoct something wonderful for thee, Giant, a gift, a magic that your'n world hath not known for centuries—I'll warrant thee. Be some time to make, aye, but mark me words; ye shall see. I be oh so grateful that ye brought back me Dene. Ye've no idea how important he be to mine heart. I don't know what I'd do without—"

"Honey, please, please," Uncle Dene interrupted. "The thing be about to start. Mayhap ye should take your'n seat." Aunt Dene agreed, kissed her goodbyes, and then made her way toward the crowd.

"Beg'n yer pardon, Giant," Uncle Dene said when his wife was out of earshot. "She hath lost much and more."

"Oh, uh. No problem," Timp said, unsure what else to say. He turned to Bjorn and whispered, "What's about to begin?"

"The thing."

"What thing?"

"We have a thing for *thee*," Bjorn answered.

"You have a thing for me? Whoa, fella. Look here, you're nice and all but—"

"Nay, Giant. We *all* have a thing for thee."

"I get it, I'm flattered, but—Wait, what kind of thing? A thing to hurt me?"

"I hope not, Giant, but—"

"Geez, Bjorn. Give me some help here. What kind of thing is it? A monstrous thing? A thing with 10 arms? A thing to come and eat me? A thing with fangs? A thing that shoots acid or fire? What kind of thing?"

"Giant, oft times ye make no sense at all."

"Me? You make no sense! You—"

"Silence, Giant. Here cometh yon hilmir."

"Bjorn!" A Viking emerged from the crowd and walked across the square, ignoring Timp's enormous, peering eye. He was huge—that is, huge by tiny blue Viking standards. He was still only the size of a large ant to Timp. His long, peppered-grey beard curled to mid chest, and wrinkles lined his sun-dried face, but he showed no other signs of aging. His muscles appeared hewn from oak, roughly modeled, knotted, and scarred. Purple tattoos reached up his arms, neck, and the left side of his face. He dressed the same as other Vikings, but his posture suggested special status. The villagers gave wide berth as he moved. This was not a man to be trifled with.

"Is he like a king?" Timp whispered to Bjorn.

"Nay. That be our'n hilmir. 'Tis more chief and lawmaker."

"Oh. What's his name?"

"Hilmir."

"And his job?"

"Hilmir."

"So Hilmir is the hilmir?"

"Aye. Now've ye've got it. You art truly ready for your'n thing."

"What thing?"

"Enough of that, Giant."

"I admit I did not think we should see thee again, Bjorn," Hilmir said, walking up and slapping Bjorn's arm.

"I expect that thought made ye happy," Bjorn replied coldly.

Hilmir laughed a humorless laugh. "Be not bitter, Bjorn."

"Bitter Bjorn. Wonderful, sire," said a small, twitchy Viking who lurked in Hilmir's shadow. "Bitter Bjorn! That hath a ring to it, sire. It does." The Viking giggled nervously, jotted down the name on his notepad, and waved it into the air. "Listen all, a new nickname appointed—Bitter Bjorn."

The crowd laughed across the square.

Bjorn did not.

"What was I to do, Bjorn?" Hilmir continued. "I must weigh the interests of mine people as a whole. If a giant should taketh the homes of our'n weakest few, be that fault mine? Would ye have me send an army to wage war against a mountain full of ice giants to salvage the run-down houses of our'n weakest contributors? Nay, I think not. Oh, I sympathize, I do, but I'd no choice but to send thee to fetch thine own property."

Timp was confused. The thithers, thees, and thines made it difficult to follow, but he was pretty sure Hilmir had just called his friends weak, and the normally pugnacious group had done nothing in retaliation. Erika didn't stab Hilmir's nose. Gunnar didn't slap himself or go berserk. They just stood there with their eyes fixed to the ground.

Only Bjorn seemed armed to defend himself against the onslaught of sarcasm and scorn. "Ye might have spared a proper soldier or two, perhaps even a Vaskrél," he said, meeting Hilmir's eyes.

"And risk losing competent members of our'n society? Nay, nay, nay. 'Twould not do at all, Bjorn. Odin blessed us when the Jötunn took *thine* houses and none others. Twas as if the heavens had reached down to cleanse our'n people of yon riffraff, leaving those who *actually* contribute to society."

"Ye over-step your'n self. I contr—"

"Settle your'n passions, Bjorn. I simply state facts. We all know ye've not been the same since the war against the Roadr Bani. I mean, what good 'tis a Vaskrél with no bee? You're not truly a Vaskrél at all then, are ye? Nay, you're just nothing."

"You're a Vaskrél?" Timp asked. He could have sworn Bjorn had said he wasn't.

Bjorn did not answer. Hilmir knew what button to press to break Bjorn's spirits and he'd just pressed it, hard. Hilmir sneered at Timp, but didn't speak. Instead, he turned his attention to the Vikings at Bjorn's side. "Ye're all nothing, but we shall get to that soon enough."

"How so?" Bjorn asked, awakened from his thoughts.

A smirk spread across Hilmir's face. "Patience, Bjorn. Patience. Ye'll learn my meaning soon enough. Never you mind. But for now, I must start this thing." Hilmir strutted away with his assistant in tow, leaving Bjorn and the other Vikings to steal nervous glances at one another.

"What a jerk," Timp said as Hilmir walked away.

"Aye," Bjorn agreed. "That jerk be mine brother."

Hilmir took his position on a small stage near the center of the square.

"So he's in charge?" Timp asked.

"He likes to think himself so," Erika said, and she and the other Vikings giggled.

"Aye, but we know who's *really* in charge," Gunnar chided.

Uncle Dene laughed so hard tears came to his eyes as he coughed and hit his cane against the ground. Even Bjorn oscillated with cackling joy. Timp didn't get the joke, but he welcomed the break tension. "Okay. Okay. What's funny?"

Fen stiffened his shoulders and pointed at Timp. "Patience, Giant. Ye'll find out soon enough. Never ye mind that," he said in a spot-on impersonation of Hilmir's grumbling voice that started the Vikings in another fit of laughter.

Timp sighed. He hated Viking jokes.

Hilmir stood at the podium waiting for the villagers to settle into the bleachers lining the square. When he was ready to speak, he shifted his posture more upright and cleared his throat. The square fell silent.

"I call this thing to order. Upon today's docket, we have the Jötunn intruder's fate, repairs for the extensive damages caused by the Jötunn, . . ."

"Great. Trapped and forced to listen to another boring speech, talk about déjà vu," Timp whined.

"What?" Bjorn asked.

"Oh, nothing. Your hilmir just reminds me a lot of DeLaney, that's all."

"Oh, aye, there be one in every village," Bjorn said.

"Seems so. We should get those two together," Timp joked, but Bjorn did not smile.

"Nay, Giant. I believe that would be most dangerous, indeed."

Hilmir rolled his eyes in annoyance at the whispering to his side and spoke louder, "Another goal of this thing is to determine the fate of the six *traitors* before thee. So let us—"

"Traitors?" Bjorn, Erika, Gunnar, Fen, O'dul, and Uncle Dene stepped back as if slapped by the tail of a gorkin—whatever that was. The village erupted in chaos. The stands filled with boos and hisses mixed with scattered cheers. People threw clumps of food, bones, and mud—At least, Timp hoped it was mud. (You never know with Vikings.) Arguments and fistfights spread throughout the stands, knocking over anyone caught in the path.

Hilmir continued undeterred, "Aye. Traitors. Traitors to your'n clans, traitors to your'n village, traitors to your'n ancestors, to your'n friends, and thine gods. Ye be traitors because ye've sided with a Jötunn. In the course of this thing, I—"

"Hey!" Timp's voice boomed so loudly that everyone in the village instantly fell silent. Even Hilmir's mouth clamped shut. Bjorn and the other five Vikings puffed out their chests and smiled.

"The giant shall clear this up, quick and easy. We be not traitors. Tell them true, Giant."

"I get it," Timp said. "A 'thing' is just a Viking word for a meeting." He smiled and nodded his head.

The accused deflated, slapped their foreheads, and groaned in unison.

Fen the Giantologist was the first to recover, "Technically, Giant. A meeting is another word for a thing."

"You lost me."

"Your'n word 'thing' comes from the our'n word 'thing' which is a gathering of people to arrive at a decision. Despite what ye may think of Vikings and our'n ways, we art oft a civil and democratic people. Everyone may have his or her say during a thing. But of course, just because one hath say, doth not mean the hilmir shall listen."

"Unless ye be you-know-who," Erika added with a wink.

"Oh, aye. Unless ye be her."

"So, in other words," Timp said slowly, "a thing is a meeting."

"A meeting be a thing," Fen corrected.

"Eh, the thing is it's called 'a meeting.'"

"As you wish, Giant."

"And a hilmir is what?"

"It's a bit like a chief, innit?"

"I don't know. I'm asking you."

"It is."

"OK, and what's your hilmir's name?"

"Hilmir."

"Your hilmir's name is Hilmir? Isn't that like having a chief named Chief?"

"Aye, now ye've got it. Well done, Giant."

"Aye, aye, major Major." Timp flicked two fingers in a salute.

"I'm no major. Mine name be Fen, and actually, I be a pacifist."

"You keep saying that, but how can a Viking be a pacifist?"

"Oh, resorting to stereotypes now, are we?"

The villagers' heads bounced between Fen and the giant like an audience following a tennis ball at the US Open.

"Okay, fine. You're Fen the Viking pacifist. Your hilmir is Hilmir, a meeting is a 'thing,' but what's the deal with this Jötunn thing?

"'Tis not a 'Jötunn' thing. 'Tis a Viking thing. It just happens to have a Jötunn present."

"Say what, now?" Timp was digging himself deeper into confusion. "No, no. I get the thing about the thing. What I'm asking, is what's this thing about a Jötunn?"

Blood rushed to Hilmir's head, turning his otherwise blue skin bright purple. "Enough! Interrupt me again, Jötunn, and I shall have yer mouth sewn shut!"

Timp thought for a moment as Hilmir eyed him contemptuously, and then the pieces fell in place. "So I'm a Jötunn. Am I the only one here that's a Jötunn? I'm just trying to narrow down the meaning."

He'd heard Erika call him that back at the house, but thought it was just a nickname, or general expression.

"Giant!"

Two Vaskrél buzzed closer to Timp's face. "Okay, Okay, I get it. A 'thing' is a 'meeting,' and 'Jötunn' is me. 'Hilmir' is him. I get it. Carry on."

Timp didn't like being threatened by a man no larger than a fingernail clipping, but being attacked by bees and having his mouth sewn shut weren't among his favorite pastimes, either. He decided to be quiet.

"Where was I?" Hilmir muttered to himself.

"Traitors," Timp answered.

"Jötunn!"

The Vaskrél buzzed down again. This time, one landed on his nose. The bee's stinger throbbed up and down, ready to stab at the slightest provocation. Timp decided to be quiet, and this time, he meant it. The villagers buried their chuckles in their hands and covered them with coughs.

Hilmir took a deep breath. "Traitors. What else shall we call one who sides with a Jötunn over the gods, who leads a Jötunn into our'n village and attacks our'n people? Traitors. 'Tis the only word for it. In the course of this thing, I shall bring this treachery into the open, but what's more, I shall prove these traitors were worthless to begin with.

"They art part of a growing pestilence within our'n village, a plague of acceptance and tolerance: acceptance of weakness, which in turn hath made our'n village weak; tolerance of mediocrity, which in turn hath made our'n village mediocre. Ye elected me thine lawmaker and hilmir. Now hear me as I make mine case:

"Let us begin with Uncle Dene, the old kook. Senile and lost, old and burned out, no longer hath he the burning flame of a warrior's heart, nor shall he die in battle to sit at his father's table in Valhöll. 'Tis a straw death for he. Worthless."

Uncle Dene nodded with his head low. Several Vikings began to protest, but Hilmir held up his hand and continued, "Then there be Fen, our'n brightest student turned dimmest fool. So long hath he studied and pined for the giants that he oft time imitates their'n speech, and adopts their'n ways. I says, if he loves them so much, mayhap he should live among them and spare us his treacherous theories. Aye, the only giantologist to fail Jötunn Psychology 101 for insisting upon the absurd notion that all giants art not evil. Humph! This attack upon our'n village shows how dangerous that thinking might be. And then there be his wife, Erika—"

Wife? Timp smiled at Erika and Fen in surprise. *So, that's why she's always defending him.* The hot-tempered, headstrong warrior Erika was married to the rational, shy, and insecure Fen. How bizarre. But hadn't they gathered six Viking houses and not five? Maybe Erika had an extra house for her weapons. Then Timp remembered that two of the houses belonged to Uncle Dene—though, he wasn't sure a pickled olive really counted as a house.

Erika glared at the hilmir with her chin held high. Fen looked back at the giant, pushed up his glasses, and blushed. The pair did seem to fit in a way that Timp couldn't explain.

"Erika, our'n best warrior, and yet another great disappointment." Hilmir continued. "She hath nary a respect for the art of war, nor respect for authority. How many 'a your'n superiors have ye hospitalized, Erika? Ten? Eleven? How many times have ye refused the orders ye were assigned? How many court marshals? The only reason ye've not been executed already is 'cause the executioner is too afraid to go near thee."

Erika pulled her shoulders back in pride. Hilmir's insults were wasted. He might as well be reading her resume. In fact, most of what he said really was on her resume.

Hilmir continued down the row of traitors, "Next be O'dul, yon village idiot. And then we have Gunnar— "

O'dul sighed in relief. Simply being called village idiot was getting off easy. A smile spread across his face. He looked like . . . well, the village idiot.

"—Gunnar, the 'berserker,'" Hilmir continued. He made a point of holding his hands up in mock quotations at the word "berserker." "A berserker who doth not berserk but instead spits and stutters all over himself while running about in circles like a drunken gorkin. Sad what shall pass for berserking these days. In days gone, the berserkers were a tribe to be reckoned with, feared by friend and foe alike, indispensable in battle. Now, look at thee."

A group of Vikings stood apart from the crowd. They wore necklaces of bones, teeth, and claws. Some wore bear-head helmets and stood in small cages, as though they were too dangerous to stand free among the crowd. Others had barred masks that prevented them from biting. A few wore leashes held by other tribe members. They seemed to Timp less like a group of crazed warriors and more like a group who had decided to play crazed warriors for Halloween. Timp suspected Hilmir was right; they were a sad impersonation of their former glory, but that didn't stop them from getting into an uproar now. They jumped and shouted, rattled their chains, and ran bones across the bars of their cages. Gunnar hopped up and down, and slapped himself. They were all going berserk.

"Save it," Hilmir yawned.

"Urgh?" The berserkers tilted their heads, and then sighed in resignation. The ones in cages sat down and played with straw. Those wearing chains studied the links. Even Gunnar stopped mid-berserk, pushed his toe into the deck, and muttered to himself. The other villagers avoided their eyes.

Hilmir was a juggernaut of malice and cruelty that crushed everyone who stood in his path, not with a sword, but with words: just the right set of words to cut out his enemy's spirit and leave the body standing. Timp had heard enough. It was one thing when his Viking friends called him names; they weren't serious, but this was altogether different. This was just mean.

Timp twisted and pulled at the ropes that bound his hands, but he could not break free. He searched for a sharp object but found nothing. Then he saw the light. Literally, he saw sunlight. The sun had risen high into the morning sky. A beam of light broke through the canopy of leaves above. Timp took his magnifying glass in his mouth and concentrated the beam onto his ropes.

"Ye should all be embarrassed," Hilmir smiled with self-satisfaction. He seemed proud that he'd destroyed everyone in the group—well, almost everyone. O'dul was fine. "Aye, this be the company ye keep, Bjorn. Me own dear brother, Bjorn—the Vaskrél without bee, the shame of me family's lineage. Through incompetence, he hath failed to secure his seat in Valhöll. Through cowardice, he watched his family die."

The audience stirred. Grunts and mumbles of dissent crawled across the square.

A thin column of smoke rose from Timp's ropes. His Vaskrél guards were too rapt in Hilmir's speech to notice. Timp pulled, but the ropes still held strong. He needed to burn them just a little more.

Hilmir ignored the crowd's hisses and continued, "Bjorn, a selfish coward who hath saved himself over those around him. Bjorn, the only Vaskrél in history to sever his own bee—"

"'Tis a lie!" Erika burst.
She charged forward, but Bjorn grabbed her.

"Bjorn?" she pleaded. Bjorn smiled weakly and assured her it was all right. It seemed he needed to hear this, felt he deserved it.

The fight drained from Erika's body. She released a heavy breath and wiped a single tear from the corner of her eye. That was all she'd give Hilmir, one tear. For a moment, she allowed Fen to hold her—or rather, she held Fen. He had many more tears in his eyes than she did. In fact, he was a blubbering mess of drool and snot, really disgusting stuff.

He buried his head in Erika's tunic, took a deep breath, and then blew his nose. A noise like a goose drowning in jello reverberated across the square. Erika rolled her eyes and shoved Fen away. The moment was over. She stood with her shoulders back and her chin held high. Her hand squeezed tightly around her spear, and veins bulged in her arm. She pretended to be annoyed with Fen, but couldn't hold back a smirk as he continued to blow his nose and cry into his handkerchief. Yes, they were a good pair.

"Aye, Erika," Hilmir continued. "Defend the one captain ye haven't tried to kill. After all, ye traitors stick together." This time, it took both Bjorn and Fen to hold Erika back. Hilmir laughed. The crowd burst into pandemonium. Some Vikings yelled and booed, others screamed and cheered. Fistfights broke out across the square. Babies cried and the berserkers went . . . well, berserk-ish (They really weren't the finest examples of berserkers).

"Father, that's enough!"

The square fell silent. The fighting stopped.

A girl stepped from the crowd and walked toward Hilmir. She appeared to be about Timp's age, but somehow seemed older. Her long dark hair was braided back into ponytails that curled down to her waist. She moved with confidence and grace, and didn't seem to care that everyone stared at her. She glanced at Timp for only a fraction of a second, but in that moment, time stopped. He forgot about the magnifying glass clenched between his teeth. He forgot about the Vaskrél, the farm, Hilmir, and DeLaney. He saw only the tiny blue Viking girl.

"Giant, be you well?" Fen asked, observing Timp.

"What do you mean?" Timp said, dropping the magnifying glass that had been in his mouth and scrambling to catch with his bound hands.

"You're all red."

Timp shook his head and swatted his face as if to brush the red away. The surrounding Vaskrél buzzed down angrily.

"I do believe Thor's bolt hath struck our'n dear giant," Bjorn murmured, and the other Vikings giggled.

"Huh? Oh, no. That's just . . . something giants do."

Fen noted the event in his journal while Timp tried to calm his nerves. He thought about cold water, about icy mountaintops, baseball, and the color blue, but not the same blue as the girl, another blue. The more he tried, the redder he got.

"Um, who is that, anyway?" he asked, as casually as he could. He placed the handle of the magnifying glass back into his mouth and rolled it between his teeth.

"*That*, Giant, be the person *truly* in charge." Erika smiled.

The girl stood before Hilmir's podium. "Father, thou art unreasonable," she said boldly, but not impolitely.

"Uh, aye. Well, um, I thought, that is, " Hilmir stammered. Timp marveled at the girl's effect on her father. She was amazing.

"Let them speak," she continued. "Perhaps matters shall become clearer upon hearing their'n side."

Hilmir started to protest, then gave in. "Aye, dear."

The villagers turned their attention to Timp and the six defendants standing trial before him.

"Well?" Hilmir barked. "What've ye traitors to say for your'n selves?"

A tendril of smoke rose from the edge of the square and disappeared while a new tendril formed in its place. The Vikings stood mesmerized by the smoke's hypnotic beauty as it curled through the air. Where was it coming from? Timp and the villagers tilted their heads, following the smoke to a small black dot that had appeared in the square's wooden deck. Timp started to ask about the mysterious spot, but his mouth held—

A villager cried out, "It's the giant. This be giant magic!" "He'll destroy us all!"

The villagers screamed and scattered like ants.

Timp tried to explain that it wasn't him, but all that came out was mumbles. He still held the magnifying glass clinched between his teeth. He looked down. He'd burned through his ropes and into the square. It *was* him. He pulled his hands apart, snapping the remaining threads, and he was free!

"Giant, why?" Fen whined.

Timp shook his head. "I didn't—" The square erupted in a blaze of fire. Vaskrél barreled toward Timp's head in attack formations.

One of the quicker bees stung Timp on the back of the neck. "Yeow!"

He sprang to his feet in an explosion of water and mud that sent a wave crashing down on the lower village. Wood planks, houses, and ships rolled under the water and disappeared. Timp swatted at bees and jumped. He banged his head on the porches, bridges, and balconies, sending them all crumbling into the murky depths below. Vikings screamed. Vikings fell.

"No, Giant!" Bjorn begged, but the buzz of the Vaskrél drowned his pleas.

Arrows, spears, and ropes shot at Timp at frightening velocity. The Vikings who'd fallen into the sea swam for safety. Timp stepped gingerly to avoid hurting them, but quickly to retreat. Every movement wreaked a new path of destruction upon the village: he avoided a spear to the face and knocked down a bridge; he ducked a diving bee and head-butted a neighborhood. He felt like a drunken Godzilla, laying waste to whole cities with every hiccup of his atomic breath. Everything Timp touched, he destroyed. There was only one thing to do. He ran.

Timp slogged through the pond as fast he could, which is to say not very fast at all. He slipped and slid and skated on slime. He splashed through duckweed and tripped over branches. Any time a Vaskrél came near, Timp dove into the water. (Okay, he tripped and fell into the water, but since he tripped and fell every time he tried to stand, it so happened that he also did so every time a Vaskrél came near.)

Despite his erratic floundering and blundering, the Vaskrél remained fixed with furious persistence. He swatted; they rolled. He dropped into the water; they waited for him to resurface. As soon as he came up, they resumed their attack. Timp dodged a dozen stings, but the Vaskrél landed a dozen more. Sting after sting burned into his flesh. Panic seized his heart, and his throat grew tight. The water deepened, and Timp's actions became sluggish. His vision blurred, and he could barely breathe. But the stinging, he had to escape the stinging. He felt lightheaded, like he might—the water was too deep to touch now. Timp sunk as the black sea swallowed him whole.

The Vaskrél hovered just above the surface, waiting. But this time, the giant did not resurface. Bubbles fizzled and popped —all that remained of the giant called Timp.

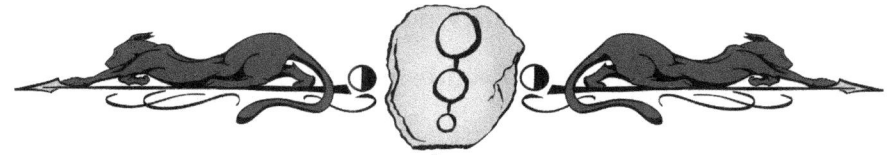

CHAPTER 29
MOLLY DOWN UNDER

Mrs. Molly's tail flicked as she watched the bushes across the pond. She'd stalked the boy down the hill to this very spot. Her thinking was clear: Once upon a time she'd had a flea, a royal flea of course—she was a Queen, after all—but a flea nonetheless. The Littletons freaked. They dragged her to see Dr. Housen, who then dipped her neck deep in smelly medicine water. Molly remembered watching the fleas swim for shore. (Okay, maybe it was more than one flea. She's royalty. Fleas love power). The point is: Even with a flea or two, Molly was nowhere near as infested as the boy. His hair crawled with pests. And if he planned to dip into smelly water to get rid of them, Molly planned to eat them as they swam for shore. *It's a win win.* There was only one problem: The boy didn't dip. He waded! *Humph, the nerve!*

He waded in and hid in the bushes. *"Probably trying to eat all of the pests himself, the greedy little servant!"* Molly said to herself.

Molly paced Timp's entry point. Green duckweed pellets undulated on the surface in a solid sheet. *Maybe I can walk on this weird green carpet*, she thought. She stepped forward boldly, and her paw plopped through the duckweed into the dark water below. Molly somersaulted back onto the bank. "*Not a carpet! Not a carpet! Definitely not a carpet!*"

She paced the shore in fury. She tried to walk around the pond, but the ground grew muddy and gross, definitely not the path a queen deserves. Eventually, she noticed a tendril of smoke rising from the bushes across the way.

"Aw, *the servant's having a barbecue! I want barbecued treats! It's not fair!*"

Molly circumvented the muddy shore and sprinted to the end of the dock for a better view. She pawed at the water, wishing it solid so she could run across and fill her belly with tender tiny-man brisket.

She didn't notice the bubbles inching her way, not at first. Bubbles popped five feet away, and then four. In Louisiana, ponds are homes to all manner of dangerous wild life: snakes, snapping turtles, alligator snapping turtles, and alligators—all of which eat small dogs, cats, and Mollys. Molly didn't know this, of course. She studied the bubbles approaching in blissful ignorance.

Pop-pop, pop-pop. The bubbles moved near. Molly leaned in. One bubble rose from the black depths and popped just at the end of her nose. She didn't know what dangers hid below the surface, but she was about to find out.

An alligator burst from the water to get Molly. Every hair on her body stood on end. She shot into the air with her legs straight and her claws out. Somehow, she found herself away from the dock and over the water. She twisted back. It wasn't an alligator at all. It was the boy. Oh, she'd have his head for this. She'd—Molly hit the water.

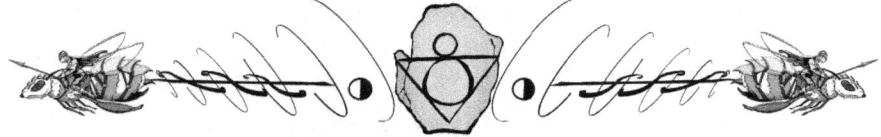

CHAPTER 30
ABANDON TIMP!

Timp hiked up the hill, his wet feet squishing in his shoes. He'd probably get blisters, but with bruises, burns, scratches, cuts, and bee stings, did it matter?

"Stupid Vikings. I hope I never see them again," he grumbled. At that moment, he meant it too.

The Vikings had brought him nothing but trouble and pain. In the 48 hours since he'd met them, he'd been held down, tied up, chased, stabbed, speared, beaten, shot, speared again, yelled at, cursed at, scratched up, thought insane, and stung (many times).

Timp continued up the hill. A breeze kicked up, and he stopped to listen. He heard nothing but the wind blowing in his ears. Suddenly he felt alone. He'd grown used to the Vikings in the short time he'd known them. They weren't friends—that was for sure—but at least they were interesting. Timp touched the scratches and stings covering his face. Nah, he was better off without them. There'd be nothing left of him if they'd stayed.

Besides, the Vikings were probably better off without him too. Now that Hilmir had witnessed them trying to stop him from destroying the village, he'd surely stop calling them traitors. Wouldn't he? Timp stopped. What if destroying the village made matters worse for the Vikings? He tried not to think about it. That was their problem, not his. Besides, it was their own fault. He never asked them to invade his life. They just appeared.

"Where are you going?" Mrs. Littleton's distant voice broke through Timp's thoughts, but she wasn't talking to him. Her shouts carried across the hill's tall, golden grass; though, she was not yet in view. "John! Where are you going?" Timp ran toward her voice. "Come back!" she yelled. "You can't leave now!"

Timp's stomach dropped. Was his father abandoning them? His parents fought, but that's what parents do. Things had been more difficult than usual lately, sure, but his father wouldn't just pack up and leave. Would he?

Tall grass surrendered to mowed lawn. His father burst out of the house wearing a pink floral apron, his hands purple with berry mush. "What is it? What's wrong?" he asked.

Timp's father wasn't leaving. He seemed as confused as Timp. But if not his father, then who? Timp followed the grass line to the orchard and found his answer. The workers stepped out of brush one by one, dropping their buckets, and walking toward the road. They were leaving, all of them.

Timp guessed who was behind this, but he wanted to be sure. He ducked into the orchard and sprinted down rows. Hidden by the tall bushes, he circumvented his parents until he reached the dirt road on the northeast side of the farm. It was just as he'd suspected: DeLaney.

DeLaney's assistants, Becca and Stephon, stood in the road next to an extended pickup, handing envelopes to the workers leaving the farm.

"So, that's DeLaney's plan, hiring away our workers so we can't make any money. That's low," Timp said to the Vikings in his ears. Then he remembered that there were no Vikings in his ears.

"Who are you? What are you doing? This is private property. Get off of our land!" Timp's mother shouted at Becca and Stephon.

"We're not on your land," Becca said as she handed another worker an envelope and helped him into the back of the truck.

"Um, excuse me, I believe this is a public road. We have just as much of a right to be here as you do. And these workers ain't slaves, honey; they're free to do whatever they want. We can't help it if we offer a better deal," Stephon added with a snap and some sass.

"Why you son of a—"

Mr. Littleton grabbed Mrs. Littleton by the waist and pulled her back as her fist swung through the air just shy of Stephon's nose. *Always with the nose!*

"What do you want?" Mr. Littleton asked, holding his wife back as she threw punches wildly.

"Oh, we've already got what we want," Becca said, closing the tailgate on the truckload of workers. She high-fived Stephon and strutted to the driver side door. "All comfy?"

The workers did not reply.

"Who are you with?" Mr. Littleton asked.

"Wouldn't you like to know," Stephon said, dusting his hands on his bottom.

Timp was surprised his father didn't recognize Becca and Stephon from the bank, but then maybe he hadn't noticed them.

"At least tell me how much they're paying you so I can match it," Mr. Littleton told the workers.

The workers stared at the envelopes in their hands, avoiding Mr. Littleton's eyes. Everyone knew he couldn't match the price, no matter how little it was.

"If you leave now, don't you ever come back," Timp's mother said, stabbing her finger at the workers from under Mr. Littleton's arm.

"Now, Pam, that's no way to be," Mr. Littleton said. "She doesn't mean it, y'all. You're always welcome back here."

"Oh, no you're not," Mrs. Littleton interrupted. "If you leave in that truck, you better not ever show your faces around here again." She charged forward but Mr. Littleton caught her.

"Y'all, she doesn't mean it."

"Oh, yes I do."

"No, she doesn't."

"Don't tell me what I mean, John."

"Sweetie, if we need people, and they need work, then we're not going to just turn them away."

"You're right. We're not *just* going to turn them away. We're also going to kick them right in the— "

"Well, as interesting as all this is," Becca interrupted, checking her watch as Mrs. Littleton kicked in her direction, "we really must to be on our way."

Becca and Stephon climbed into the truck.

"Do something," Mrs. Littleton urged.

"Don't worry," Mr. Littleton said. "They're just following the herd. It's mob mentality. We just have to break them into individual people. It's like Scout in To Kill a Mocking—"

"John, they're leaving!"

"Oh, right. Watch." Mr. Littleton cleared his throat and nodded to the workers, who fidgeted uncomfortably. Becca and Stephon leaned out of the windows and waited with twisted grins.

"Guys," Mr. Littleton said. "We're like family. Frank, you know. We helped you move into your new house just last winter. And Marisa, last summer when your car broke down, we picked you up every day. I'm not saying you owe us anything, but at the very least, we have to be able to depend on one another. I know it's been tough, but we've always paid you fair wages. We've always kept food on your tables. We're going to make it through this, I just need you to help us through the summer. What do ya say?"

The truck peeled away, leaving Mr. Littleton coughing in a cloud of ochre dust.

"Nice work," Mrs. Littleton said, patting Mr. Littleton on his shoulder. "Just like Scout Finch."

"Well, I guess you can't believe everything read," Mr. Littleton said.

"That's right, blame the classics."

Timp watched his parents wrap their arms around one another. After a deep breath, they parted and took a few steps toward the house. "Timp, you can come on out now."

Timp climbed out from under the bushes. "How did you know?"

"Timp George Washington Littleton, what in the blue blazes have you gotten yourself into?"

"I . . . um . . . fell in the pond."

"Heavens to Betsy! Are those bee stings?" Mrs. Littleton held Timp's chin and inspected his stings.

"Just a few dozen."

"Are you okay? Do you need to go to the hospital?"

"I'm fine. Not the worst day ever."

"Hrmm," Mrs. Littleton huffed. Timp's parents had a way of seeing through him. He sometimes worried they could read his mind. He cleared his thoughts just in case. His mother didn't press him further. "Well, we better get you inside and cle—"

She paused with her head tilted, ear to the air, and brow furrowed. Timp and his father listened. They could still hear the truck rattling in the distance, but they also heard another vehicle. It was rare for cars to visit the farm. Timp and his father exchanged shrugs. Timp's mother checked her watch.

"What is it?" Mr. Littleton asked.

"I'm sorry," she said.

"Sorry about what?"

"Last night, when I called them, I didn't know that today was going to go like this."

"Called who?" Timp asked. His mother bit her lip guiltily. "What have you done?"

A white BMW shot through the lingering cloud of dirt like the white horse of the apocalypse. Timp recognized the car immediately.

"I take it back," he said. "This *is* the worst day ever."

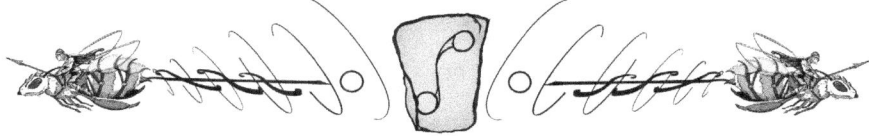

CHAPTER 31
THE GUEST FROM HEL

Timp cursed the Vikings as his cousin Trevor leaned against the back of a white BMW playing games on his cell while Aunt Rose struggled to dislodge a large suitcase from the trunk.

"Hi ya, errybody," she said as she yanked and pulled. "Hi there, Timp. Long time no see, stranger. I hear you're going to have some company this summer. Are you excited, sugar?"

"Excited doesn't even begin to describe how I feel, right now," Timp said, shooting his parents an evil glance. His mother shrugged in feigned innocence.

"You need a hand with that, Rose?" Mr. Littleton asked.

Aunt Rose was exhausting to watch. Her mouth ran as fast as her hands, and both would lap a Formula One race car. She yanked, pulled, and punched the luggage in her trunk. Her son, Trevor, was her opposite. He rarely moved and seldom spoke above a grunt or a belch. On the occasions when Trevor did speak, Timp invariably wished he hadn't.

"Why, my lands, I just think you two are gonna have the best gosh darn time of your sweet little ol' lives," Aunt Rose said. Timp imagined she pulled the bags so desperately out of fear that his parents might change their minds about taking Trevor in.

"Do you need a hand with those bags, Rose?" Timp's father asked again.

"Why, it was just so gosh darn nice of y'all to invite little Treevsie-weevsie over. I swanee, it'll be the best thing in the whole little ol' wide world to get him out here, breathing this fresh, and—Ahhh!" The suitcase unstuck, and Aunt Rose fell back onto Timp's father.

Trevor played his game.

"Well, I swanee, aren't you just quick on your feet and nimble as a thimble. I say, I woulda just died right here on the spot." Aunt Rose stood up, adjusted her hair, and checked her lipstick in the corners of her mouth with her pinky. "Where was I? Oh, yes. Trevor! Get off that car right this instant, and come say 'hello' to your little ol' cousin, Timp."

Trevor grunted hello, but kept his eyes fixed on his cell.

"Yes, it's just so sweet of you to take care of my little Trevsie-weevsie, just sweet as strawberry pi—"

"Well, Rose. I actually need to talk to you about that—" Timp's mother tried, but she couldn't fit a word in edge ways.

"Oh yes, I'd just love that, darli'n. We should talk, but I can't just now, suga. I've got an appointment at the . . . um . . .

doctor, hair salon, nails . . . um, yes, all of those, honey. You be good, Trevor. Do whatever Uncle John and Aunt Pam tell you, now, ya hear?"

"We actually lost our employees, today," Mrs. Littleton continued.

"Awe, suga, I'm sorry to hear that. I would just die right then and there on the spot. Now, you give me a call and you tell me all about it, ya hear? Gotta go—them appointments and all. Trevor won't be any trouble at all. You just sat him down right in front of that ol' TV and he's just as snug as a bug on a rug, but you give me a ring if ya need me, m'kay? Kay. Love ya lots."

Aunt Rose peeled off in a cloud of dirt and exhaust. Timp tried to place when she'd gotten back into the car and started the engine. She'd done it so quickly, he hadn't even noticed. He replayed the scene in his mind: She kissed Trevor on the cheek, and in one fluid motion of talking and walking, she somehow reached the driver side door, opened it while still rambling and pointing off in the distance, then started the car, chatted it up with her body half in and half out, and then she was gone. Timp could almost admire the artistry of it all. Like a great magician, Aunt Rose was a master of misdirection. Only instead of pulling a rabbit from a hat, she pulled a Trevor from her car. The smoke from Aunt Rose's disappearing act settled to reveal his cousin playing on his cell.

Worst. Magic. Trick. Ever.

"You got Playstation?" Trevor asked without looking up from his game.

Mr. and Mrs. Littleton shrugged. It was that kind of day.

"Right this way, Trevor," Mr. Littleton said. "Let's get you settled into Timp's room. Timp, grab Trevor's luggage."

Trevor's suitcase must have been filled with bricks. Timp hoisted it onto his hip and started duck-walking toward the house.

"Oh yeah, this will be just the best ol' time in the whole little ol' wide world," Timp muttered in his best impression of Aunt Rose's nasally voice.

The Vikings would have laughed.

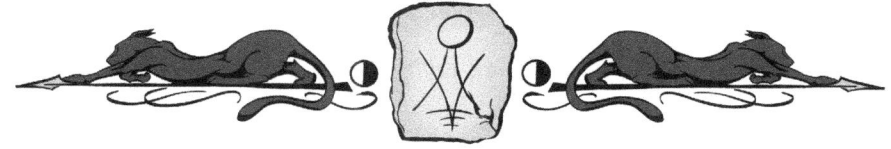

CHAPTER 32
PEST PATROL

Molly paced the dock, dripping wet and cursing. Eventually, her fur began to dry. Then the patrols began.

At first, one bee flew back and forth along the dock's edge. Molly thought nothing of it. Bees were common on the farm, and though she had never seen one drink water, she was sure it happened. Then more bees appeared. They too flew along the water's edge, but in the opposite direction. This, Molly felt, was peculiar bee behavior. But what did she know about bees? Molly ducked down and wiggled toward the bees' flight path. When one buzzed by, she watched it with her large—and she would say purrrfectly perceptive—kitty-cat eyes. But what she saw made no sense. She was certain she saw one of the little blue grumpies alive—not only alive, but riding a bee!

"Any sign of him?" a grumpy asked another as they reigned in their bees nearby.

"Naw. Nothing, yet," answered a rough and gravely grumpy woman.

"He left some alive? That good-for-nothing servant boy can't do anything right. Well, I guess if you want something done, you have to do it yourself," Molly growled.

"Well, the hilmir says we gotta find him. Says we ain't to stop 'til the giant's dead. Says the debt must be paid in flesh, says he. Says it's the only way to stave off Ragnarök."

"Sounds like the hilmir be saying an awful lot these days," the woman said spitting over the side of her bee.

"Yep."

"Reckon the giant drowned?"

"Hope so," the man said with a spit over the side of his bee. "That Jötunn burned me ma-in-law's house down."

"Heck, Clyde. Who you talk'n to? I met yer mother-in-law. I reckon that giant did ye a favor."

"Oh, no he did not," the grumpy named Clyde retorted. "Now, she wants to move in with us!"

"Ohhh, I see. You ain't mad the giant burned down her house down. You mad—"

"—that me mother-in-law weren't still in it! That's right."

The two nasty little vermin laughed until tears poured from their eyes. When their mirth subsided, one of them casually said, "Say, Clyde, you reckon yon cat-beast is 'bout to attack us?"

"Why, yes, Ethel. To point of fact, I do."

Ethel spit over the side of her bee.

Molly sprang from the grass in a fit of teeth and claws.

"I'll get you little blue pests! I'll teach you some manners! I am a queen! I'm a . . . Ahhhh!"

Clyde and Ethel slid their bees out of the way, and Molly flailed past.

"Hope that cat swims better'n she flies," Clyde said as Molly splashed into the water.

"I'll say," Ethel agreed with another spit over the side of her bee. "Wanna keep patrolling?"

"Reckon we should."

The bees flew away as Mrs. Molly Fish-Kisser sunk into the scummy pond below.

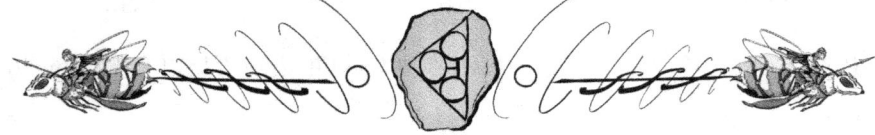

CHAPTER 33
ONE PEST FOR ANOTHER

Timp watched Trevor play with his cell over a plate of chicken and mashed potatoes. He couldn't believe his parents had allowed Trevor to bring the game to the dinner table. They never let Timp bring anything to the table. He couldn't even read at the table, which made no sense at all because they nagged him constantly about reading more often.

When Timp commented on the game, his mother hushed him, "Trevor is company."

For her, no further explanation was needed, but the answer left a sour taste in Timp's mouth—even worse than broccoli. And to make matters worse, he swore he saw just the faintest smirk crack Trevor's lips. Timp stabbed at the broccoli in the serving bowl.

"Timp, get your broccoli, and pass it along."

Timp looked at Trevor's plate. Trevor had no broccoli. He just passed the bowl along without so much as a sniff. Timp was sure his mother had noticed, but he decided to point it out just in case. "Trevor didn't get any."

"He's company," Timp's mother explained again.

Timp *definitely* saw Trevor hiding a smirk this time, but he knew better than to say anything more. Instead, he muttered under his breath, spooned out the bare minimum amount of broccoli that he thought he could get away with, and passed the bowl.

"Timp," Mr. Littleton said in a serious tone. It was the same tone his father had used two nights before, a tone that meant Timp wasn't going to like whatever he was about to hear. "Timp," he repeated through Timp's sighs and eye rolls, "Tomorrow, I have to go into town and see about hiring some new workers. I was hoping you could get an early start, feed the animals, and put in a good day with the berries for us."

"What about Trevor?" Timp asked, his eyes burning a hole in Trevor's broccoli-less plate.

"Trevor's company," Timp's father said.

Et tu, Dad-e? Timp had been born in the South, he'd been raised in the South, but there were some facets of Southern hospitality that he couldn't grasp. As near as he could figure it, in the South, you can get away with murder as long as you do it while you're a guest in someone else's house. After all, then you're company.

Southern hospitality annoyed Timp because he was never the recipient. When the Littletons traveled, they left the south. In Colorado, they put him to work. When they returned, they put him to work. While he'd never visited the North East or the West coast, he felt certain he knew what would happen in both places: they'd put him to work. Timp clinched his jaw so his curses didn't leak out. His parents took this silence as acceptance. Tomorrow, he'd be put to work.

Something large smacked the dining room's sliding glass door. "*Noooooo! Why is the fat one allowed inside and not me? Why does he get to dine in my halls? I'm a queen! A queen! A queeeeeee . . .*" Molly slid down the glass with a screech. For once, Timp knew exactly how she felt, even if he didn't know what she was saying.

"What has gotten into her lately?" Mrs. Littleton said, more to herself than anyone else.

Dinner passed. Timp choked down his broccoli. Trevor played his game and enjoyed an extra helping of dessert. (After all, he was company.) Then Trevor played with his cell all the way down the hall. He'd hardly spoke throughout dinner, and only grunted replies when Mr. and Mrs. Littleton attempted to elicit polite conversation, but as soon as Timp flipped on his bedroom lamp, it was as though he also flipped on the switch to Trevor's mouth—the trick now would be shutting it off.

"You got Playstation?"

"I have a Playstation 2."

"A two? That's like 100 years old! Ugh, I figured that'd be the case out here in the boonies-ville, so I brought my own." Trevor yanked Timp's Playstation 2 out of the TV stand and threw it to the side, cables and all.

"Hey!" Timp said, as he picked up his discarded console and tried to reattach a broken piece. "If you brought one, why'd you ask if I had one?"

"'Cause, if *you* had one, we could play each other on separate TVs, but since you don't, you'll just have to watch me."

"Oh, joy."

"I'm the best. I have 45,000 Ghost Zombie Kill Points. Hey, move."

"Gho- with the zom- with the what now?" Timp stepped aside and tried to regain his footing.

"Ghost Zombie Kill Points, idiot. It's from Ghost Zombie Apocalypse. You ever played it? Probably not since they don't have it on the two. You'd also need Internet. Do you have Internet out here in hicks-ville?"

"Yes, Trevor, we have Internet."

"Probably dial-up."

"Now you listen here—"

Trevor giggled and went on. "I'm the world's best at Ghost Zombie Apocalypse. Well, I haven't beat it yet. But seriously, I'm gonna compete. I really am. If my Mom will drive me to Houston, that is. It's an FPS."

"FP—what, now?"

"Ugh, First Person Shooter."

Trevor looked at Timp as though Timp was from another planet, and for a moment, Timp thought he might be. Trevor spoke in a way that somehow made him feel inferior. Timp learned in school that when confronted with a situation like this, the best possible thing you can do is lie. So, even though Timp was a terrible liar, he struck the most cool, confident, and aloof expression that he could muster and replied, "Oh, yeah, I know all about those."

"Good, cause you'd have to be the biggest loser in the world not to know about those. And you're not a loser, are you Timp?" Trevor's lips curled up over butter yellow teeth and he snorted a drip of snot back up his nose in what Timp guessed was laughter.

"No, Trevor. I am definitely not a loser."

Trevor directed his attention to untangling the mountain of wires and electric plugs from his backpack. "I got into FPS gaming with Red Sun Alien Invasion 3D: The Quest for the Centurion, but the pissy-baby down the street ruined that. Mom got all worked up about collective play after a few of my friends and I started trolling this pissy-baby from school. My buddy Nick hacked his account and changed it so any time the pissy-baby's avatar spoke, a bubble popped up that said 'I'm a pissy-baby.'" Trevor squealed in delight.

Timp did not.

"Anyway, then the puss tried to off himself—just wanted some pissy-baby attention—but his mom called my mom, and she made me get rid of the game. It's all good though, 'cause to make it up to me, she got me Ghost Zombie Apocalypse, and Meal Deals on Wheels of Terror: Murder, Mayhem, and Food Delivery. That game was balls."

Timp sat on his bed, watching Trevor carry on. How could his parents let this troll into his room?

As Trevor snorted back a drip of snot and droned on about his game collection and bullying classmates online. Timp tuned him out. He touched a few of the bee stings on his face and felt annoyed that his parents had forgotten all about them. He could have died! He could have died, and he didn't even get extra dessert, but Trevor did. That made sense. Southern hospitality and all. Timp's head weighed more than he could stand. He lay back, realizing for the first time how utterly exhausted he'd become.

Trevor ran wires and plugs all over the room, hooking up his system and talking the whole time. Timp no longer listened. He took a deep breath and slid his head down his headboard to his pillow: his soft, heavenly pillow. His head had just stopped sinking when his bedroom door opened with a knock. Timp cracked one eye to find his father holding a tattered brown sleeping bag, a musty old camping pillow, and calamine lotion. They hadn't forgotten after all.

"Hey-ya fellas. Timp, I brought you your sleeping bag."

"My what now? Sleeping bag?" Surely, he meant Trevor's sleeping bag.

"Well, yeah. I knew you'd want to give Trevor here your bed, since he's company."

"Oh, you knew that, did you?" Timp said before he could catch himself.

"Timp, could I talk to you in the hall a second, buddy?"

Timp knew he'd crossed a line. He noticed Trevor smirking as he passed, and for a second, he thought about kicking the ghost-zombie troll face, berserker style. But he didn't.

In the hall, his father popped open the calamine lotion and started rubbing it on Timp's face, checking for stingers. "Look. I know it's tough, sharing your space, but Trevor is company, so we need to do what we can to make him feel comfortable, okay?"

"Yeah, he's company. He's not the king of Persia."

Timp's father smiled. "No, he's not. If he was the king of Persia, your mother and I'd have to give him our bed." Timp's father waited for a laugh, but the joke was lost on Timp, so he explained, "Because it's king size."

Timp slapped his forehead and calamine lotion splattered across his palm.

"Get it? Get it?" his father asked as he elbowed and poked Timp.

"Yes. Yes, I get it," Timp said, trying to remain grumpy and being all the angrier that he couldn't.

"And he doesn't seem that bad," Timp's father said nodding toward Timp's room. "At least he's quiet."

Timp looked at the door. "Yeah, he's quiet as a mouse."

Back in his room, Timp arranged his pallet on the floor to the bustling sounds of machine guns, zombie screams, ghostly moans, and hand grenades. Trevor's system was up and running. Timp figured once the game started, Trevor might stop talking, but Trevor was a multi-tasker.

"You see, the zombies are tricky because sometimes you get fast ones, and boy, are they freaky, but the ghosts are tough too. They fly through the air, and you can't shoot them, cause they're ghosts, right? But then they possess people and you can shoot them," Trevor laughed and sucked back snot as he fired a rocket at a school bus. Children screamed. Timp did not get the joke. "You lose points for killing innocents. You're supposed to send in the priest to exorcize the ghost and then trap it, but where's the fun in that? Way easier just to shoot the people and trap the ghost as it escapes."

"Wait, you're shooting innocent bystanders? Why?" Timp asked, more than a little disturbed.

"Haha, cause it's fun." Trevor had a maniacal giggle that made Timp uncomfortable. "The problem is, then they come back as zombies, and you have to kill them again. That, or shoot one of your teammates in the leg so the zombies catch him, instead of you."

"Is that part of the game?"

"It is when I play it, but man, does it piss Nick off." Trevor cackled as his crazed eyes bounced across the screen.

Timp loved video games. He even loved shoot'em up games, but there was something about the way Trevor played that felt off, like he didn't play for fun. He played for practice. He went on for hours, talking about various parts of the game, strategies, characters, and trolling. He talked about his friend Nick, and how cool he was, and how they bullied newbs online. Somewhere in the middle, Timp stopped listening. He lay his head down on the musty, old camping pillow and fell asleep.

That night, Timp dreamed.

He seldom remembered his dreams. They were shadows in his mind that retreated at first light, but this dream felt different, clearer. Even as it happened, Timp knew he'd remember the dream come morning.

Timp was flying, flying but unafraid, which was unlike Timp since he hated heights. He felt none of the fear that arrested him when he climbed the old oak tree next to the water tower.

No. He felt . . . exhilarated, free. He felt like he was someone else, someone great and mighty, someone brave.

Then, he heard the buzz. *The Vaskrél!* Fear shot through his heart, and he almost woke. He reminded himself that he was inside a dream, and tried to control that dream. He concentrated on stopping the buzzing. It was his dream. He should have control. He wanted to feel powerful and brave again. But as the buzzing slowed, he started to fall. His dream turned into nightmare. He fell, spinning around and around until he didn't know which way was up and which was down. He saw the moon, the sea, the moon, the sea, the moon reflected in the sea, the moon, and the sea again. The sky became the sea, and the sea became the sky, and then cold water, endless deep. Blackness. Only blackness.

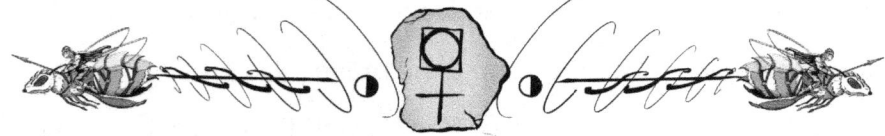

CHAPTER 34

ALL WORK AND NO PLAY MAKES TIMP A DULL BOY

Timp stepped onto the porch and into the thick morning air. The sun would rise in a couple of hours to burn away the fog and dew, but for now, the farm was comfortable and serene. Despite the unbelievable heat that lay ahead, Timp almost looked forward to working. He could use a day away from Trevor, away from his parents, and away from the Vikings—a day to relax, but, above all else, to heal. Timp would not get to relax that day.

An oily black stain marked the spot in the carport where his father's truck usually sat. Mr. Littleton had gone in search of new workers. Timp knew it was hopeless. DeLaney would have paid off everyone nearby, and no one else would be willing to drive all the way to Blueberry Springs to work for so little.

Shower water ran through pipes that knocked against the outside walls, and Timp knew his mother would be out shortly. He scooped a cupful of dry cat food and dumped it into Molly's dish.

Molly snored in her cat bed. Her fur was unkempt, like she'd swum through Hel to get here. Her whiskers flicked as she moved through kitty-cat dreams. Timp wondered what those dreams might be, but then decided she probably just dreamed about chasing mice.

In truth, Molly dreamed of a large banquet held in her honor. She stuffed her mouth with plate after plate of little blue treats, some cooked into pies, some skewered on tooth picks, some cut up and smeared onto bread like jelly jam. Molly's legs twitched and Timp smiled, blissfully unaware of the psychotic fantasies floating through the cat's head.

He fed the other animals, and then grabbed some buckets and straps and went to the orchard. He began picking berries and soon fell into his usual perfunctory rhythm, moving hand-over-hand and rolling his fingers to knock away the stems, before he dropped the berries into the bucket with a satisfying *thunk*. No sooner had the last berry left the tip of Timp's fingers than his dexterous hands reached back for the next handful.

The day began to pass, and Timp's mind began to wander. He tried not to think about the Vikings. He wanted this day to relax, to heal, but guilt nagged his conscience. He thought this feeling would have dissipated by now, but whenever he closed his eyes, he saw Bjorn's disappointment. Bjorn had been the worst. He looked as though Timp had planned to betray the Vikings the whole time, like he really was just an evil giant bent on destroying their village. Surely, Bjorn knew better . . . right? Surely, he knew Timp didn't intentionally set that fire. Fen too. They all knew. They had to. Timp was their friend — or something like a friend — a frienemy, at the very least. Timp didn't want to answer that, because then he'd have to ask what happened to his friends after the smoke cleared. Had they burned? Did the hilmir arrest them as traitors? Did he execute them? No. Hilmir saw Timp wasn't part of their gang. Surely, Hilmir must have freed them. Right?

Uncertainty clawed at Timp's chest and throat. He'd made a mess of those tiny little lives, but then, they'd made a mess of *his* life too. He had the burns, stings, cuts, scrapes, and bruises to prove it. And to make matters worse, his parents thought he was crazy, then they moved Trevor the disgusting, ghost-zombie-alien-slaying troll into his bedroom. Timp's life had fallen apart since the Vikings. He was glad to be rid of those pests . . . that is, if he was rid of them. Timp remembered the Vaskrél. How long would they keep searching for him? What would they do if they found him? Questions flooded Timp's mind as he worked down the rows of berry, but one question bubbled up no matter how hard he tried to tuck it away: *What about the girl?* Hilmir's daughter, had she survived the fire? Did she believe Timp was an evil giant? What did she look like again? Timp tried to piece together her features in his mind with as much detail as possible, but he couldn't quite capture her. All he managed was a feeling that made his heart race. Would he ever see her again?

Now you've gone too far. What do you care? You don't know her. But for some reason, Timp felt like he did.

What about the girl? Maybe he could go see her. No, what about the Vaskrél? But what about the girl?

Timp wiped the sweat from his brow. He'd been so lost in daydreams that he hadn't noticed how hot it was getting. Soon, the berries would become too soft to pick, and he'd have to go inside to help his mother until the berries cooled that evening. Timp picked up his pace, but was suddenly struck by the feeling of being watched.

He watched out of the corners of his eyes as he moved from one bush to the next. Sure enough, every time he moved to another spot, a bee several bushes down the row moved over too. Bees were common on Blueberry Springs Farm. In fact, like all farms, they depended on them. He was too far away to see the rider. Maybe it was just a regular bee and the following, a coincidence. Timp varied his speed. He skipped bushes to see if the bee maintained the same distance. It did—a Vaskrél scout, Timp knew it. Probably the same Vaskrél who buzzed him on the hill. They were preparing an attack. No doubt, the scout had already called the other Vaskrél. Any moment now, they'd pour over the bushes and strike him down. Timp contemplated attacking the scout before the others arrived. At least he could take one down with him, but the Vaskrél was still two bushes away. By the time Timp reached it, the bee would fly out of range, or lead him deeper into a Vaskrél trap. He couldn't risk it. There was only one thing Timp could do. He ran. In fact, you might say he ran home to Mommy, but that was purely a coincidence. It was time to go in and help her anyway.

The scent of freshly baked blueberry pies filled the air. Timp was relieved that he could just enjoy the smell instead of rushing to the oven and juggling hot pies for fear that the Vikings might murder him with a swarm of killer bees. Yep, life was a lot easier without the Vikings, or so Timp kept reminding himself. Timp's mother glanced up from the kitchen counter, but said nothing. Timp thought they were past this, but he guessed she was still mad about their argument two days before, or maybe she was upset about Molly being hung up in the barn, or maybe she was mad because—it was best not to guess. Suffice to say, she had plenty to be mad about.

"Mom?"

Tears muddied her eyes. Before he could say another word, her arms wrapped around him in a choking hug.

"Heyoooo," Mr. Littleton said as he walked through the door. "I'm glad to see you two getting along."

"Hey, hon," Timp's mother replied. "Find any workers?"

He didn't need to answer. His expression said it all.

"It's DeLaney," Timp blurted. "I bet he's hired everyone in town."

"I told you to stop with that," Timp's father said. "It's no mystery or conspiracy that no one wants to work for free. Once I told them we wouldn't be able to pay them until the—"

"But I'm telling you—"

"Timp!" Timp's father rarely raised his voice. It had a sobering effect.

How could he not see that DeLaney was behind all of this? Was he that naïve? Mr. Littleton returned Timp's glare with tired, worn-out eyes.

Finally, when she could stand it no more, Timp's mother broke the silence. "Just tell him, John."

An unspoken conversation moved back and forth between his parent's eyes. It drove Timp crazy when they did this. He barely understood them when they used words, and here they were having a full conversation with a few exchanged glances.

"Okay, fine," Timp's father groaned. "Timp, Mr. DeLaney is . . . " Timp wondered if his father was deciding what to say, how much to say, or how to say it, " . . . Well, he's family."

"The Hel you say?"

"Timp!" His mother gasped and then tried to hide her laughter.

"His last name isn't even Littleton," Timp said, hoping to bypass his lapse of profanity.

"It's complicated," Mr. Littleton said.

Timp took a moment to absorb this new information. How can family be complicated? You're related or you aren't. Is he a family robot sent out into the world to experience being human? Maybe he's a human-animal hybrid, grown on the farm. Do I call him Uncle Chimera? But the only question that broke through the filter of Timp's mind was: "How do you know he's not behind all this?"

"Because, I told you, he's family," Timp's father repeated. It was as if that explained everything, the same way "he's company" explained why Trevor got the royal treatment. His parents believed these principles were infallible laws of the universe. Timp thought about Bjorn and Hilmir. They were family, but Hilmir was ready to have Bjorn labeled a traitor and maybe even killed. Family can be crueler than strangers. How did his father not know that?

Timp started to protest, but his father cut him off, "He'd never do anything to hurt us, Timp. Especially not you."

"Why *especially* not me?"

"I didn't say 'especially.'"

"Yes you did, you said 'especially.'"

"Well, I just meant because, you're a kid . . . and," Timp's father stumbled around, the way he sometimes did.

Timp's mother filled in the blanks. "Because you're our son."

"Why would that make a difference?" Timp asked. *Maybe I'm the experiment, and he's the scientist. I was grown in a lab. That explains a thing or two.*

"Because he's family," Timp's father returned with a triumphant smile. There they were, full circle. Timp knew better than to keep pushing. Arguing with his parents was like chasing Vikings around a mobius strip. It was a never-ending exercise that may or may not end with a spear in the nose—okay, his parents had never stabbed his nose with a spear, but this all sounded very suspicious.

"What kind of family?"

"Like an uncle . . . or something."

"Or something? What does that even mean? If he's my uncle, why haven't I ever met him?"

"He's very busy," his mother said.

"What about birthdays?"

"Busy."

"Christmas?"

"Busy."

"New years?"

"Very Busy."

"Why'd you never tell me about him? Why was he a secret? Why—"

"Why don't you tell Trevor it's time for lunch."

A never-ending, one-sided loop.

Timp had rather hoped Trevor ran away during the day. He listened and heard gunshots followed by ghost and zombie screams. Trevor was still there.

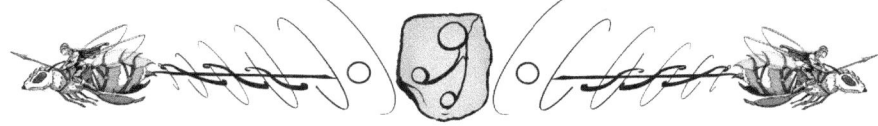

CHAPTER 35
THE BUZZ ON THE STREET

The next day found the Littletons in the orchard. They couldn't afford to lose another day searching for help, and everyone had to pick if they stood any chance of reaching even half their quota for the Summer Fun Fest Farmer's Market on Sunday. Everyone had to work 50 times harder than usual. That is, everyone but Trevor. (After all, "he's company.")

But even with all three Littletons working as hard as they could, Timp knew it was impossible to harvest one tenth of their usual haul—not without help. His father was more optimistic. Mr. Littleton planned to pick through the heat of the day, despite the risk to the berries and heat stroke. He believed that hard work paid off, and he planned to prove it.

"I might even strap on a headlamp and pick through the night." He was determined.

Timp's father was crazy enough to do it too. His optimism encroached insanity. The sky could be falling and Mr. Littleton would open an umbrella shop.

Timp's mother was a more accurate barometer with which to measure the family atmosphere. Her clinched jaw and silent resolve told Timp that trouble hung in the air. She shared no optimistic words, no hopeful clichés, nor platitudes. What good would they do? The Littletons were past mere conversation, past arguing and planning. Now was the time to work. They needed berries to get money. They needed money to keep the farm. They needed to work. She was a fighter, not an optimist. She'd work just as hard as Mr. Littleton, just as tirelessly, but not because she thought they could get enough berries. She'd do it because she'd never let anyone break her. She'd go down fighting.

Timp watched his parents as they walked. He saw them as people, rather than parents. But, not only people: Vikings, fighting to protect their future. Timp admired them . . . even if they were a constant pain in his Asgard.

"Okay, let's divide and conquer," Mr. Littleton said. "Timp, why don't you start at the bottom of the hill by the pond —"

"No!" Timp shouted, and then caught himself. "I mean, how about I start at the top of the hill instead?"

Timp wanted to be as far from the pond as possible. His parents exchanged shrugs. Timp just hoped the top of the orchard was far enough. He'd been lucky to escape the Vaskrél scout the day before, but there'd be others.

The first half of the morning passed without incident. Timp picked nine buckets and was going on ten with no sign of the Vaskrél. He saw a few bees, but all of them far away, and none followed him when he moved from bush to bush. Timp relaxed, but just as he lowered his guard, his enemy came crashing down.

It began with a passing buzz rather than an explosion of fury. Timp looked around, but saw nothing. Then he heard it again, a buzz in his right ear. He searched, but again saw nothing. He waited. His eyes darted left and right. He listened, ready to flee at the first tiny sound of buzzing wings, but he heard only crickets and cicadas playing their rhythmic songs. Timp turned to walk away, when a bee popped him between the eyes. He jerked back and shook his head. The Vaskrél entangled itself in his hair. The buzzing against his ear triggered panic. He swung his bucket with wild abandon. He slapped himself, bounced up and down, and head-banged like a bobble-head glued to a paint mixer. A Donald Duck blathering string of curses poured from his mouth. Gunnar would have called it going berserk. Timp was scared out of his wits.

When he stopped, the Vaskrél was gone. No, not gone. Timp felt it, that prickling on the neck feeling he'd gotten when he was being watched, only this time, it was much stronger. He scanned the bushes until he found the source. Several yards away, a Vaskrél sat, facing him. Somehow he knew this was the same Vaskrél as yesterday. He still couldn't see the rider, but Timp knew that he was there, and that meant there'd be others. Given his encounter with this Vaskrél the day before, Timp knew exactly what to do: he ran . . . again.

He ducked and weaved through the bushes. The remaining berries left in his bucket rattled around and flew all over the place as rows of branches slapped his face. Timp listened for buzzing at his back but could hear nothing through the snapping and cracking of twigs and branches in his ears. He ran until he found himself on the other side of the farm, a distance Timp judged to be far enough away that not even a Vaskrél could have followed. He panted and heaved to catch his breath. Sweat poured from his brow and his stomach churned. His right hand held his now empty bucket, and for a moment, Timp thought it'd be a great place to vomit. He restrained himself. He stood so the breeze hit his face and neck, sweeping away the heat, sweat, and grime. His nerves settled, but he didn't enjoy this feeling for long before something insidious nagged at the back of his mind. Once again, he felt he was being watched.

"That's impossible," he said, but he saw that it wasn't.

The Vaskrél hovered several yards away, ready to charge. Timp's heart sank. He'd run so far. He'd ducked through rows and weaved under branches. He'd run across the farm! How could the Vaskrél have followed? It wasn't fair.

Annoyance compounded into anger. Who did these bullies think they were, pushing him around? They were tiny. He was a giant! This time, Timp didn't run. He was too hot, too tired, too out of breath, and too fed up. This time, he stood his ground.

"You think I'm scared of you?" Timp said, feeling braver than wise. He still couldn't see the rider but he knew he was listening. "You think a tiny thing like you could hurt a giant like me?"

The bee hovered.

Timp thought about the Vikings chasing him away, two days before. He thought about his friends accusing him of burning their village. He thought about DeLaney trying to take over the farm, and how a part of him hoped that he would. He thought about the workers abandoning his parents and the looks on their faces. And the guilt he felt for wanting to join them. He thought about Trevor overtaking his room. He thought about *all* of the wrongs of the world and the thoughts filled him with rage. Tears welled in his eyes. Timp knew there was no point in holding them back.

"Well come on then!" he yelled. "Come and get me!" The Vaskrél tilted, preparing to charge. Timp wiped the tears from the corners of his eyes and beat his chest. "I said come on!"

And then, Timp got his wish.

The Vaskrél charged in a whirl of speed that sobered Timp from his rage. He flailed back, and his foot caught the bucket that lay abandoned on the ground.

It was just as he'd dreamed two nights before, Timp was falling—

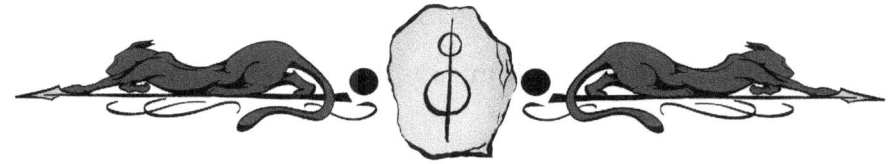

CHAPTER 36
MOLLY VS. CLYDE AND ETHEL

Mrs. Molly Bee Watcher lay on the porch stretching her paws and . . . well, watching bees. One zipped by, then another. *"Nasty, rotten little pests,"* she growled.

It'd taken hours of restless grooming to get her fur to lie down after her dip into the pond. *"I looked like a common alley cat,"* she whined. *"But I'll make them pay. I'll make them all pay."*

She stretched to her feet and hopped off of the porch. She stalked through the grass until she reached a group of bees hovering a few feet off the ground.

"Hel's bells, Clyde. I don't believe it. There's just no way," one nasty, little bee rider said.

"I tell ya, that's what I heard, Ethel. And the sooner, the better, says I."

"I don't know, Clyde. Don't you reckon that's a bit extreme? I mean, death? Alls the giant done was tore up some docks and a couple bridges. Ain't no-one got hurt. Nothing serious, no ways."

"Just telling you what I heard. Besides, he's a giant," the grumpy Clyde said, "The hilmir says them giants gonna bring about Ragnarök."

"Ragnarök? Thor's Hammer, Clyde. Hilmirs been playing that fiddle for a thousand years."

"Aye, granted, but this hilmir says it's for real. Claims he seen it in the runes."

"Hel's bells. Reckon if that's true, Clyde, then we gotta kill 'em."

"Reckon so, Ethel. Reckon so."

Molly didn't know who they wanted to kill, and she didn't care. She squat on her haunches and prepared to attack. Oh, how delightful those bumpkin pests would taste, and this time, they were over land.

Another bee zipped in. "Gather, all. Hilmir be posting a bulletin, this moment."

"Right now?"

"Aye, right now. Let's go!"

The tasty grumpies took off, and Molly sprang into the air, grasping desperately as her appetizers flew away. They flew toward the pond. Molly's hackles rose, and she spit as she gave chase. Molly was on the hunt.

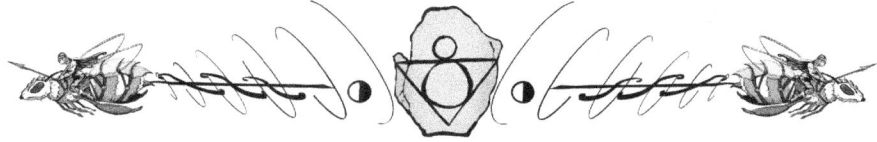

CHAPTER 37
GOOD MORNING, SUNSHINE

Timp awoke with berry branches reaching over his head, and the sun burning through green and yellow leaves. He felt odd, peaceful and content. The world seemed new and beautiful. He felt so completely full of love that, for a moment, he wondered if he'd knocked himself a little silly. It wasn't that he *minded* being happy; he just had no idea *why* he felt so elated.

Timp searched his surroundings. He vaguely remembered being attacked by a Vaskrél but saw no sign of the scout now. He noticed a slight tickling on his cheek and reached up to scratch. The Vaskrél flew up. Timp's exuberance cracked, and anxiety seized his heart. His impulse was to crawl back through the bushes, but something about the bee's hovering seemed strange. Unlike the aggressive flying Timp witnessed in the village, this Vaskrél didn't threaten attack. Instead, it peered into Timp's eyes with curiosity.

Timp held out his hand and the Vaskrél landed in his palm. He cringed when it landed, ready for the sting. When none came, he studied the Vaskrél closer. The bee had no rider, and it wore no body armor. This was no Vaskrél at all. It was just some weirdo bee. Timp held out his hand to let it fly away. The bee fluttered in the air for a moment, and then landed back in his palm, where it rubbed its face against his curled fingertips. *What a weirdo bee!*

Again, a feeling of love and joy overwhelmed Timp's heart. He felt so cheerful that giggles burst from his lips, causing the bee leap into the air with a start. When they broke contact, the feeling faded. The bee hovered before his eyes with its head tilted:

"It's okay," Timp said.

The bee charged Timp's face. He stiffened, but chose to trust a crazy notion that had formed in his mind: maybe this bee didn't want to hurt him, but even if it did, what was one more sting?

The bee didn't sting. It rubbed against Timp's cheek like a cuddling pup. His heart leapt in exaltation. He almost couldn't sit still. He slid his finger gently across his cheek and the bee climbed aboard.

Timp studied the bee while the bee studied him. It was smaller than most bees. Fur pointed in all directions in a yellow and black ball of unkempt chaos. He ran a finger across the bee's head, and it arched its back, allowing him to pet its thorax and abdomen. Timp found himself thinking of the bee more like a puppy than an insect. This bee wasn't a weirdo. It was special. . .

Timp decided to keep it.

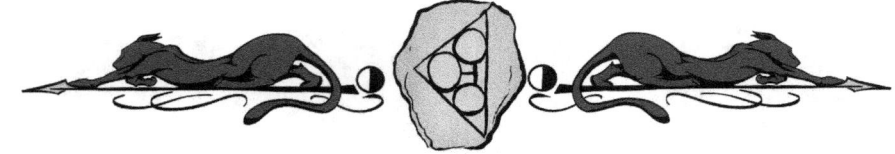

CHAPTER 38
MOLLY ON THE PROWL

Mrs. Molly Prowl Master pawed bitterly at the edge of the murk. She'd followed the bees as far as she could. She'd crawled over and under branches, weaved her way past snakes and briars, and still, she was not close enough to reach the village center. A small neighborhood hung high above. The branch was much too thin to support Molly's purrrfectly queenly figure. The rest of the village hung over the water a few feet away. Mere feet, but for poor Molly, it might as well have been miles. She was many things: a queen, a master huntress, a feline fatale, but a swimmer, she was not. She'd had enough of that to last nine lives.

"*Nasty, rotten, little pests,*" Molly cursed as she dipped a paw into the filthy water and yanked it back, licking it clean all over. "*Think they're so smart.*" Lick. "*Think they know what they're doing.*" Lick. "*I'm a queen.*" Lick. "*I've dined with kings and—*" Molly paused her ranting and raving when she heard one of the grumpies shouting.

"Father! Father!" The grumpy whined as she ducked and weaved through other pests working to reconstruct their village. "Father!"

"Here," a voice replied.

The tiny blue girl stomped toward her larger and plumper father. They both looked deliciously tasty. Molly wished she could jump over and eat them, but the thought of falling back into the water sent shivers through her fur.

"Father, what is the meaning of this?" the girl demanded, holding up a torn piece of paper.

"That, me dear, be an announcement of public execution."

"'Tis marked four days hence."

"Aye, mine daughter's ability to read is unsurpassed."

"And when do you propose to hold a thing determining their guilt?"

"We hath conducted that thing. The accused proved their'n guilt by interrupting the proceedings to burn down our'n village."

"They knew not the giant would lay fire upon the village. They were as surprised as we. You could see it upon Uncle Bjorn's face."

"'Tis irrelevant. They became party to the attack the moment they brought the Jötunn among us."

"They deserve a trial! Their side must be heard!"

"Ailsa, daughter, ye be mine blood, and I hold thee most dear, but as hilmir, my responsibilities art to our'n people."

"Ye've a responsibility to democracy, to the *ways* of our'n people."

"I've a responsibility to see justice served!"

Molly purred. This was a juicy piece of drama. Dinner could wait. Besides, grumpies probably tasted better all worked up and salty.

"Justice? Doth justice include murdering thine own brother?"

"Aye! When me brother brings a giant into our'n realm, when that giant destroys half the village, then aye, justice includes executing me own brother! He must be made an example of—" The grumpy called "Hilmir" snatched the paper from his daughter's hand. "This be what happens to traitors."

Ailsa snatched the paper back and held the image before her father, "He be our'n blood. He's your'n brother and my uncle!"

"And I be hilmir! But I'd not be for long if I favored mine kin over justice."

"You could hold a thing to gain the village's vote."

"'Tis too late for that! Mine decision is made. The date is set, and they are to be executed. All of them."

Hilmir stormed away, and Ailsa's shoulders dropped. She let the paper fall from her hands, and the wind carried it to rest on the water at Molly's paws. The bulletin depicted six tasty blues, and their date of execution in four days.

"*What a waste of dinner.*" Molly's eyes glowed. She decided then that far more than six pests would be executed. Oh, yes. She'd execute every last bacon-delicious one of them and sooner than four days. She'd do it now.

"Fingar?" the little blue girl said without taking her hands from her eyes. A nearby worker stopped pretending to hammer and listened. "Fire the *cat*-apult."

"Aye, ma'am," Fingar said and then reached for a lever.

Molly noticed the emphasis of the word "Cat" in "catapult" a second too late. Fingar pulled the lever and Mrs. Molly Kitty-Cat Cannonball flew into the air with a screech. Villagers paused their hammering and sawing to watch the flailing cat rocket by, but when Molly landed in the middle of the pond with a distant splash, they resumed their work. They had a village to build, a giant to find, and six traitors to execute.

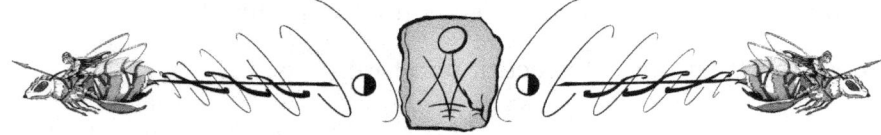

CHAPTER 39
THE BEES-KNEES

Timp spent the rest of the morning with his bee. Whenever they touched, the world seemed more vivid and more real. Colors appeared brighter and details sharper. He felt smarter, quicker, at the top of his game, and though Timp couldn't be certain, he sometimes felt as though time slowed to a crawl. He dreaded the thought of being apart from his bee, and he sensed the bee felt the same. What if it was addictive?

Timp pondered the visceral effects of the bee. What if the emotions he felt were not his own, but those of the bee? It was a crazy notion, for sure. But was it? *Psychic Bees!*

He remained in the orchard throughout the heat of the day. His parents probably thought he was working extra hard, but in truth, Timp had forgotten about work altogether. He was too busy trying to communicate with his bee . . . telepathically.

As evening approached, Timp still hadn't managed a word out of his bee, nor had it seemed to understand a word he thought. The bee seemed unable to follow even the most basic telepathic order. When he tried to send the bee to fetch a berry or blade of grass, it just lovingly stared back. When he envisioned the bee rolling over, it nuzzled his pointer finger. He decided adopt a more traditional approach. He sat the bee down and gently used his finger to teach simple commands, beginning with "sit."

The bee learned quickly. In a couple of hours, it could not only sit, but also lay down, and roll over. This was way easier than telepathic shenanigans. With each success, Timp tossed the bee into the air and cheered. The bee looped happily, and then snuggled his cheek. Finally, Timp decided to teach his bee to come when he called. There was just one problem: the bee had no name. This oversight needed mending.

"Roofus?" The bee made no reaction. "Woodrow?" The bee stared back in adoration. "Felix?" He wasn't sure, but the bee might have hissed at that one.

"Timp?"

For a moment, Timp thought the bee had spoken *his* name. He studied its almost microscopic mouth.

"Timp?" Timp knew that voice. His mother called from the back porch. Timp checked the sky, surprised at how dark it'd become. It was time for dinner.

"Well, come on, whatever-your-name-is," he said as he scooped the bee onto his shoulder. It nuzzled his neck, and his heart warmed with bliss as he strolled toward the house, empty bucket in hand.

Dinner didn't begin as quietly as it had in previous nights. In fact, it began with a beating.

Timp found his mother standing on the porch with a disapproving look at the empty bucket in his hands. "Tell me that isn't all you did, today," she said. Timp studied the ground in embarrassment. "You know we all have to work extra hard."

"I know. I'll do better," Timp said, pushing a rock with his toe.

Timp was surprised that his mother didn't press him further. In fact, she looked guilty and sad, and then angry. "Not that it matters," she muttered, more to herself than to Timp.

Several buckets lined the porch banister. It was a meager harvest that his parents had picked. At this rate, the Littletons wouldn't have enough berries to bother going to the Summer Fun Fest Farmer's Market at all.

Summer Fun Fest: Timp dreaded the thought. He hated working there on a good year, but this one would be humiliating. Bee-Brain Wokowski would no doubt brag about his honey harvest and tell giggly stores about the mating habits of his bees. Peachy Pam would show off her apples—Timp stopped. *Peachy sells apples. Why the heck do we call her "Peachy?"* He shook away the thought. The point was, they'd be the only ones showing up with next to nothing, and no doubt, they'd lose the farm. The thought didn't make Timp as happy as he'd expected.

"Come on. Let's get you inside and cleaned up for dinner." His mother held her hand up and rain her fingers through his hair.

"Let me guess: chicken, mashed potatoes, and broccoli," Timp said.

His mother slapped him. She slapped him hard across the side of the head.

Timp jerked back in surprise. He couldn't remember the last time his mother had slapped him. Maybe never. Then, she slapped him again, this time on the side of his neck, and again on the ear. Timp tried to block her with his hands, but she pushed them away. "Bee!" she said, and Timp remembered.

"No! Don't!" Bolts of panic splintered through his brain with the horror of each resounding slap, and Timp knew then that he'd been right: the feelings he'd felt in the orchard were not his own. They were the bee's.

"NO!" he yelled, but his mother kept swatting and slapping. The bee tried to fly away—left, then right—only to be hit back again. Its wings buzzed in terror. "NO! Stop! That's my —" The bee broke connection. "—pet."

"What do you mean that's your pet?"

Timp crawled around the porch on all fours, scanning the ground for his fallen bee.

It was nowhere to be found, this relieved and worried Timp. It must have flown off, which meant that it was alive, but was it hurt? Was it gone forever? Did it blame him for his mother's attack? Did it feel betrayed like the Vikings? Timp tried to block out such worries and find it.

"Timp? I'm talking to you."

"I mean it's my pet. It's my pet bee," Timp said, after his fourth or fifth sweep of the area.

"Pet bee, who ever heard of such a thing. Is that why you're all stung up? From playing with bees? Timp Buster Keaton Littleton, I swear. What has gotten into—"

"What the devil is going on out here?" Timp's father barreled out of the house.

"*Your* son tried to bring a bee inside." Timp's mother stuck out her bottom lip and blew away a sweaty curl that had fallen before her eyes. "Said it was his pet."

Timp's father laughed. "Well, it wouldn't be the worst thing he's brought into this house."

"One time! I bring snakes into the house one time, and you never let me forget it!"

"And the raccoons."

"Also only once."

"And the possums?"

"Just one. The babies don't count. How was I supposed to know it was carrying babies?"

"It's a marsupial!"

"Well, lesson learned. And who had to get them out of the couch cushions, huh? Me. That's who. Have you ever stuck your hand into a couch, searching for naked baby possums? I have! It's terrifying."

Timp and his parents laughed at their feigned fight. They needed the laugh. But the fun didn't stop there. Mrs. Molly Pond Diver walked up, soaking wet with cowlicks pointing in all directions. She looked like a scraggly alley cat.

"Molly! What happened to you?" Mrs. Littleton laughed. Queen Molly ignored the question and strutted on by. She walked straight into her straw-lined cathouse and kicked up hay until it blocked the door. "*Stupid. Rotten. No. Good. Grumpies.*"

During dinner, Timp told his parents all about his bee and the tricks he'd taught it. Timp could see his parents dismissed the tale as a wild flight of their son's imagination, but they enjoyed the distraction enough to play along more than usual. "Well, if it comes back, you can keep it," Timp's mother said with a wink to his father.

"Can I, really?"

She may have been patronizing Timp, but he didn't care. The thought made him happy. It was the first time they'd ever offered to let him to keep anything he'd brought home. Snakes, possums, raccoons, rats, lizards, and tarantulas were strangely unwelcome in the Littleton household. He knew the only reason they said he could keep the bee was because they didn't believe he'd ever see it again, but Timp was glad to have their promise locked down, just in case—and in front of a witness! Timp looked over at Trevor, who fired round after round of semiautomatic plasma rays at ghosts, zombies, and innocent bystanders. The light from his cell reflected in his wide, sadistic eyes, and spit foamed in the corner of his mouth. Timp wondered why his parents let *that* pest inside the house, but he decided it unwise to say so. You had to quit while you're ahead in the Littleton household. He resolved then and there that, first thing in the morning, he'd find his bee.

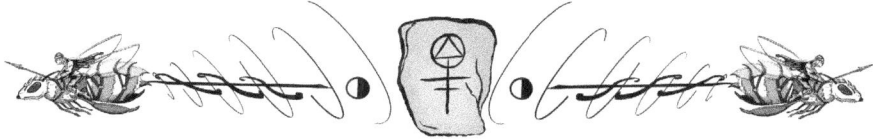

CHAPTER 40
BEE-LOVED

Timp awoke at 3 a.m. bleary eyed but determined to find his bee. He checked the porch again, just to be sure it wasn't waiting there or hurt, and then moved on to the top rows of the orchard where they'd met.

He picked berries while he searched, so not to disappoint his parents.

He filled bucket after bucket and moved down the rows. The sun climbed through the sky, and the smell of hot grass and sweat permeated the air, but there was no sign of the bee. Timp's imagination tarried on the worst. Maybe it *was* hurt, or worse yet dead. Maybe it'd flown away and died . . . alone . . . in the dark . . . and without a name! Panic and frustration fired electric static through his mind until relief came as a gentle nudging at the back of his neck. His heart leapt. He ran his hand along the back of his neck until he felt the bee climb onto his fingers then pulled his hand around and checked the bee over like a protective parent. "Bee, are you okay? You had me worried." He ran his finger around the bee's thorax, checked under its wings, and scratched its belly when it rolled over.

The bee appeared unharmed.

Timp sighed with relief. "I didn't know if you were lost, hurt, or worse. Don't ever do that again. Don't ever, ever, ever—" Timp felt the bee's mood descend into sadness, so he quickly changed his tone. "But I love you, bee, just the same."

This made the bee happy; though, Timp sensed a guardedness that had not existed the day before. The bee's uninhibited adoration seemed marred by—Timp searched his feelings for the right word—distrust. Timp frowned. He still felt the bee's love for him, but that love now felt tainted. He wanted to protest, but stopped. He had betrayed his friend's trust. He'd brought the bee into harms way—unintentionally, yes, but carelessly, nonetheless. Timp promised to work hard to regain the bee's trust.

"I'm sorry. I won't let anything happen to you, ever again," Timp promised. He meant it too, but he couldn't predict the future. He couldn't control the world around him or know of things to come. At least for now, the bee felt warm and content (which made Timp feel warm and content too. Strange, that).

"Today we have two things to do," Timp said. "First, we have to pick lots and lots of berries, and second—" Before Timp finished, the bee flew to the nearest bush and started pulling on a blueberry. The bee wasn't strong enough to actually pluck the berry, but it tugged with loyal determination. Timp laughed. "That's the idea. Just like that. And second, we have to give you a name." The bee whirled in a blur of excitement.

Timp picked berries as he brainstormed. "How about Frank?" The bee fluttered its wings in frustration. "Arnold?" Buzzed in annoyance. "Theodore?" Tanked to the ground and played dead. "Dexter?" The bee jumped up and charged as if to sting. "Okay! Okay! Not Dexter!"

Timp wondered if he was on the wrong track altogether. He scoured the list of names queued in his mind and struggled to remember everything he knew about honey bees, which, as it happened, was next to nothing. He thought about the beekeeper who sold honey at the Farmer's Market. Mr. Wokowski was an odd, nervous sort of fellow who Timp avoided like broccoli lest he get pulled into meandering lectures about the mating habits of bees. (Had Timp known how important those lectures would be, he'd have paid closer attention.) But Timp did recall the beekeeper saying something about honey bees. He said that all honey bees are worker bees and all worker bees are . . .

"Are you a girl bee?" Timp asked, surprised by the revelation.

The bee flipped in joyous loops of confirmation while Timp blushed at his oversight. The bee landed on his hand, and he felt her exhilaration surge through his emotions.

"So, we need a girl's name," Timp affirmed, and the bee buzzed in agreement.

A girl's name, this stumped Timp something fierce. "Bee . . . Bee . . . Bee . . . Beatrice?" The bee ignored him. "Beelzebub?" She buzzed in aggravation. "Bee Arthur?" If bees could groan, she would have. "Beezoar." For the second time that day, Timp thought she might sting him. He ducked as she charged back and forth impatiently, and held up his bucket as she swirled to strike. There was only one way out of this, Timp shouted the next name that came to his mind, "Bonnie! Bonnie! The bee stopped, hovered in the air, and tilted her head. Timp remained on guard, in case she attacked. "Bonnie Bee?"

She circled Timp's head and looped around and around. Timp knew this pattern well. He held out his hand, and she landed on his palm. Her emotions surged through his body. Sure enough, she was happy. Bonnie had a name.

Timp and Bonnie spent the rest of the day picking berries and talking. He taught her many new tricks, which Bonnie learned quickly, and she tried to teach him some new tricks, but Timp didn't learn a single one. In fact, he didn't even realize Bonnie was trying to teach him anything. He just walked along, picking berries and feeling her happiness flow through him with nary an idea that she might be trying to communicate something important. He'd forgotten all about the Vikings, and it never occurred to him that Bonnie might know anything about them

274

that he didn't. Eventually, Bonnie gave up trying to train her giant and contented herself just to be with her boy.

They returned home late for dinner. Timp wanted everyone settled at the table before he introduced them to Bonnie. Maybe then he could avoid another incident like the night before. As they neared the house, Timp felt Bonnie grow nervous.

"It's okay," he assured her. "Nothing bad is going to happen to you."

Timp hoped he was right.

Bonnie's wings buzzed as they walked through the door. Timp cradled her in his hands and did his best to sooth her . . . and himself. (Her fear was contagious). His mother sat at the dinning room table, poking at her mashed potatoes. Trevor sat across from her, pounding on his cell with his tongue sticking out until it almost touched the dried snot crusted around his nostrils. Timp's father dished broccoli onto a plate at the stove.

"Hey, kiddo. Got your dinner." Mr. Littleton held up the steaming plate, and then froze when he saw that Timp was holding something.

Timp rolled his eyes. "It's not a snake." *One time!* His father relaxed. "It's a bee." Mr. Littleton stiffened again. Timp sighed. "She won't hurt you."

Mr. Littleton followed Timp into the dinning room and sat down next to Timp's mother while Timp positioned himself at the head of the table to present Bonnie. All eyes were on Timp.

Even Trevor had stopped gaming to give Timp his undivided attention. He slid his hands onto the table and uncovered his palm.

"May I present Bonnie Bee," Timp said rather grandly, and then added, "because she's a bee."

Bonnie trembled beneath the enormous new faces. She crawled onto the table, ready to fly away at the first sign of danger. No one moved.

"Bonnie knows all kinds of tricks, including how to sit, lay down, roll over, flip, and play dead." As Timp said the commands, Bonnie obeyed.

His parents gasped. "My lands." "Never in all my—" "Why, that's the darnest—"

Timp smiled, now he had them. "You said I could keep her."

"Keep her? Hell, son, we should put her on Broadway!"

"Or sell her to the circus," his mother added.

None of these ideas had occurred to Timp, but he had an absolute opinion about them right away. "No. She's not for sale." He scooped Bonnie into his hands, and held her close. He'd never seen that look in his parent's eyes before, and he didn't like it.

"But son, this is amazing. I've never heard of a bee who could—"

"No. She's not some kind of a circus freak. She's mine. And besides, she could get hurt. I promised I'd protect her."

"Timp, it's a bee," Timp's mother said in a tone that suggested Timp was being silly or childish. "We need the money."

"No!" Timp was growing angry, but more than that, he felt ashamed, and he didn't even know why. He'd expected a different reaction. Of all people, they should understand. They were the ones always telling him. "Money isn't everything, Timp." "No man is poor who has his own land, Timp." They said things like that all the time. He turned his shoulder away from his parents, keeping Bonnie as protected as possible. "There are some things worth more than money, even all the money in the world. Don't y'all understand that? Why doesn't *anyone* understand that?" His voice shook, it made him mad to use their words against them. His eyes began to burn. "You sound like *them*." Timp pointed with his chin at the surrounding farms, keeping Bonnie held close against his chest. His parents knew who he meant. They sounded like DeLaney. They sounded like everyone else, everyone trying to take their farm and cookie cut the world out of greed. They dropped their heads. The conversation was over. Timp had won.

Timp had never won an argument against his parents, before. It didn't feel as good as he'd imagined.

His eyes wandered to Trevor, the one person who had not spoken throughout this ordeal. Trevor stared at Timp's hands with eyes that made Timp instinctively draw away. He'd seen that look before. It was the same expression Trevor had mowing down other players in Ghost Zombie Apocalypse.

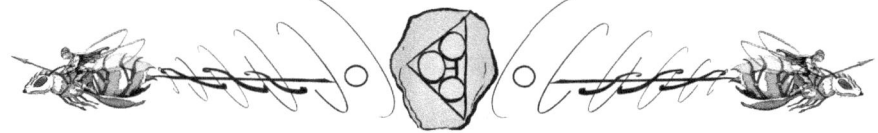

CHAPTER 41

NOBODY PUTS BONNIE IN THE CORNER

That night, Timp grabbed the matchbox that had held the Vikings only days before and lined it with cotton. He adjusted his pallet on the floor and sat the box on a shelf next to his head.

"You'll sleep here," he explained, showing Bonnie the matchbox. He could feel her growing more comfortable with her new environment. She crawled out of his hand and inspected the box. At first, she seemed confused, but then she pushed down, burrowed a hole into the cotton, and peeked her head out with approval.

But as Bonnie grew more comfortable, Timp grew less so. Something felt wrong. He tried to place what it was, and then he realized that the room was silent. No machine guns rattled. No hand grenades exploded. No rockets whooshed from speaker to speaker only to crash into ice cream trucks. No ghosts moaned. No zombies screamed. All of the sounds Timp had grown accustomed to over the past few days were conspicuously absent.

In fact, Trevor didn't have the TV on at all. He stood behind Timp, silently, leering over Timp's shoulder.

"Can I touch it?" Trevor asked, eyes fixed on Bonnie.

"No," Timp said, partly to payback Trevor for never letting him play his Playstation, but also because Trevor was giving him the creeps.

"What are you going to do with it?" Trevor asked.

"With *her*, not 'it,'" Timp corrected.

"We should pull off its wings," Trevor said.

Timp's scalp crawled back, and his eyes rounded white as a chill shot down his spine. He opened his mouth and managed an almost inaudible "What?"

"We should tear off its wings and see what it does—or no, its head! Yeah, we could tear off its head and see if it still moves."

"Are you crazy?" Timp scooped up Bonnie, matchbox and all, and held her against his chest. He'd never noticed how big Trevor was before. He'd noticed Trevor was overweight, sure, but he'd hardly seen Trevor stand and never so close. Timp now saw that Trevor stood at least a foot taller than himself and out weighed him by more than a hundred pounds.

Trevor licked his lips, "I wonder how long she'd live without a head."

Timp wanted to puke. "Well, we're not going to find out." He tried to push by Trevor, only to get slammed into the corner. Bonnie crawled onto Timp's hand, and her fear cut through him like razorblades. Timp wondered if he should scream. He heard his parents arguing on the other side of the house. He heard the back door slam and then slam again. His parents were outside now. Timp was on his own.

He felt small and alone in Trevor's shadow, but he also felt guilty. He'd promised to keep Bonnie safe. Instead, he'd delivered her into the hands of a psychopath. He didn't mean to, of course, but he should have known. He'd heard Trevor brag about bullying his neighbor. He'd seen Trevor giggle and fire rocket launchers at stray cats or kill his teammates in co-op mode just to watch, but that was in a video game—even Timp laughed at video games—this was real life!

Bonnie trembled in his hands. Timp's stomach boiled with her anxiety. He wanted beg her forgiveness, but her emotions overpowered his thoughts until he could no longer form words. Finally, he found one. *Fly*, he thought. He thought it loud and he thought it hard, but Bonnie remained.

Timp made a tight hollow ball with his hands to protect Bonnie and head-butted Trevor in the arm. It wasn't a powerful hit, it was awkward and clumsy, but he hoped it would let him push on by. It didn't. Trevor pinned Timp into the corner with his elbow, and pressed Timp's face against the wall until Timp thought his jaw might crack from the pressure. Timp's hands came apart and the matchbox fell. Bonnie clung to Timp for protection as Trevor reached for her with his free hand. He hesitated. Timp knew what Trevor was thinking. He wanted to grab the bee, without being stung. He wanted it unharmed so he could torture it at his leisure, to see how long it could live without its wings, or its head. Would it really die if he ripped out its stinger? Trevor's mouth wired into a crooked, sadistic smile. *Fly! FLY!* "FLY!" Timp screamed in his mind and then with his mouth.

Bonnie sprang into the air. As Trevor tried to grab her, Timp pushed away from the wall with all his might and elbowed Trevor in the gut. Trevor keeled over with a satisfying "*Umph,*" then shook his head and stood back up. Bonnie banged against the bedroom door, trying to get out. Timp jumped over the bed and grabbed the doorknob. No sooner had he cracked the door an inch, than Trevor slammed his meaty fist into the wood and shut it again.

Timp elbowed Trevor again, and then circled around and kneed his groin. He'd fight dirty if it meant saving Bonnie. Timp opened the door as Trevor fell back Bonnie flew down the hall, bumping into paintings and the wall as she searched for a way out. Timp tried to guide her to safety, but Trevor grabbed his ankle and yanked him back like a rag doll. Timp wrapped around Trevor's calf and bit down. They elbowed, kicked, hit slapped, and stomped their way down the hall.

"To the right! Not that right, your other right!"

Bonnie flew into the living room, dining room, and then the kitchen. With Mr. and Mrs. Littleton still outside, the house was an open war zone.

Trevor grasped for Bonnie's tail. Timp fought to keep up. He tackled Trevor, getting kicked in the head on the way down. They wrestled and rolled on the hardwood floor. Trevor broke free, stood up, and kicked Timp back to the ground. Timp rose to stand, but Trevor turned around and slapped him across the cheek with a resounding *Smack!*

Time stopped, and the air grew cold.

Bonnie rotated until she hovered at eye-level, staring straight into Trevor's wide, fish-like eyes. Her head bent forward and her stinger was out. No one slapped her boy. No one.

Trevor froze, evidently reconsidering his career as a bee-dissecting mad scientist. He stepped back, almost tripping over Timp, who lay on the floor holding his ribs and watching Bonnie. A broken clock rattled inside Timp's mind. Slowly, the universe tried to piece itself back together. He was trying to remember something Mr. Wokowski, the beekeeper at the Farmer's Market, once told him about bees. He said bees' stingers are barbed. Once they go in, they can't come out without killing the bee. But that meant that if Bonnie stung Trevor, she'd . . .

Bonnie charged Trevor's head.

"No!" Timp cried.

Trevor squealed as he stepped back into Timp's side, and tumbled to the ground.

Bonnie missed and circled around for another attack.

"Stop!" Timp shouted. He covered Trevor. Not to protect him, but to protect Bonnie. "Don't sting him!"

Bonnie stopped.

Trevor shoved Timp away with a belch and climbed to his feet, wheezing, and dripping with sweat. Timp stood up and positioned himself between Bonnie and Trevor.

Trevor started for Bonnie and Timp shoved him back.

"Go, please," Timp begged.

Bonnie tilted her head. Timp didn't need their connection to understand her confusion. Why was he siding with Trevor? Why was Timp protecting the enemy? Why was he choosing this horrible, disgusting troll over her? Why didn't her boy love her? She didn't understand. How could she? Timp wanted to hold her and explain it. He wanted her to know why it had to be this way, that he wasn't protecting Trevor, he was saving her, that bringing her inside had been a mistake, but he couldn't do any of that. He couldn't risk her falling into Trevor's warped, sadistic hands, not again. Timp's mother and father opened the back door.

"Go!" Timp shouted. He'd brought her into harms way after he promised that he wouldn't. She was better off outside, better off without him. He grabbed a book that had fallen off the shelf during the scuffle and held it over his head. "I said get out of here!" Tears burned his cheeks.

His parents stood dumbfounded with the door open. Bonnie hesitated and turned back.

"You need to go." Timp dropped the book and covered his tears with his arm. He was glad he couldn't feel Bonnie's emotions now: confusion, betrayal, disappointment, anger, and heartbreak. Pain.

Timp wiped his eyes. When he looked up, Bonnie was gone.

His parents watched her disappear into the dark night sky and then turned to face a house in shambles. "Timp David Byrne Littleton, you just won't be happy until you burn this house down!"

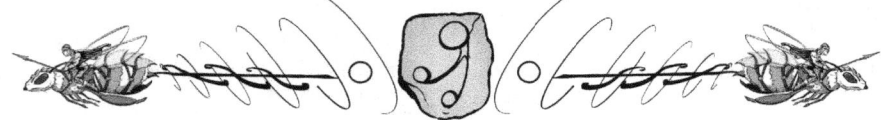

CHAPTER 42
THE PUGILIST, THE DAY AFTER

Timp slept through the following morning. After his fight with Trevor, he swore he'd have nothing more to do with that house-pest. (Trevor was a house-pest and not a houseguest, because houseguests eventually go home, and Trevor—it turned out—could not.)

Aunt Rose had taken her newfound freedom and ran. Immediately after dumping her wretched son in the Littleton's driveway, she'd hot-tailed it to New Orleans and booked passage on a singles cruise to Jamaica. She was now sunbathing in the Caribbean, sipping mojitos, and giggling at inane stories about bachelor parties told by tanned boy-men with plucked eyebrows. Timp learned all of this during the nuclear fallout that became known as "The Great Bee Kerfuffle." He'd demanded his parents send his psychotic cousin home, only to have them produce a series of postcards explaining that they couldn't. Each card depicted scantily clad Caribbean men with messages penned in his aunt's handwriting: "Yummy!" "Yes, Please!" and "I'll have two." The postcards made Timp regret ever learning to read. His mother said there were others, but those were "not for children's eyes." Timp was happy to take her word for it. The salacious notes didn't matter, their underlying message was clear: the Littletons were stuck with Trevor for an indeterminate time to come. So, Timp scraped up his sleeping bag and musty pillow from his bedroom floor and lay claim to the living room couch intent on sleeping for a year.

The sun had other plans.

Daylight broke through the curtains and burned Timp's sleep-filled eyes. He glanced at the old cuckoo clock on the wall as he rolled off the couch: 9 a.m. His parents probably had rose before dawn and headed to the orchard. He was surprised they'd let him sleep in and thought about lying back down to sleep some more, but the murmur of zombie screams echoed down the hall. His eye twitched. He decided to go out and work.

He slogged through his morning ritual and stepped onto the porch where humidity assaulted his lungs: another scorching hot day. Molly sat in the corner studying Timp, and Timp studied back. Her fur shot out in all directions, filled with knots, tangles, and unruly cowlicks. Timp's bruised cheek still showed finger marks from last night's slap, his face and neck were pocked with stings, and he had more scratches and bruises than he could count. They made quite a pair.

Timp grabbed buckets and straps and walked down the stairs. He half expected Bonnie to meet him there. He imagined her jumping into his hands as soon as his feet touched the grass, but she didn't. He walked toward the orchard, hoping she'd land on his shoulder by the time he arrived at the blueberries, but she didn't. Maybe she'd show up just as he began picking berries and nuzzle his neck like she did before. But this time, she didn't.

"Booonnnnnnnnnnnnnnnnnnnniiiiieeeeeee," Timp called in long drawn out cries. He no longer cared if the Vaskrél heard him, but began well away from the pond, just in case. Surely, they'd given up their search by now. The Vikings had probably forgotten about him too. He was just a battle tale they told: "The Day We's Met a Giant." Timp imagined Uncle Dene sitting in his olive with Bjorn, Erika, Fen, Gunnar, and O'dul, laughing at the time giants tried to bake him into a pie. Timp wished them well. He didn't know they were prisoners, slated for execution in two days.

By noon, Timp had traversed the farm and gathered twelve buckets of berries, but he found no sign of Bonnie. He skipped lunch and searched on. He called her name to the trees and sky, but only cicadas answered.

That is . . . until they didn't.

Timp turned onto a long row of bluebells that curved gently around a hill. He found himself closer to the pond than was wise, but he was getting desperate. He called Bonnie's name and the farm fell silent. No cicadas sang. No crickets chirped. No wind blew. Despite the heat, a chill ran up Timp's spine. Again, he felt he was being watched.

"Bonnie?" Timp hoped.

Two bees hovered near an outcropping of berries several bushes away. Timp didn't get a Bonnie feeling. Were they regular bees or Vaskrél scouts? Timp decided not to wait and find out. He ran. Watching the bees at his rear, he ran into a someone.

"Dad, you gotta start watching—" But person standing above Timp was not Mr. Littleton. "DeLaney?"

"*Mister* DeLaney," DeLaney corrected.

"Mister De Pain in my Asgard," Timp muttered as he stood and dusted himself off. He wished the Vikings were around to hear that one. It seemed the kind of thing they'd enjoy. Timp buried his Viking thoughts and realized he'd run clear to the edge of Blueberry Springs. "What do you want?"

"Relax, boy. I'm not here for you or your paltry farm—"

"I wouldn't care if you were," Timp muttered.

DeLaney eyed Timp suspiciously and then continued. "Not that I've forgotten how you made me look in front of the board, but we'll worry about that another day."

"Whatever, dude," Timp mumbled distractedly, as he checked under the row of blueberries for Bonnie.

"Today, I'm making sure everything is ready for my construction crew to clear the neighboring farm."

That got Timp's attention. "The Plimptons'?"

A bee buzzed near Timp's ear. At least he thought it was a bee. It sounded like a bee. Was it a bee? Bonnie?

"It's not the Plimptons' anymore, boy. It's the bank's land now. I heard they ran back to Oklahoma. Good riddance. Their land is going to make me very rich."

"Well, good on you, bud." Timp stiffened as something landed on his shoulder, crawled across his collar, and then onto his neck. "Bonnie?" he whispered, and then he heard them.

"Hey ya, Clyde. You reckon this him?"

"Hel's bells, Ethel. How'd I know? Gotta get around and see his big ugly giant face."

"Well, what're ya wait'n for? Fly around and look."

"What ya think I'm trying to do, Ethel?"
Vaskrél scouts. Timp tried to remain as nonchalant as possible and brush away the bee that flew into his peripheral.

"Hey! He swat'n me, Ethel!"

Timp focused on DeLaney. He needed to get rid of him so he could fight off these bees. "Yeah, yeah yeah. Money, farms, world domination. Why don't you get with it then?"

"Oh, I will. Don't you worry about that. But first, I need to check the lay of the land against some blueprints." DeLaney unfolded a leather-bound tablet and began pinching and zooming architectural drawings and comparing them to the Littleton's farm. The whole show annoyed Timp to his core.

"Don't you already know this farm? I mean, you've spent a lot of time here, right?"

A smile spread across DeLaney's face. "What've they told you about me?"

"They said you're my uncle or something." Timp swatted at the bee, but the Vaskrél barrel rolled out of the way.

"Yehaw! Missed, you tricksy, li'l Jötunn devil." Timp really hoped DeLaney would leave soon, before—

"Aye. I reckon that be our'n Jötunn, all right. I'll go ahead and call the others."

A horn bellowed near Timp's ear, and birds flocked from the trees. Crickets and cicadas stopped singing, leaving only the faint buzz as a cloud of bees rose from brush in the distance. *The Vaskrél swarm!*

Time was running short.

"Uncle! Is *that* what they told you—"

"Look: uncle, not uncle, I don't care. Take the farm. You can have it. You know what I'm going to get? Gas station nachos and Dr. Pepper Icees. So have at it, buddy. The enemy of my enemy is my . . . not enemy. Right? Either way, I win." Timp was starting to dance around and look nervous.

DeLaney stood speechless. He clearly had fancied a more dramatic altercation. The Vaskrél circled. Timp shuffled nervously while DeLaney started anew. "Family is such a complicated construct, but why dig up ancient history when you can build something new. Indeed, take a good look, boy. Next week, it's the Plimptons'. In a month, it'll be Blueberry Springs Farm. Surprising how easy it was too. All I had to do was hire away your help." DeLaney grabbed a fistful of berries. "You must feel lost at sea: surrounded by water yet dying of thirst. Small. Helpless. Pathetic. I have to be honest, I hoped for a better fight. But then, John always was weak."

Timp knew DeLaney was just trying to get a rise out of him. He hated that it was sort of working.

"Aye, let's see how you like this one, Jötunn!" One of the Vaskrél scouts stung Timp on the back of the neck.

"Ow!" Timp slapped, and missed.

"Yehaw! Look who decided to join the rodeo, Clyde."

"Yep, I do believe that cowboy's bitten off more'n he can chew, Ethel."

The Vaskrél snaked closer. Timp had to end this. "Look! I told you. I don't care if you take the farm. Dr. Pepper Icees, dude. What'd I say? I got bigger fish to fry in the sky, brah. Now, I gotta get my going on!" Timp was scared nonsensical. He turned away from DeLaney and ran.

"No one is bigger than me in this town, boy. No one!" DeLaney laughed at Timp's back, and then sort of muttered to himself. "Might have over done that. Bit anti-climatic, though."

Timp knew DeLaney wanted revenge. Knew he wanted to push his buttons. But the Vaskrél swarm was way bigger and more deadly than DeLaney. If DeLaney got the farm, they'd be his problem. The way Timp saw it, that was a win.

The Vaskrél shifted in Timp's direction as he tore through the orchard with buckets flailing. He barreled past his parents, who didn't even look up from their work. They were getting used to the new Timp.

The bees were on him, now. The head of the swarm reared back, a snake ready to strike. Timp ducked. The Vaskrél's lead guard rolled over his right shoulder and circled back for another attack. He turned toward the house, hoping the Vaskrél wouldn't follow. They did.

Molly sat on the porch, grooming out the last cowlick left from her most recent bought with the grumpies. Timp pounded past, nearly knocking her over.

"*Hey! Watch it, servant! I'm your que—*" Molly's eyes went wide in face of the Vaskrél swarm.

"Seize the guard-beast, as well!"

The cat turned tail and— "*Hold that door!*" but it was too late. Timp slammed the door and leaned against it, catching his breath.

Molly slid down the door. "*Traitor. I'll get you for this. Traaaaaiiiiiittttttooooooorrrrrr!*" The buzzing of bees drowned her cries.

Timp decided he would have lunch, after all.

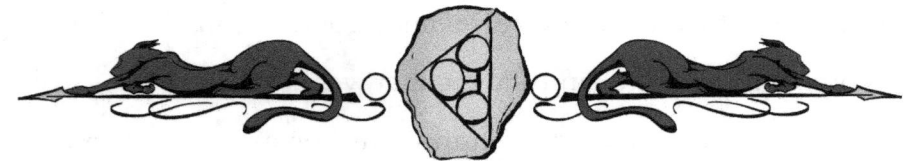

CHAPTER 43
ATTACK OF THE U.S.S. QUEEN MOLLY

It took until Saturday for Mrs. Molly Mane Tamer to assert her dominance over her cow-licked welts. She'd hacked up several satisfying hairballs in the process and was now regal once again. Queen Molly was ready for revenge.

She surveyed her kingdom. That stupid, treacherous servant boy had awoken early that morning to wander the orchard and moan. "*Oh, that incessant bellyaching.*" He'd been at it for two days, crying the same thing over and over: Bon Bon, Boon, Bonnie . . . something like that. Molly didn't know what a Bonnie was, but she hated it. She hated it so much. If she ever met one, she'd eat it for sure (just as soon as she finished off those little, blue grumpies).

Molly slinked toward the pond. Those rotten pests had attacked her at her home. Now, she'd get them at theirs. She'd developed a new plan of attack: the land side of the village was barricaded and covered with *cat*-apults—she'd learned that the hard way—but knowing how much she hated the water, those tasty little idiots would never expect a seaside attack.

Molly imagined herself leaping into the middle of the village and tearing open those tiny blueberry houses. How shocked they'd be as she ate her way through every last one of them and laughed with arms and legs hanging out of her mouth. "*A seaside buffet.*"

All she needed was a queen's vessel (or a chunk of wood to use as a raft). Molly searched the pond's bank for a log big enough to support her queenly figure. She wanted to be sure that there was no chance her purrfectly groomed fur touched that disgusting, nasty, water ever again. She wasn't some shabby alley cat, after all. She had to keep up appearances, and that meant choosing a proper vessel.

On the far side of the pond, Molly found a large log stuck in the muddy embankment. She pressed against the damp bark with her front paws, but the log didn't budge. She jumped on it and kicked off with her back legs, and then turned around. Her vessel was grounded. Molly would see about *that*. She stepped back, stuck her bottom in the air, dug her claws deep into the dirt, and charged. Molly and the log tumbled down the embankment: ground, sky, water, ground, sky, water, ground, sky, *water!* She shoved out her front paws, clawing up mud and grass until she slid to a complete stop with her nose inches from the pond's surface. "*That was close.*" She purred in celebration until she noticed something strange. Her feet felt weird. It was like they were in—

"*Water!*" Molly flipped into the air and landed with all paws safely on dry land. "*Gross! Gross! Water! Gross!*" She licked her feet and dragged them in the grass, flipping blades of yellow and brown into the air. When her paws felt dry, and she was certain she hadn't contracted some filthy water disease, Molly remembered the log.

The log lay at the bottom of the embankment half in and half out of the water. "*Puurrrfect.*"

Molly stepped gingerly onto the wood and tested its buoyancy. It bobbed up and down but stayed afloat. The vessel seemed sturdy enough. She shoved off the shore with her back paws, and stood on the log with her chin high, taking in the breeze of . . . nothing. Molly opened her eyes. She hadn't moved. The log remained stuck in the pond's edge.

"*Must everything always be so difficult?*" Molly growled.

She hopped back onto the shore, planted her hind legs in the clay, and pushed off with all her might. She sprang onto the log as it broke free of the bank and slid into the water. She'd done it! She was sailing. She was . . . sailing in the wrong direction. Molly shifted her weight thinking that'd steer the log toward the grumpy's village. The log rolled. She stepped forward, stepped back, and then latched on with every claw she had to hold it steady. That stopped the rolling, but it did nothing to correct her course. Mrs. Molly Lost At Sea cried a pathetic meow as she drifted toward the center of the pond.

åSeveral hours later, Molly perfected the art of dog paddling (though she'd insist it was "cat paddling"). The log ship inched toward the grumpy's village. Soon, she'd stuff her belly full of delicious pests.

As she floated into the shadows surrounding the village, Molly crouched on the log and prepared to pounce. Sparse rays of light sliced through the leafy ceiling, making the darkness around them seem black as night. Molly relished the protective darkness. The grumpies had no idea what was coming.

But before she reached the village, she came to six tiny cages, floating in a row. Inside each cage was a tiny blue grumpy. *Mmm, Appetizers,* Molly thought, *and neatly packed in to-go boxes. How sweet.* She reached out to grab one, but then she noticed a small boat paddling in her direction. *More treats.* If she struck now, she might lose the ones in the boat, but if she waited, she could almost double her haul. Molly ducked into the darkness to wait.

A grumpy stood at the boat's bow with a smaller grumpy at his side. Behind them, two hulking lumps of blue and purple rowed and grunted the ship forward. As the boat reached the first cage, the man at the bow grabbed a bucket full of slop and held it up.

"Last meal, Bjorn. I fear they were all out of steak."

He dumped the slop onto the man within the cage.

Molly licked her lips. *Mmm Now it's covered in gravy.*

The gravy-covered grumpy named Bjorn said nothing, stuck his bottom lip out and sucked the slop out of his mustache.

The grumpy in the boat laughed maniacally, and reached for another bucket. Molly recognized the man as "Hilmir." *I like this one,* Molly thought. She wasn't alone.

"Excellent shot, sire. And a most inspired joke," the grumpy's assistant said.

Hilmir commanded the rowers forward and the boat groaned to the next cage.

"I should think ye all might be grateful. Most traitors would be denied a final meal." Dump.

He's covering them all in gravy. Wonderful. What a wonderful idea.

"Next."

The boat paddled on. Some little, blue pests dodged the slop, others opened their mouths to catch as much as they could, but none of them said a word. Finally, the boat reached the last cage. This one contained a woman, larger and angrier than the others.

"'Tis truly the finest slop in all the village," Hilmir said, but as he prepared to toss the bucket onto the grumpy woman. She shoved her hand between the bars, and flipped the man's bucket so that he dumped the slop all over himself instead. The other blues howled with delight.

"Keep yer slop, Hilmir," she spat. "I hear 'tis the finest in all the village."

Hilmir wiped chunks of carrots, potatoes, and leeks from his brow and shoulders, and flicked them into the water. "I shall miss thee, Erika," he said in a tone that made Molly suspect he would not miss her in the least. "In fact, I should like to keep thee around as long as possible. Aye, I believe I shall have you executed *last*. That way, ye can watch as we break your'n husband's limbs one by one, and chop his head from his body."

Two cages down, a rail-thin grump—hardly big enough to eat—brought his hands to his mouth, but failed to suppress a whimper. It was barely audible, even to Molly's keen ears, but the sound bolstered Hilmir's cruelty. "Then I think it shall be the serpent pit for Bjorn, perhaps the gorkin for the rest, and maybe a dragon for you." Hilmir reached through the cage to pat Erika's cheek.

"Touch me, and lose thy hand," she growled.
Hilmir chuckled, but retracted.
I'm starting to like this one too, Molly thought, eyeing Erika.

"Aye, a dragon for you, indeed. But fear not. It shall all be over first thing tomorrow morn. Any pieces left shall be dumped into the endless sea. Perhaps the Midgard Serpent will have use for thee."

It took Molly a moment to grasp the meaning of Hilmir's words. Surely, he wasn't planning on throwing these six delicious morsels away. Why cover them with yummy gravy just to toss them into the pond? *What a waste!* They should feed them to poor, hungry Molly. She's a queen, after all.

Echoing her sentiment, the grumpy named Bjorn said, "Why not save yerself the trouble and feed us to the giant's vicious guard-beast?"

He pointed his thumb back, and Molly realized that, in her excitement, she'd floated out of the shadows. She stood at the end of the log licking her chops over the cages for all to see. Strangely, they didn't seem concerned.

"Nay. Nay, that simply wouldn't do," Hilmir said. "If I did that, I may not get to try out me new Cat-bat."

"Cat-bat? Cat-bat? What's that?"

Hilmir signaled to some unseen enemy high above, and an enormous branch swooped down, and smacked Molly, sending her yowling through the air to plunk into the middle of the pond with a distant splash.

"Typical. Just Typical."

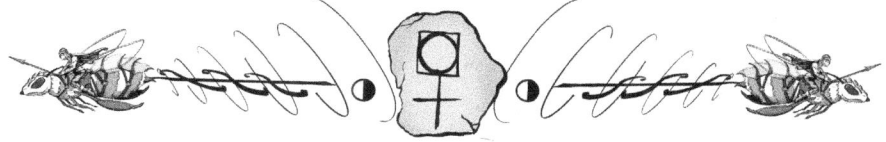

CHAPTER 44

THE SEARCH FOR BONNIE. THE SEARCH FOR BERRIES

Timp searched for Bonnie well into the night and continued his search the next morning. He traversed the farm, from the highest hill to the lowest ditch. He checked beneath the water tower, since she knew that was his favorite spot, and then circled the pond, whispering Bonnie's name as loudly as he dared that close to the Viking village. When he found a bee gathering pollen and drinking nectar, he no longer withdrew from fear that the bee might be a Vaskrél, but instead ran toward the insect and talked to it in an excited chatter. The bees found this behavior most peculiar. Some fled. Others defended themselves, in which case, Timp fled. But there was no sign of Bonnie Bee.

"Still nothing?" Timp's father stood several feet away with buckets full of berries strapped to each hip. "I'm going in for lunch. You wanna go?"

A familial silence fell as Timp and his father walked toward the house. Mr. Littleton scanned the farm in slow, deliberate wipes, as if taking it all in for the last time. "Are you worried about losing the farm?"

"Shoot no, son," Mr. Littleton lied. "We have the rest of today to pick, and who knows, maybe if we work hard, we'll have enough berries for a good haul for the market tomorrow. And maybe we can put out a tip jar, and you can sing and tap dance. You can sing, right?" His father nudged him with his elbow. Timp could not sing. "Yep, I think we're going to be fine. Just fine. Just . . . fine."

They climbed the steps to an empty porch. Normally, the porch was covered with buckets of berries waiting to be cleaned and packaged, but not that day. The area to the left, reserved for crates of prepped berries and other blueberry products, was also empty. Mr. Littleton sighed, and Timp knew his father didn't believe his own optimism.

After lunch, they returned to the orchard and picked berries throughout the rest of the day. Even Timp started to give it his all. They slathered themselves in sunblock, but in the fight against a two dollar bottle of lotion and an enormous sphere with a mass 333,000 times planet Earth burning with nuclear fusion so hot that it can melt planets, the sphere wins every time. By dinner, the Littletons stood with their faces, necks, and shoulders burned red. Hot, misshapen berries mashed into the bottom of their buckets. Normally, they'd throw those berries away, but the situation was dire. "No berry left behind." Those berries would be 20% off.

At the end of what seemed like the longest day in a history of long days, the Littletons took stock of their harvest. Empty spaces marked their failure while cicadas mocked them from the abundant orchard. Timp heard DeLaney's laugh. "Dying of thirst in a sea of water." Suddenly, Timp didn't feel quite as excited about the prospect of moving.

"Let's get some rest," Timp's mother said, breaking the silence. No one moved. They stared at the minuscule stacks of packaged products on the kitchen counter and floor. "Come on. We have an early morning tomorrow."

The Farmer's Market would come before dawn whether the Littletons willed it to or not. They'd rise at three in the morning to load the truck, drive to Shreveport and sell what few berries they had, and that'd be the end of it. Time was up. DeLaney had won. It annoyed Timp how *easily* he'd won. He didn't drop bombs or invade with an army like a Viking would. He just exploited Mr. Littleton's trust and hired away their help. Simple. Too simple, really. Timp sighed. What did it matter anymore? Bonnie was gone, and the Vikings hated him. Timp looked out the window at an orchard teeming with blueberries, and hidden wonders. The orchard was full of life, and Timp felt empty. He had no bee, no friends. *Let DeLaney have it*, he thought.

At least this way, Timo didn't have to spend the rest of his life hiding from those blasted Vaskrél.

Timp's mother shook her head. "There's no reason to get up at three tomorrow. We should sell out in an hour or two. Might as well sleep in a bit."

No one argued.

Exhaustion eroded Timp's anger, and soon he lay on the couch, snoring away the hard day's work and dreaming of Bonnie. The hours wore away and the moon climbed high as he dreamt that Bonnie came back and forgave him. She flew down and landed on the end of his nose. She crawled around for a second, nudged him a few times, and then took out her stinger, and—"Yeow!" Timp jumped up with a start. He heard something small smack against the wall at the end of the couch.

"Bonnie?" Timp whispered at the wall.

No answer.

He rubbed his sleep-crusted eyes. Had it been a dream? It felt so real. He noticed something stuck in the tip of his nose. His eyes crossed, but he couldn't make it out. A stinger? A splinter? He pulled the object out to get a better look: a spear. Erika!

Always with the nose, Erika! She'd brought the war to him.

Timp's eyes darted around the room, anticipating the direction of a Viking attack. He listened for the familiar buzz of 1,000 angry bees, but the house was quiet, too quiet. He sat on the couch, a frozen statue, moving only his eyes and listening until

304

silence rang in his ears louder than the buzzing of any Vaskrél. He vaguely remembered hearing something smack against the wall, so he slid in that direction. "Erika?" A tiny grappling hook flew over the couch arm and caught purchase in the fabric. The rope moved back and forth with light, almost inaudible grunting. Someone was climbing.

"Erika?" Timp whispered again, but the person who climbed over the ledge was not Erika.

"For what purpose do I find thee *here*?" the Viking asked with a huff.

The question caught Timp by surprise. "Me? What are *you* doing here?"

On the arm of the couch, with dress torn, arms crossed, and looking none too pleased stood Hilmir's daughter, Ailsa. She glared at Timp as if deciding whether to answer such a preposterously nosy question. Timp waited. He felt nervous under her gaze. His cheeks flushed red, and his heart banged against his sternum, but he waited. Finally, the tiny Viking girl sighed, dusted her hands on her hips and announced, "I am Ailsa, first and only daughter of yon Hilmir, descendant of Thor, and the next keeper of The Book of Secrets. I am warrior, scholar, and traveler. 'Tis in *that* capacity in which I come here today, Giant. I've traveled two days and equal nights to meet thee: two days through dragon infested jungles, two days of hiding from mine own and moving in secret, two days of such filth and hardship that a pampered giant such as your'n self could scarcely imagine, and after all of this, I enter this dry, ice-mountain dwelling that you dare call home, and where do I find thee? *Here*, far removed from where twas I'd been told your'n cave hollow should lay. Now, 'tis your'n turn to answer to *me*, Giant. For what purpose do I find thee here?"

Man, these Vikings sure like giving speeches, Timp thought. *Well, when in Rome, or is it Asgard?*

Timp had not been properly introduced to Ailsa at the thing the week before. After such a grand speech, he knew any introduction he gave would be inadequate, but he tried anyway. "I am no giant. I am Timp, son of . . . my parents, and descendant of, um, well, their parents too, I guess. Imagine, you, how far back this goes—their parent's parents, and theirs before them, and so on and so forth all the way back until . . . well, way back when, to be honest, in the days of old and drive in movies. And, Oh! I am the keeper of this pillow. Yep, 'tis true, I vow, and the sleeper of this couch, and I'd like to thank yon Academy, as well as my co-star—"

"'Tis quite enough, Giant," Ailsa interrupted. "I cannot bear to watch thine bumbling any longer. Ye misunderstand my question. I've on my person a detailed map of these mountain caverns. Upon this map, I show that your'n dwelling should be along such corridor as lay there behind me, and yet as I stand *here*, I find thee here as well. And inside of your'n hollow, where *you* should be, I find instead a most odiferous giant even larger, uglier, and more grotesque than your'n own disgusting giant self, Giant. So I ask thee a final time, why art thee *here*?"

Timp pinched the bridge of his nose. How could so much noise come out of something so tiny? It took him a moment to process what this little blue chatterbox was yammering about, but slowly the pieces fell together. "You mean Trevor?"

"I am sure I did not get its name." The girl said rather snottily. "It snored a unmelodious tune, while slobber dripped from its gaping mouth, and the smell, let us agree that scent was quite repugnant."

Timp laughed. "Yeah, that's Trevor all right. But he's not a giant. He's—" Timp thought of many colorful adjectives to describe Trevor, but then he remembered Trevor's Internet bullying, and a smile curled up his cheek. "—a vicious troll."

"A troll?" Ailsa's eyes widened with rapt attention. Timp liked her attention.

"Oh, yes," he continued, furrowing his brow to appear more knowledgeable. He was glad to finally know something that a Viking didn't—even if it was complete hogwash. "Trolls are big filthy beasts who invade our houses—er, that is, our mountains—and take them over."

"You mean that troll hath forced thee from your'n own home? Why did ye not fight back?"

"Oh, I did, of course. See these bruises here, and here. Oh, and there's one here too. I'm lucky that's all I got, really. Trolls can spit acid, you know? It'll melt the flesh right off of your bones. And their skin stinks so bad that if you touch any part of them you'll never be able to wash the smell off. You'll stink for the rest of your life."

"That's terrible," Ailsa gasped.

"Yes, it is, Ailsa. Yes, it is. Trevor is an awful, terrible troll." Timp felt proud that he'd impressed his guest—after all, she was company.

A comfortable silence fell. Then Ailsa shook away her thoughts and resumed her usual authoritative tone. (Though, Timp noticed she now sounded kinder and more patient . . . at first, anyway.) "Giant, I come to thee with a quest—nay, not a quest, an opportunity—an opportunity for thee to right the wrongs thou hath created."

"Wrongs I created?"

"Aye, wrongs to Bjorn, to Erika, to Gunnar, to O'dul, to Fen, aye, and to the Denes. Wronged all, Vikings who might have once called you 'friend.'"

"Humph! 'Friends,' yeah right."

"Misguided their trust may have been, they tell me you are not entirely the monster of legends. They claim you may have thoughts and feelings capable of empathy—or at least the ability to feign empathy until ye get close enough to destroy our'n

308

village, a vile and clever ruse, Giant, but the mere pretending friendship tells me ye understand what kindness *should* be, and; therefore, may possess some understanding of right from wrong."

"Wow, that's some logic for you."

"Indeed, 'tis for this reason I appeal to thee, Giant. I call upon thee to correct the wrongs thou hath bestowed upon mine village, to your'n friends, and to all mine people."

"Sounds like I've wronged a lot of folks," Timp said, then thought, *which is pretty amazing considering it was y'all who beat me, burned me, tied me up, and stung me with bees.* But Timp didn't dare say that part out loud. He still found Ailsa a bit intimidating (which was horribly depressing given that she was no bigger than an ant).

"Aye, Giant, ye have. And now my father, yon Hilmir, has declared Bjorn and his co-conspirators traitors." She waited a moment to gauge Timp's reaction, but Timp knew Hilmir considered the Vikings traitors. This news didn't surprise him at all. Ailsa rolled her eyes and sighed. "Which means they're to be executed!"

"Executed? Why? When? How can he do that?"

"He may do as he pleases. He is the hilmir and none shall oppose him. That is, none except perhaps you, Giant."

"Me? What can I do?"

"You have brought the hilmir's wrath upon your'n friends. Owing to your'n deeds, they were imprisoned, beaten, and tortured for days on end. Now, come first light, they shall all be executed unless you help them. You've but a few short hours, Giant, and you ask, what ye may do? I shall tell thee: You charge into yon village and set right the wrongs thou hath caused. Ye go with me and save their'n lives, because if you do not, Giant, they shall all be dead by first light."

"Geez, no pressure or anything."

"Indeed." (By account of the many ways that Vikings could convince someone to do something, the fact that Ailsa hadn't used an axe or sword, and had only used one tiny spear, was low pressure.)

Timp rubbed the whelps from past stings. "What about the Vaskrél?"

"Let us hope they do not kill you before you save our'n friends, but if they do, perhaps ye shall sit at the Great Table of Valhöll."

Timp wasn't comforted. He'd rather grow old and buy his own table.

Ailsa assured Timp that she could help him avoid the Vaskrél. She explained her plan, and while Timp wasn't thrilled about returning to the Viking village, it seemed a good plan overall. Plus, Ailsa made a strong case for the importance of saving lives, moral responsibility, honor, and all that. Timp put on his shoes, placed Ailsa on his ear, and started out of the house.

As he passed his parents' door, Timp was surprised to find their light on and the door cracked. It was nearly midnight. In five short hours, they'd have to rise for the Farmer's Market. The light from their room cut across the kitchen, dividing Timp from the path to the back porch. He moved slowly. He skirted the back of the kitchen, trying to remain in the shadows, but there was no way to avoid the light. The beam struck his face, and he stopped. He didn't mean to pry, he only wanted to make sure his path was clear, but the scene inside his parent's room arrested his attention, and his mission fell to the back of his mind.

Timp's father sat at the end of the bed with his elbows on his knees and his head resting in his palms. His mother paced the room. "How are we going to afford that, John?"

Mr. Littleton rubbed his forehead and pinched the bridge of his nose, "Well, if we make enough at the market tomorrow to afford a moving truck, then maybe we can stay with your parents for a while, just 'til we get back on our feet."

"But this is our home."

"I know. I'm sorry. I let you down."

"Giant, are those trolls, as well?" Ailsa asked in Timp's ear.

"What? No," Timp whispered. "Those are my parents." He watched as his parents held onto the only thing they had left: each other, and he listened to his mother assuring his father that it wasn't his fault. Timp knew who was truly to blame. He was. He knew DeLaney had been behind it all, and he'd done nothing. And for what? A few potential neighborhood friends and some Dr. Pepper Icees? He hated DeLaney for what he'd done to his family. He hated all of the DeLaneys of the world, including the hilmir. But he hated himself more. "Let's go."

Outside, Ailsa resumed her know-it-all chatter. "Of course, when you say those were your'n parents back there, thou doth not mean they actually gave birth to you, not since all giants are born from the darkest, most vile sin pits of middle earth, and—"

"What are you blathering about?"

"Giants. Everyone knows that when a Viking sins an evil giant is hatched from the foulest pits deep within the mountains, where they feed upon the wicked thoughts of youngling girls and boys until they grow strong enough to venture out and devour whole villages. That is why you must be moral and true, lest an ice-giant eat your'n kin."

"That's the most ridiculous run of claptrap that I've ever heard in my life. Those were my parents back there, and without getting into too many details about the birds and the bees, they did give birth to me. Just like your parents gave birth to you; I assume."

"Oh."

"'Oh' is right." Timp's anger at DeLaney, Hilmir, and himself burned into his stomach like hot coals. He wasn't sure why it bothered him so much that Ailsa thought of him as a monster sprung from a cave. He didn't care when the other Vikings called him a vicious, cannibalistic beast—In fact, Timp kind of liked that everyone was afraid of him. But Ailsa was different. He expected more from her, and deep down, he worried it might be true.

As he walked in silence toward the pond, the world withdrew. Timp heard no crickets, no cicadas, no coyotes, and no frogs, only the dry crinkle of grass under his feet. It was as if every creature in the world except Timp had the good sense to know danger was near. He walked, lost in thought. He didn't even notice that he was being followed.

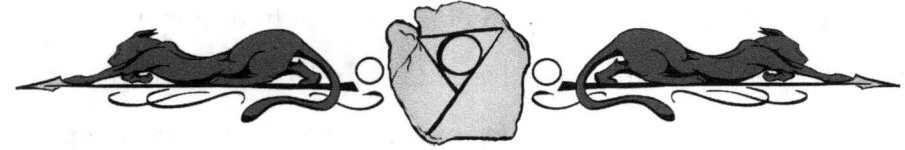

CHAPTER 45
IN THE HEART OF DELICIOUSNESS

You have to wake up pretty early in the morning to outsmart Queen Molly Grumpy Hunter, Molly thought from the high grass several yards away. *And considering that this is about as early as you can get without it being late, I'd say that makes it just about impossible to outsmart me!*

Molly licked her paw and rubbed it over her ears. Her fur lay down and then popped back up with a dull throb of a stubborn welt. Molly growled. Those pests were going down. She'd rip through every last one of them. That is, if she could get to their village. Her servant boy would take care of that. She need only follow him into the heart of deliciousness.

Molly licked her chops as she imagined devouring whole families of little blue grumpies. She awoke to find herself standing alone. *"Boy, wait. Boy!"* She ran down the hill to catch up. She wasn't going to miss this opportunity. If revenge is a dish best served cold, and dessert is a dish best served cold, and Molly wanted grumpies for dessert; then she'd have her revenge-cake and eat it too . . . cold . . . like revenge . . . and dessert . . . and cake— *Ugh!* She just wanted to eat some grumpies, okay?

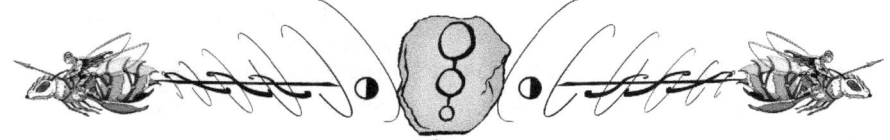

CHAPTER 46
BACK INTO THE LION'S DEN

Timp stepped lightly as he and Ailsa approached the pond. Ailsa had not spoken since their argument by the house. She seemed to be weighing all she'd learned about giants.

"Giant, I owe thee an apology," she said as they reached the embankment. Timp began removing his shoes and listened. "My people know giants to be large beasts, as vicious as they art stupid, but—"

"Wow, this is some apology," Timp interrupted.

"*But* I must confess, you seem different."

"Oh. Thanks?"

"It almost makes me sorry that—" Ailsa stopped. "What are you doing, Giant?"

"I'm taking off my shoes so they don't get wet."

"We need not go through the water."

"I thought the dry side of the village had been blocked and fortified?"

"Aye, but I know the way."

Timp brightened. He'd been dreading the thought of wading through the dark, snake infested pond ever since Ailsa had first told him her plan. The fact that there was a dry route into the village made Timp so happy that he didn't question further.

Ailsa directed him into the orchard. The moon was bright, and Timp could see well enough to walk without getting whacked in the face by blueberry branches—"Ouch!"—but it happened anyway.

"Quiet, Giant!"

"I'm trying. How much further?"

"Just a bit."

"Ouch."

"I said 'silence.'"

Molly stalked close behind— "*Like a ninja. That's what I am, a cat-like ninja cat, stalking delicious little blue grumps. Mmm, they'll taste so good. Fit for a queen, which coincidentally, I am . . . and a ninja. I'm both.*" But, of course, Timp heard none of her yammering.

"Okay, Giant, we've arrived," Ailsa whispered.

"Where? I don't see anything," Timp whispered back.

"There, straight before you."

A small round break in the brush formed a jagged hole, a black abyss in an otherwise bright night. Branches hung down like sharp teeth ready to devour anyone who dared enter.

"In there?" Timp suddenly had second thoughts about this plan.

"Aye, in there. 'Tis the only way."

Timp knew every inch of this farm, and he had never seen this hole before. Limbs, branches, and twigs lay atop one another in intricate patterns forming a tunnel leading into a domed hive buried in the thicket of blueberry bushes.

"We expanded security after your'n attack. 'Tis new," Ailsa explained, sensing Timp's hesitation.

Expanded security? They'd built a fortress around their village.

"Fear not, Giant. I've taken steps to ensure your'n path be clear."

"Oh. I see." Timp did not move.

"Well, what are you waiting for, Giant? Let's be on with it."

Timp stepped toward the hole. His stomach churned and his throat pulled tight. He willed himself forward despite his body's protests and the nagging in the back of his mind. He got down on his hands and knees and peeked inside the thicket. It was dark and quiet. What did he expect? He reminded himself that dark and quiet was good. Dark and quiet meant the Vikings were asleep. Less light and less noise meant less danger—or so he told himself. Timp crawled forward. His hands broke through the dry leaf-cover with a crunch.

"Quiet, Giant. You mustn't wake the village."

"I know," Timp growled between clenched teeth.

"If ye know, then make it so," Ailsa retorted.

Timp swallowed the stream of curses that tickled his tongue and pressed on.

Be quiet, Timp told himself. *Be quiet.* He quickly learned that if he pointed his fingers, he could slide them at an angle between the leaves to make less noise. As he inched forward, the terrain changed from dirt to mud, and then sank into silt and slime. *Gross.* The damp beneath the leaves soaked around his hands and knees. "How much further?"

"The prison chambers art housed in the back of the village. 'Tis but ten rôsts, or I believe you would call them miles."

"Ten miles?" Timp exclaimed, then remembered that ten miles to a Viking who was small enough to fit in his ear was probably only twenty feet to him.

"Silence your'n self, Giant."

Timp rolled his eyes and crawled on. The tunnel turned to the right, along the pond's edge. Timp followed.

Molly stalked in the shadows behind. *"That's right, lead me to those delicious, little blue treats. There's a good servant."*

Timp did not hear. He listened for Vaskrél buzzing, not kitty-cat purrs.

"'Tis the village just ahead."

319

The tunnel opened into a circular chamber. At the far end of the chamber, reaching over the pond, was a large, densely laden, blueberry bush—the village. Golden lanterns lined the streets and provided a dim layout of the sleeping city. Six dots floated in the water, several feet from the newly constructed docks. Timp knew those must be the prison cells.

"*Oh, yes*," Mrs. Molly Grumpy Masher purred upon seeing the village. "*An all-you-can-eat paradise.*" Molly inched forward in her usual kitty-cat ninja pose—her head down, and her butt way up in the air.

Timp started forward, but Ailsa stopped him.

"Still yourself, Giant. The Vaskrél patrol shall pass any moment, then ye may enter the clearing, but you must be quick."

Timp watched as two bees buzzed around the bush.

"*Mmm, appetizers. Servant, I demand you bring me one this instant,*" Molly said, and Timp realized the cat was there.

"Keep that beast away," Ailsa commanded.

Timp pulled Molly behind him.

"*How dare you touch the royal fur without my permission. I'll have your head for such high-handed familiarity.*"

But as usual, Timp understood nothing Molly said.

He held his breath and ducked lower into the leaves and mud, praying the Vaskrél wouldn't hear Molly's grumbling. The Vaskrél passed and continued his route. Timp breathed once again.

"Servant, what are you doing? Go catch them!" Mrs. Molly Vaskrél Muncher mewed.

"Shhh, back, Molly. Back," Timp shushed.

"Don't shush me, human! They're getting away!"

Molly sprang onto Timp's shoulder and leapt into the chamber with a battle cry worthy of a Viking charge: *"My Hors d'œuvres!"*

Time slowed.

Timp's mind exploded with shouts and screams, but his voice failed him.

Ailsa's did not.

"No! Not yet!" she cried, as Molly flew through the air with drool trailing her toothy, kitty-cat grin.

But, if time slowed as Molly leapt, the following seconds worked double-time to catch up. The room erupted in chaos. As Molly's paws touched the ground, a net exploded from beneath the leaves, sending mud and debris smacking against the chamber walls.

The net swallowed Molly whole. The furious feline swung through the air cursing and hissing about appetizers, servants, and betrayal.

It was now or never. Timp clawed his way forward and jumped to his feet. The chamber was just large enough to stand. He pushed the net out of the way, sending Molly swinging in circles around the chamber. *"I'll get you for that, servant. You're all going to pay. I'll eat you all. I am a Queen! A Quuueeeeeeennnn!"*

"Giant, what are you doing? Stop!" Ailsa yelled from Timp's ear, but he ignored her pleas.

He called Bjorn's name as he ran toward the floating prison cells. There was no point in secrecy now. The village was coming alive. Molly's screeches and curses alone would wake every Viking between there and Valhöll. Timp knew it was a matter of seconds before the Vask—

Vaskrél poured into the chamber with a terrifying buzz. Timp had to grab his friends and get out of there, fast!

"Bjorn?"

Between Molly's screeches and the Vaskrél's buzzing, Timp heard nothing else. The prison cells were too far into the water to grasp from the shore. A veteran berry picker, Timp didn't think twice. He grabbed the bush by the stem and swung over the water. A thousand Viking screams joined the cacophony as the village bent under Timp's weight. His efforts paid off. He grabbed the string of floating prison cells.

"Bjorn? Erika? Fen?" Timp held the cages to his ear.

"Aye, all are present, Giant," Bjorn said, remarkably calm. Timp enjoyed a feeling of accomplishment for half a second before Bjorn brought him back to reality. "Perhaps 'tis time ye get us out of here."

Timp shoved the cages into his pocket, swung himself back to the shore, and let the branch go with a snap. Bridges, awnings, porches, and houses crumbled as the bush popped back and forth with the sweeping screams of the Vikings who lived there. The only Vikings not screaming were those puking over the railings.

Ten thousand lanterns ignited throughout the village, enabling Timp to see, but the light brought no comfort. Thick limbs fell into the water behind him, blocking any hope of a watery exit. The only way out was the way he came in. Timp turned toward the tunnel to find a wall of bees staring back at him in attack formations. He thought about diving through, but as if reading his thoughts, they pulled a small wooden peg, and a heavy wooden gate crashed down, sealing the chamber. Timp was trapped.

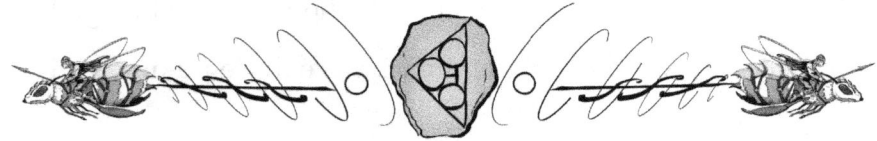

CHAPTER 47
TRAPPED, AGAIN

Timp had been lucky to escape the Vaskrél before. He'd heard horror stories about people dying from bee stings, but he'd always assumed it was people with allergies toward bees. Facing them again, Timp knew they could take down anyone or anything, especially him. *Killer bees, there are worse ways to go.* Then he thought about it for a second. *No, no there aren't.* But he was ready, all the same. Ready to claim his seat next to his forefather's table in Valhöll. Was that right, forefathers? Was he going to sit at a table next to Washington, Jefferson, Adams, and Franklin? Or were those founding fathers? Timp was sunk. He had no idea whose table he was about to sit at. He should have listened when the Vikings explained it . . . not that it mattered now. The bees swirled in a black cyclone before him, awaiting the order to attack. Timp was ready. Whoever's table he was about to sit at, he hoped they had something other than broccoli.

"Well, come on," Timp said. "What are you waiting for?"

The Vaskrél did not attack. Molly swung like a pendulum in the middle of the chamber, growling curses, and casting a dark shadow over the walls as she moved. Four bees flew forward, carrying something the resembled a small Viking ship between them. As they flew into the light, Timp saw that the hilmir stood at the platform's bow with a triumphant grin.

"Well done, Ailsa," Hilmir clapped.

It took Timp a moment to realize what the Hilmir meant. Understanding stung worse than any bee. He thought about the tunnel limiting his path, about the net that grabbed Molly, the branches that now blocked the pond, and the gate that cut off his exit. He thought about Ailsa's scream as Molly jumped into the chamber: "No! Not yet!" At the time, Timp assumed that Ailsa had screamed out of fear that the cat would give them away, but Timp now realized she was warning the Vikings not to release the net because he wasn't in range.

"You set me up!"

Ailsa ignored him and stepped to the forward most point of Timp's ear. "Father, remember our'n bargain: the giant in exchange for the traitors."

In exchange for the traitors? Timp wondered if they'd known about the trap. He couldn't bring himself to believe they would betray him too.

"Aye. Aye." Hilmir waved his hand dismissively. Timp thought he seemed a bit disappointed. "I shall set them free as soon as we pull them from the giant's dead body."

"Thank you, Father."

Timp couldn't believe what he was hearing. It was one thing to lie to him, to make him crawl through mud, to betray him, to trap him, and to lead him to his death, but it was something altogether different to talk about killing him so casually. They acted like his life didn't even matter. That was just plain rude. *At least show a little Southern Hospitality.*

Well, if they wanted to play hardball, then Timp would play hardball. He reached up to his ear.

"What are ye doing, Giant?" Hilmir panicked.

Timp grabbed Ailsa between his fingers so she couldn't escape and held her forward as she kicked and beat his fingers.

"Get back or I squeeze." He drew out the word "squeeze" as long as he could to give the Vikings time to imagine Ailsa's guts running down his fingers.

It worked. Everyone stared wide-eyed and slack-jawed at the giant. The Vaskrél seemed to freeze in midair.

"I said back!" Timp said with a stomp. "I'll do it. I'll squish her like a bug, and then I'll shove her in my mouth and roll her around 'til her screams come out my nose!"

"*Do it, servant! Do it!*" Molly snarled.

Timp applied only the slightest bit of pressure between his fingers and Ailsa screamed. The air sucked out of the room with ten thousand Viking gasps.

"Aye, back! Back!" The hilmir ordered, and the Vaskrél obeyed. "Release me daughter, Giant, and I shall promise thee a quick death."

Timp laughed. He'd heard the line a hundred times in movies and always thought it ridiculous. Dead was dead. What kind of bargaining chip was a quick death? Especially when the girl still gave him a chance to get out alive. "Afraid I'm going to have to pass on that one, Hilmir." Timp pointed his hand toward the exit as if holding a TV remote and gave Ailsa another light squeeze, making her scream again. "Now, open that gate!"

In truth, Timp barely squeezed at all. He suspected Ailsa was hamming it up for her audience, but that garnered no favor from Timp.

Hilmir nodded and the gate began to lift.

Timp smiled. It felt good to be the one holding the cards for once—even if that card was a tiny blue girl. But then, as suddenly as fortune had shined upon Timp, it turned its fickle light away, and he found he no longer held anything. A Viking spear, larger than any he'd seen before, shot from the corner of the room and embedded deep into his thumb. It hit the quick, shooting electric pain to the bone. *Of all places!* Timp shouted and opened his fingers without thinking. Ailsa dropped like a stone. Her screams jarred Timp from his pain.

"Ailsa!" He whipped his hand around and caught her just before she smacked against the ground. He held her up in his palm to get a better look. "Are you all right?"

"No thanks to you," Ailsa grumbled as she dusted herself off and checked her side for broken ribs.

"No thanks to—? You set me up! You—" Before Timp could finish, a Vaskrél swooped down and snatched Ailsa from his open palm. He grasped after them frantically, but the bee was too fast and flew out of reach. Timp gritted his teeth and cursed his absent-mindedness. He'd lost his only bargaining chip. The gate crashed down with a clank. He'd lost the one thing keeping him alive.

The Vikings fell silent; even the buzzing of bees dropped away. Molly swung in bitter antipathy as Timp searched for a way out. He banged his shoulder into the chamber wall, but the wall didn't give. He tried again and again, until his shoulder ached and blood showed through his torn shirt. The Vikings watched. Then out of their silence came laughter—wicked, self-satisfied laughter.

"Now, you're mine," Hilmir croaked.

Timp turned to find a column of black and yellow bearing down on him. The Vaskrél, there were so many of them . . . so, so many. Timp scanned the room for a way out, any way out. If he was smart enough, fast enough, or strong enough, then surely there was a way. He thought about holding Bjorn and his friends hostage like he had Ailsa, but the hilmir had planned to kill them anyway. What did he hilmir care if Timp threatened them? *Think, Timp. Think!* But all he could think about was a thousand bees crawling in his ears and stinging and stabbing their way down his throat. How long would it take for him to die? Would he go into shock? Would his eyes and throat swell shut, making him blind and defenseless, before he suffocated? It was too horrible to imagine.

He looked at the limbs blocking his way to the pond. Beyond those limbs was freedom. Only five feet away, but it might as well have been a hundred miles. The Vaskrél would be on him before his feet touched water. Even if he did reach the limbs, they looked too heavy to move and climbing over would slow him down. It was hopeless. Hot tears streamed down his burning cheeks. He slammed into the wall again, but it didn't budge. And again. Not an inch. He slammed over and over, but it would not give.

He clawed his way up the walls only to slide back down the mud covered sides.

He thought again about charging through the village, climbing over the logs, and diving into the pond. But, following his eyes, the Vaskrél moved around and blocked his path.

The Vaskrél revved their wings, anticipating the attack. Timp was a caged animal, desperate and powerless. He released a sound somewhere between a whimper and a moan while the hilmir laughed the sadistic cackle of a deranged zookeeper taunting a lion through its cage—power by circumstance.

"Nowhere to go, Jötunn. Nowhere to hide."
Hilmir's words felt like an icicle in Timp's spine. He knew the hilmir was right, but he was too proud to beg and too stubborn to give the creep the satisfaction.

Timp's terror melted into cold acceptance. For a moment, he felt half Viking. He wiped his eyes, stood up straight, and looked down at the hilmir. "I've hawked loogies bigger than you," he said, and while his captors shrugged at one another in confusion, Timp showed them exactly what he meant. (Now, Timp was not the kind of boy to go around spitting on people. He had manners, after all. He never joined the other boys when they spit out of the school bus window, no matter how fun it looked. Spitting was a nasty habit, and Timp generally had nothing to do with it; however, in this particular circumstance, he thought it over and decided that if someone planned to kill you, then good manners were already out the window . . . much like spit from school bus. So, it had a poetic justice in a way—at least, that's how Timp rationalized it.) He snorted all the snot he could muster, hawked it down into the back of his throat, and fired the projectile at the hilmir.

To say that the hilmir panicked in the face of an enormous, flying snot rocket would be an understatement.

"Dive! Dive! *DIVE!*" He shouted to his Vaskrél convoy, but he was too late. Timp's aim proved true. The loogie slapped the hilmir off of his feet and smacked him against the wall, where he oozed to the floor, speechless, shocked, and heartily disgusted. The villagers roared with laughter, and for a moment, Timp thought he'd won the day. But the slimed hilmir was still in command. After regaining his faculties, his embarrassment boiled into unbridled rage. "*Kill the Jötunn!*"

"Bring it!" Timp roared. "I've got plenty of loogies for everyone." He hawked his throat again, even though he knew that he was dry. It had the desired effect. The Vaskrél paused their attack and looked back at the slimy hilmir. Timp laughed. Even the bravest Vaskrél stood fearful before the mighty loogie.

"What are ye waiting for?" Hilmir barked. "Kill him! Kill him, now!"

They charged.

Timp's world turned black with bees. The first sting shot lightening down his spine. The second felt like a hot match head being stabbed into his ear. He wondered how many stings a person could take. How many had he received the week before? 10? 20? Did those still count? Another sting, an icepick twisted into the back of his knee.

Vaskrél swarmed around and around. Their armor protected their barbed stingers from becoming stuck in Timp's skin, so that stinging wasn't a deathblow for these bees; it was another note in a venomous symphony of torture. Timp couldn't hope to outlast them. They'd sting until his last breath. Panic seized his senses. He slapped and swatted. There were too many. He threw himself against the wall. There was no escape. He slipped and fell to the muddy ground, and clawed his way to the gate as sting after sting rolled over his skin like laps of fire burning the flesh from his bones. His ears rang with the buzzing, and his eyes watered and swelled until he could barely see through the tiny, wet slits. This was the end. His head felt dizzy and his body felt weak. His throat felt dry and swelled until he could barely breath. He mustered his strength for one final earth-shattering scream. It was a scream only the dying can make, a scream where the soul declares to God and the universe: *No! I am not ready!*

Timp screamed.

And then . . . something happened.

The temperature dropped 30 degrees, and time spread into an endless sea. Timp was nothing more than a tiny raindrop, rippling in the ocean. Bees fluttered their wings as if flying through air thick as jelly. They danced in a delicate ballet. Was this death? Had it finally happened? No. The Vikings felt it too. They paused their attacks. At first, they were confused, then scared. Finally, it was their turn to scream—and how they screamed.

A volcano of leaves erupted in the room. Water, mud, and detritus filled the air, blacking out almost all visibility. Timp saw only blurs of the village crumbling to the ground, shadows of Vaskrél thrown across the chamber, and slapped against the walls. Molly swung in wide circles, yowling in her net. The ground beneath his chest shook with such fury that Timp feared it'd open up and swallow him whole. Vikings fought to get away, but they were all victims of their own trap. Their dropped limbs blocked their ships from a watery exit. Their gate blocked the Vaskrél from hauling away villagers. Their chamber contained them all, and something was tearing the room apart. A section of the wall broke away and flew into the air, shattering into a million pieces and assaulting Timp with water and debris. Something was after them. Timp couldn't see what it was, with his eyes swollen and wet, but whatever it was, it was fast, powerful, and very, *very* pissed off.

A tornado!

North Louisiana was no stranger to tornados, and it wouldn't be the first time one touched down on Blueberry Springs Farm. The sky had been clear, but that didn't mean much. Tornados came out of nowhere, clear sky or no. Timp had traded one horror for another. He tried to crawl toward the broken gap in the chamber wall, but his elbows shook under his weight. His stomach lurched, and he grew sick as his body tried to purge itself of the toxic bee venom coursing through his veins.

But it was too late. He'd been stung too many times. Timp collapsed amidst the panic and screams, amidst the water, mud, and leaves. Timp collapsed amidst the horror.

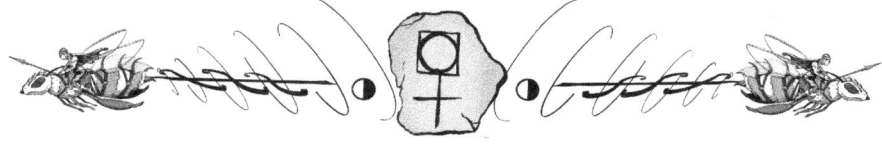

CHAPTER 48
THE WAKE OF THE STORM

Timp floated on a bed of clouds a hundred miles above the earth, but he didn't feel cold; he felt warm and safe, as if something or someone protected him and guided his every move. Ten thousand candles lit the world in golden radiance, and the most beautiful music filled the air. Timp's heart filled with a profound bliss. He felt the way he imagined people felt when they died and went to heaven—*Died and went to heaven!*

Timp jumped up and sent a hundred Vikings tumbling to the ground.

"He's awake!"

Timp's bliss flipped into guarded anger as he scrounged for a limb or stick that he could use to smash the Vikings.

"All's well, Giant. All's well. Begging you, please. We mean you no harm," Hilmir's assistant begged, as other Vikings ducked for cover.

"Mean me no harm? You tried to kill me!"

"Er, aye. Twas ill form. Sorry."

Sorry? Sorry? They'd stung him more times than he could count, and now they were sorry? Timp sat nonplussed. Part of him wanted to crush them all and make them pay, but a bigger part of him was just plain confused. He looked about the chamber, searching for answers when he realized: "I can see!"

He poked around his eyes with his fingers. Still sore, but the swelling had gone down considerably. His skin was covered with sticky, pink goo, and there was something else: "I'm in my underwear!" Timp scrounged for as many leaves as he could gather. They weren't fig leaves, but they managed to hide his Spider-Man boxers. "What's the big idea?"

Hilmir stood with his arms crossed and a pouting expression, avoiding Timp's gaze. His assistant continued to do the talking. "Um, aye, Giant. Our'n apologies. Twas necessary to undress thee in order to tend your'n wounds. Oh, but rest assured, we averted our'n eyes."

Tinkling giggles spread throughout the room.
Timp grabbed his pants and began dressing. The stings on his chest and legs had been covered in the pink poultice. How long had he been out? It was still dark. He must not have been asleep for long, but there wasn't a cloud in the sky. Not one.
"I guess the tornado passed," Timp said, more to himself than to anyone else.

"Tornado?"

Timp tried to explain tornadoes as best he could, but as he did, the villagers began to snicker. He expected that sort of reaction from Vikings. They probably thought tornadoes occurred whenever the mighty Odin broke wind. Timp tried again to explain barometric pressure and wind shear, but the harder he tried the louder the Vikings laughed.

"Sir Giant, sir, begging your'n pardon, but the disturbance thee felt did not come from any cloud," the assistant interrupted nervously. "Twas from yon."

Timp followed the Viking's finger to Bjorn, Erika, Fen, and:

"Bonnie!"

Bonnie Bee leapt through Timp's open arms, flipped in a loop, and then nuzzled his chest, nearly knocking him over with her force. His heart filled with bliss. He felt warm and protected. Any hatred toward the Vikings dissipated. His body felt one with the world around him, just as it had in his waking stupor moments before, and he understood that what he'd felt was Bonnie's love and protection.

With Bonnie, Timp took stock of the shattered and broken chamber. Molly swung bitterly in the net with her fur a mess. Sections of the chamber had been torn away, and the Viking village was in ruin. Entire sections of village hung by a thread. Bridges lay crumbled over docks, and staircases spiraled into nothing. Shattered fountains shot water into houses, and one

Viking sat on the toilet staring at Timp where once there'd been a private wall. The village needed many repairs, proving that Timp hadn't imagined the storm, but Hilmir's assistant said there was none. "What happened?" Timp asked Bjorn.

"Your'n bee happened," Bjorn answered in a tone of newfound respect.

"What?" Timp looked down at scruffy Bonnie and then the carnage surrounding him. "She's just a bee. How could—"

"See!" Hilmir awoke from his pouting silence. "The fool knows not! He understands not the first thing about it. 'Just a bee,' he claims. I say again, 'tis a mistake. We should kill him. We should kill him at once!"

At these words, Bonnie leapt up and buzzed her wings. Every Viking in the room jumped for cover and shook with such fear that Timp had to clap his hands and laugh.

"Silence, Father," Ailsa said, "before you doom us all."

Hilmir huffed, spat, and then resumed his pouting. Bonnie eased back onto Timp's shoulder. The villagers relaxed.

"Will someone please tell me what's going on?" Timp groaned.

Fen stepped forward, pushed up his glasses, and cleared his throat. "Giant, no doubt you've guessed that your'n bee 'tis no normal bee." Timp admitted the thought had crossed his mind. "Yon bee is special. We've long awaited the coming of a new Gullvindr."

"Gullvindr," all the Vikings echoed in unison.

"We not know this be a Gullvindr!" Hilmir said.

"Silence, Father," Aisla shushed, while Hilmir stomped his foot with a huff.

"I thought they were called Vaskrél or ving-bats or something," Timp said.

Fen closed his eyes and took a deep breath for patience. "A battle-bee is called a vígbý. One chosen to ride upon a vígbý is called a rider, and we honor our'n riders who reach singularity with their'n vígbý by ascribing them the title 'Vaskrél.' Therefore, a Vaskrél be both rider and vígbý as one."

Timp stared blankly at Fen, so Bjorn chimed in. "A vígbý's soul be linked to a rider; therefore, a Vaskrél be neither bee nor rider, but two pieces joined to form a whole: warrior and protector as one. It takes years of training for Kindred Kind to achieve the status of Vaskrél."

"I'm lost. What does all of this mean?"

"Means ye get our'n respect, dummy."

"Yeah, I can tell it's working."

"When a vígbý be born, the bee's soul is incomplete. Its powers be unstable, so it seeks a kindred soul for balance, a 'Kindred Kind.' Once found, they form a life bond—the stronger the bond, the stronger the bee's power." Bjorn surveyed the ruins and smiled. "And given the look of things, Giant, I should think only the gods of Asgard hold more power than your'n vígbý."

"You're saying my bee did all this?" Timp gestured to the destroyed room surrounding him and the broken village.

"I say that your'n bee, is so powerful that she be not your'n bee at all, but rather you are'n her human."

"The Hel you say," Timp said in disbelief.

"The Hel I do say, Giant, and ye shall believe after we begin training." Bjorn beamed with pride.

"Training? You go too far!" Hilmir burst. "He be Jötunn! And that bee is an abomination!"

"Hey!" Timp and Bonnie buzzed in irritation. "What's he mean by that?"

"Gullvindrs art most rare. Only a truly powerful rider may form that bond."

"And there be nothing to suggest this giant holds such power," Hilmir shouted. "'Tis a mistake, says I. This be not the one true Gullvindr, but just another female vígbý who sits upon an empty title. Rare, she might be, but not extraordinary. And this fool be not the chosen one. He's nothing more than a Jötunn! The truce doth not extend to Jötunheimr. I say again: we kill these abominations where they stand, and we kill them, now!"

"Father," Ailsa's voice echoed off what remained of the chamber walls, "he is Kindred Kind. Gullvindr or no, both he and his vígbý fall under our'n protection by the Truce of Stinger and Shield, and that reaches beyond the powers of the hilmir."

"Mayhap he is Kindred Kind, but he be not Norse kind. I forbid any Vaskrél from sharing our'n secrets with this Jötunn. And the Vaskrél *are* within my power, Daughter." Hilmir turned from Ailsa to meet Timp's eyes. "Who will ye get to train thee, Giant? None of *my* Vaskrél, I assure ye of that. You think this be a blessing that hath befallen you? Without control over your'n vígbý, ye shall surely fall into madness. Fen hath told ye not what becomes of riders who fail to achieve Vaskrél status: madness, Giant, torturous madness. They lose themselves and their'n souls. Nay. This be not a blessing upon you, fool. 'Tis a curse. Ye are the cause of Ragnarök, not the salvation from it."

The Vikings avoided Timp's eyes as silence spread before him.

"I shall train him," Bjorn said, stepping forward.

"And I," said Erika.

"He has my brain," said Fen.

"And mine," added O'dul.

"In's that's case, he's doomed," Gunnar muttered and then added, "but, ye have mine talents, Giant."

"And our'n wisdom," added Uncle and Aunt Dene.

Timp scooped them up and placed them on his shoulder next to Bonnie. They stood together, unified and defiant. Timp's heart soared. He finally had friends, and he only had to almost die twice to get them. Being 12 was tough.

Hilmir laughed. "You, Bjorn? An ex-Vaskrél has-been, with no bee to call his own, training a giant with a vígbý no bigger than him's own boogers? Ridiculous."

"There art ways around the giant's size, Father," Ailsa said

"No! No! No! That magic is sacred! I forbid anyone from opening the Book of Secrets for this Jötunn!"

Ailsa studied her feet and avoided her father's eyes. Even from where Timp stood he recognized that posture, and so did Hilmir. "Daughter, what have ye done?" Hilmir asked.

"I may have . . . already helped Aunt Dene open the book."

"You— Have I no power over mine domain?" Hilmir jumped up and down, shouting curses, and going berserk in general.

"Twas my doing," Aunt Dene said, coming to Ailsa's aid. "I owed the giant a life debt for saving my Dene. I thought t'would make a fine gift. Twas before the Gullvindr."

Timp had no idea what they were arguing about, but the hilmir seemed annoyed, and that pleased him.

"How many?" Hilmir demanded.

"Three," Aunt Dene said, and then brought her chin high. "Three magical beans."

Timp burst with laughter. "You're arguing about beans?"

"You believe not in magical beans, Giant?" Fen asked.

"Oh, I believe. Beans, beans, the magical fruit: the more you eat the more you toot. The more you toot, the better you feel.

So why not have beans in every meal?" Timp finished his song with a broad smile.

None of the Vikings returned the smile.

Hilmir's face reddened and began to shake before erupting. "You see? This be no Viking! 'Tis be but a blathering, singing idiot! Without the consent of the hilmir, only a Viking may take the magic from the Book of Secrets, and this Jötunn be no Viking."

"He could go iViking," Fen said. "The title of Viking be not limited to the Norse. All he must do is—"

"I know what be needed to go iViking! He'd have to complete the rights of passage, the least of which is to defeat the gorkin, and I . . ." Hilmir trailed off, stroking his beard in thought. Slowly, a wicked smile spread across his face. "Upon second thought, I shall allow your'n giant to face the gorkin and attempt to win the right to go iViking. After all, as ye say, going iViking be not exclusive to our Norse brothers and sisters, alone. Aye, he should be given a chance to prove his worth. That is, if he agrees."

"Do thee, Giant? Doth thou agree?" Fen urged. "Will ye face the gorkin and go iViking?"

Timp had no idea what they were blathering about, so he answered as he always did when completely lost: he agreed. The Villagers cheered their approval.

"But I forbid ye from opening the Book of Secrets, again," Hilmir iterated, grasping for some semblance of authority. "If yer giant passes the trials of iViking, he shall have what ye've made, but no more. There shall be no more magic in this village so long as I am hilmir. It cost us far too dearly last time. And he'll receive no training before the challenge. After all, Bjorn, did I not forbid all Vaskrél from training this Jötunn? How is it that ye think you can volunteer to train him?"

"You spoke so your'n self, brother. Without a bee, I am no Vaskrél at all. As you say, I am nothing. Therefore, my training him shall not violate your decree." A wry smirk spread across Bjorn's face.

Hilmir turned red with fury, but stilled his nerves. "Fine. If he earns the right to go iViking, ye may train him." The villagers cheered and Hilmir leapt from his platform onto Timp's shoulder. He pulled Bjorn near so that the Viking villagers couldn't hear, but Timp heard. "Ye train yer giant, Bjorn. See how far it gets thee. He shall never achieve Vaskrél, neither he nor his vígbý shall wear the armor, not while I'm hilmir. Ye'll watch as your'n pupil fall into insanity, just like ye watched the last you trained. That is, if he survives the trial. I hear tell gorkins may be tricky beasts, Bjorn." Hilmir laughed his wicked laugh.

"A gorkin is nothing to a giant," Bjorn retorted.

"Aye. Aye. Right ye are, brother. Right ye are." Hilmir stepped from Timp's shoulder back onto his platform, where his Vaskrél convoy flew him and his assistant out of the chamber.

"What was that about armor? And what was that about your previous pupil going crazy? And me going crazy? And what's a gorkin?" Timp asked.

"Never you mind all that for now, Giant," Bjorn said, still watching the hilmir's convoy. "Untold dangers lie before thee, Giant. Great battles loom upon the horizon. Many will perish. Your sanity shall be tested. But you've earned many a true friends this day, and we shall stand at your'n side."
"Bjorn?"

"Rest your'n self, Giant. Ye shall need it if ye are to go iViking and begin your training come morn."

"I can't start tomorrow. I have to go to the Farmers Market, aww but it's no use. We don't have enough berries. And we're going to lose the farm, and—"

"Rest yourself, Giant. Be one with thine vígbý. Enjoy thy victories. They are but passing moments in a life full of struggles and failures."

Bjorn shot Timp a wink and a smile, and held up his hand in Timp and Bonnie's honor. The room erupted cheers. Timp looked down his shoulder at the celebrating faces of his friends: Bjorn, Erika, Fen, Gunnar, O'dul, Uncle Dene, and Aunt Dene. Even the Vaskrél cheered. The clapping and joy rang so loud and earnest that Timp could hardly believe the same Vikings had tried to kill him only moments before, but he was too bemused to hold a grudge.

After the celebration ended, Timp walked home feeling rejuvenated with purpose. He sank deep into the couch and started to doze. Bonnie had been understandably nervous about going inside the house, so the Vikings promised to give her safe quarters inside their village. Even from the great distance between the pond and the couch, Timp was sure he could feel her connection, two pieces becoming one, the Kindred Kind. The Gullvindr.

"Hello? Hello? Is anyone there? Hello? What about me?" Molly swung back and forth, trapped in the net within the dark empty chamber. *"Humph! Typical. Just typical."*

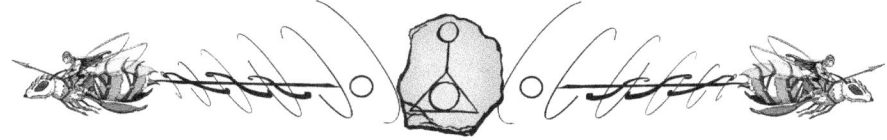

CHAPTER 49
A BRAND NEW DAY

Timp awoke the next morning even more tired than when he'd gone to bed—or in his case, gone to couch. He'd slept for an hour or two, but it was a restless, dreamless sleep. At least he was pretty sure it was a dreamless sleep. If he'd dreamed anything, he dreamed that he wasn't dreaming, which was just as bad as not dreaming at all. It seemed that no sooner had he shut his eyes than he opened them again. It didn't help matters that he opened them to someone grabbing his head and shouting.

"Timp Anthony Great Scott! What happened to your face?"

Timp jumped up to his mother leaning over him, mashing his cheeks together, and inspecting him like a mother hen. She'd come to wake him for the Farmers Market and was shocked to find him pockmarked and covered in pink goo. It took Timp a moment to register what was wrong. He put his hands to his eyes, still sticky with poultice. "Bees," he remembered.

"Bees? Bees! When did you get stung by bees?"

Timp didn't answer, but got up from the couch.

"When were you around bees? John! John, get in here!"

Timp went into the restroom, making sure to close the door tightly against to the yells behind him.

After he brushed his teeth and washed off most of the sticky pink goo, he stepped from the restroom to find his parents standing with arms crossed and feet tapping. A half-asleep Trevor played games on his cell.

"See," his mother said. "He looks like a human pincushion."

"My lands, you're right," his father said. "What in the devil's name have you gotten yourself into, Timp?"

Being a bad liar, Timp did what any intelligent liar would do; he told a half-truth, "I stepped on a bees nest. It's no big deal. It doesn't hurt."

After Timp reassured and then re-reassured his parents, they worked their way toward the door, picking up the items they needed for the Farmer's Market as they moved.

"Are you sure you don't need to go to the doctor? What was that pink goo all over you? Why were you out?"

"I feel fine. The goo helped."

Timp's parents rolled their eyes as they opened the door and stepped onto the porch.

"What were you doing outside last night?" Mr. Littleton repeated; and then he stopped. He stopped so abruptly that Timp walked into his back.

"Oh, Timp," Mrs. Littleton said. Both she and his father stood with jaws hanging open. "How did you ever?"

"My Lands."

Even Trevor stopped playing his game—if only for a moment—to behold the sight before them.

Row after row of buckets, overflowing with blueberries, covered the Littleton's porch, lined the steps, and reached into the yard. Timp tried to pick up his jaw and act as nonchalant as possible, but it was a hard sell. There were more buckets than all of their workers, working all day, every day could have picked in a month. The sight was so unbelievable, so beautiful, that there was just one thing to say:

"We're gonna need to take two cars," Mr. Littleton said.

"Or three."

"Timp, you got your license, yet?"

"I'm only 12."

"That's unfortunate."

Timp rubbed his stings. He thought about the Vikings and his summer so far just to make friends. "Tell me about it."

THE END… FOR NOW

Timp and Molly's adventures continue in
Timp and the Blueberry Vikings, Book 2:
When Worlds Collide.

EPILOGUE

The limousine idled on the Market Street bridge with horns honking angrily at the rear. The driver checked his mirrors nervously, sneaking apologetic waves to the furious drivers that passed, but he didn't dare move the car. DeLaney had death in his eyes, and the driver didn't want those eyes on him.

DeLaney stared out the window at the Farmer's Market below with a sneer fixed upon his face. His assistants waited, stiff and quiet.

"That boy made a fool out of me," DeLaney said after an awkward eternity. Becca and Stephon followed his gaze down to the Blueberry Springs Farm tent where the boy who'd set the bank into chaos weeks before peddled blueberries to a crowd. "He told me he was on our side, that he hated that farm as much as me, and I was fool enough to believe him . . . maybe because I know that feeling all too well. But look at him now, selling the biggest haul the Littletons have had in years. Where'd they get it? Who picked it for them? That's what I want to know."

DeLaney turned to his assistants for an answer but received stutters, mumbles, and wide-eyed stares. Disgusted, he returned to the window. "We hired away their workers. We paid everyone in town *not* to work for them, and yet they succeeded. More than succeeded. With a haul like that, they'll pay the overdue notes they owe and this month's mortgage as well. Do you know what that means?"

"We'll . . . have to find . . . another plot of land?" Stephon hazarded.

"There is no other land! I spent years buying the properties surrounding that farm! I lined up investors and contractors, gathered permits, and lobbied to rezone the area just to flatten that farm! Did you really think that was an accident? I saved Blueberry Springs for last!"

Becca and Stephon gibbered, but DeLaney wasn't listening.

"After all I've done, do you think I'm going to give up now?"

"No, sir," they pounced in unison, pleased to know an answer.

DeLaney took a breath to calm his rage and began laying out the steps as if to reassure himself further. "We have one more month. If they miss their last payment, the bank can foreclose, and we can still take the farm. We'll have to work double to break ground on time, but we can still do it. We just have to stop their remaining harvest."

He glanced at his assistants and then his look became distant as his rage swelled back into his face. "That boy is behind this. I can feel it. John could never pull anything like this off. The boy played me like a fool, the deceitful, arrogant brat. He picked those berries. Now you're going to find out how, and then you're going to stop him."

A chill ran through the limousine. The assistants agreed and DeLaney commanded the car forward. The driver shifted the limo into gear with one last apologetic wave to the furious drivers that passed.

ACKNOWLEDGEMENTS:

A special thank you to my brother, Brandon, who encouraged me to dust off this project and finish it. Without him, the bee-riding vikings never would have taken off. And thank you to my mother, Lynnee', who read (and finished) an early draft. Truly, a mother's suffering knows no bounds. Thankfully for me, neither does her love and support.

Thank you to Bert Pearce, who left over 700 comments, edits, and notes in a desperate attempt to make me sound halfway literate. You're an awesome friend and a grate edifer. (That's going to drive him nuts.)

And finally: thank you to you. There are a lot of books you could have read and you chose this one. Thank you for your time and support. This book was independently published. If you enjoyed it, please share or recommend this book to others and visit theShawno.com for updates on future projects.

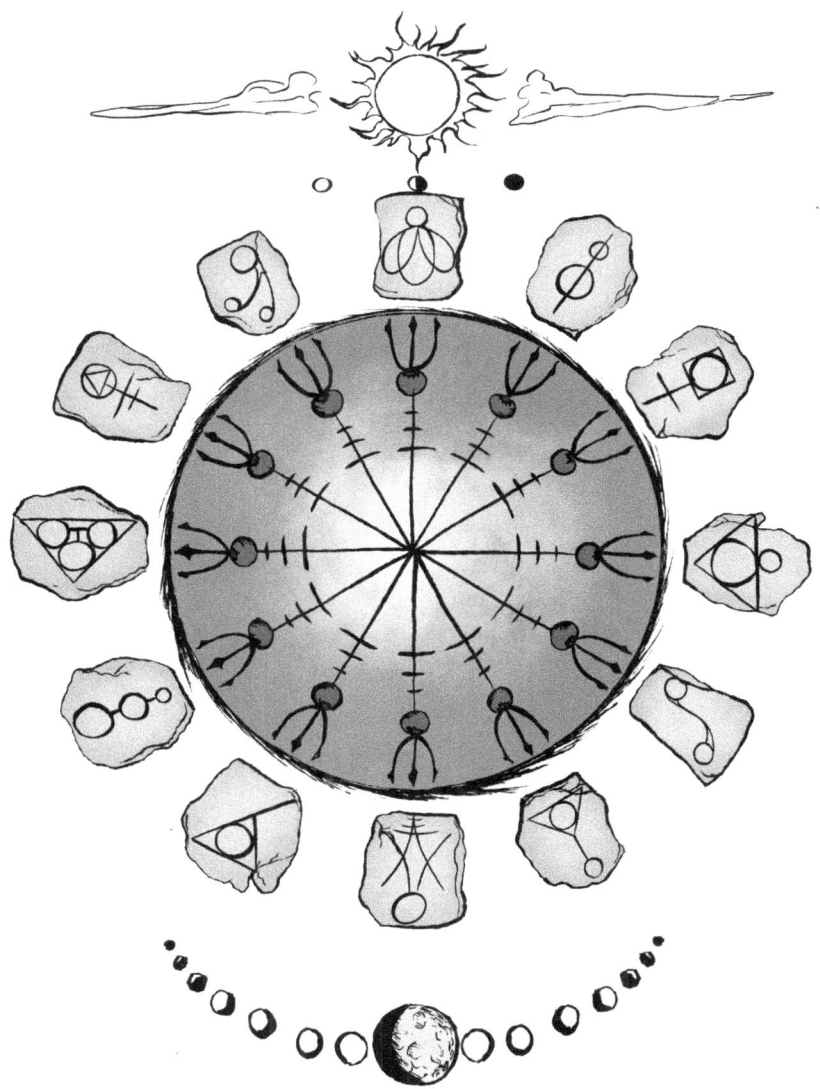

www.ingramcontent.com/pod-product-compliance
Lightning Source LLC
Chambersburg PA
CBHW070635180626
46817CB00006B/2125